Exit Point

By

Artemis Greenleaf

Other Books by Artemis Greenleaf:

Marti Keller Mysteries series:
The Hanged Man's Wife (Book 1)
Dragon by Knight (by "Coda Sterling")
The Magician's Children (Book 2)

Earthbound
Cheval Bayard
Confessions of a Troll

Anthologies with Stories by Artemis Greenleaf:
Space City Six
Tides of Impossibility (2015)

Acknowledgements

As always, thank you to my wonderful family. This endeavor would not be possible without your love and support. I also appreciate the invaluable editorial and structural help of my critique groups and beta readers. You know who you are, and I couldn't do this without you. This is my NaNoWriMo book from 2009.

PUBLISHED BY:
Black Mare Books
Houston, Texas
www.blackmarebooks.com

ISBN: 978-1-941502-91-4
Exit Point
Copyright © 2014 by Artemis Greenleaf

Dramatis Personae

Table of Contents

ACT I

Chapter 1
Pool Party

I moan softly as Tyler's warm lips move down my throat to the little hollow above my collar bone. At least I think it's Tyler. Could be Kevin. It's really dark out here and I've had a lot to drink. He smells nice, anyway.

"Sorry, baby," I say, pushing him off me. "But I have to go pee."

"Can't you hold it, Mimi?" he whines. I was wrong. It's Josh.

"No." I dodged a bullet there. I'm not desperate. Well, at least not that desperate. Yet.

I don't know where my shoes are, so I stumble across the rough concrete barefoot. Between the flaccid glow from streetlight in front of the subdivision pool cabana and the misty half-moon, I have enough light to find the bushes. Don't know why I'm bothering. Nobody can really see me anyway.

I squat in the bushes for a while after I'm done, trying to figure out a way to stay out here with my friends, but avoid Josh. I look at my cell phone to check the time. It's 12:59. We haven't even been here a whole hour yet. Maybe if I tell him I think I might hurl, he'll back off. I decide to go back to the party, such as it is. If I start making a lot of noise, Lexie, Tyler, Sierra and Kevin might come crawling back from wherever they're hiding and I won't be stuck all by myself with Mr. Lame-O.

The moon ducks behind a cloud. I know no one can see me, at least not well, but I can't help feeling that someone is watching me. It's really creepy. I know it's only my imagination, but I can swear there is a shadow near the beer cooler. Who sees shadows in the dark? Better get going before Loser comes looking for me.

I'll grab a beer on the way. May as well look like I might be at the puking stage.

I start to shuffle my feet when I get near where I think the cooler is. It growls across the cement as I crash into it. Probably have a bruise on my shin tomorrow, but I don't feel anything now. Señor Tequila has seen to that.

I rummage around in the mostly melted ice in the cooler and grab the second to last can in there. The penultimate can, as Mrs. Weismuller would say. Junior English class seems a long time ago and far away. It's June, and the last heavy perfume of the honeysuckle is cloying in the damp night air. The cooler lid thuds into place when I let it go.

Instead of feeling my way in the dark, instead of paying attention, I am designing my Senior Prom dress in my head. So of course, I trip over the cooler.

I stumble and topple over, putting out my hands to break my fall. I get a whiff of chlorine, then feel cool silk slide over my skin as the pool gobbles me up. I start to open my mouth to yell, and water rushes in. I snap my lips together. I may as well be swimming in ink. I can't tell which way is up. Kicking my legs and flailing my arms, I launch myself headfirst into something hard. I feel hot blood spreading under my scalp, then nothing more.

Chapter 2
Deb

O h, give me a break," a female voice whines. "Mimi? Mimi's a dog's name."

Who is that, and where did she come from? I open my eyes and see a pale Goth girl – my age, more or less – sitting cross-legged on a metal bench. She's got a purple barbell through her left eyebrow, a ring in her nose, and maybe ten silver graduated hoops march from her right earlobe up to the top of her ear. Her hair is black with blonde roots and streaks of purple. Like that hasn't been done before.

There is nothing else around. Just her and the bench. No trees, no light poles, no buildings. It reminds me of that play we had to sit through in American Lit, where the actors came out wearing flesh-colored unitards and there wasn't any scenery or props.

I've had weirder dreams than this, though.

"Could you at least sit up?" the girl says.

I feel as if I'm floating in space. I can't feel any floor or earth underneath me. I think 'sit' and suddenly I'm sitting there on the not-ground. Oddly enough, I'm dry, and my shoes are back on my feet. "What is this place? Who are you?"

"Deb. I'm Deb, okay? This place? It's complicated. You can call it the Astral Realm, the Other Side, or Limbo, your choice, okay?"

"Am I dead?" I don't feel dead. But then again, I don't know what dead feels like.

"Maybe. Maybe not. That depends on you."

"What's that supposed to mean?" I ask. I'm already getting tired of this. If this is a dream, it's pretty lame.

Deb sighs and looks up to the not-sky. "Like, everybody goes down to the Earth Realm with some job they're supposed to do, okay? Maybe it's one big thing, or a bunch of little things, or maybe one little thing – doesn't matter. The point is, there's always a reason. And you know what? There's something you and I have to do together. Only I died before it happened. Until it happens, we're both stuck."

"Yeah. Why would I do anything with you? I don't hang with freaks."

Deb smiles and runs her tongue over her teeth. "We get into a fight. In the food court at the mall. I get to kick your ass."

"And this is important how?" I'm so not believing her.

"Okay, there's like this woman having lunch there. She sees the fight and then gets the idea to start the Rhiannon Foundation. For troubled girls. One of the chicks who gets a scholarship from the foundation goes on to become president and she figures out a way to stop World War III from starting up in, you know, like the Middle East area."

"You know, that's sad and all, but it doesn't affect me. I don't live there," I say.

"If Theresa Mitchell doesn't become president, the person who does will start a nuclear war," Deb says.

Why does it matter to her? She's dead. I decide to humor her.

"So you're telling me that if you and I don't get into a fight at the food court at Silverton Mall, the whole world will be destroyed? And you expect me to believe that?"

Deb shrugs. "If you, like, want to get out of Limbo, you have to help me contact the foundation lady. But you're not going anywhere until it happens. Live or die. Your choice."

I close my eyes, and I feel I'm sinking. When I open them again, the nothingness has started to fade, like a curtain being pulled back at the theater. It looks the same as any bus stop on any city corner. A three story building rises behind the bus shelter. A street light erupts out of the sidewalk next to the bus stop sign. Oddly enough, this one isn't covered in stickers. It isn't exactly light or dark, just a grey twilight. I look more closely at the buildings. They're made out of stucco or adobe, and all are various shades of yellow, tan and gold.

A man wearing a striped knit scarf walks by. I swear one end of the scarf rises up and peers at me. When I look again, it's just a scarf, bouncing as the man walks along.

I wonder if it's about to rain. The only thing I can smell is water.

Deb stands up. Her black extra-strappy cargo pants hang low on her hips. She's got a skull and crossbones dangling from her belly button. I'm afraid to know what else this girl has pierced. "So, you coming or what?" she asks.

My brain tells me not to go with this nutjob. She looks like a freak and she's spouting completely insane stuff. Nothing good ever happens when you hang out with crazy people. But there is some part of me that believes her. Don't see that I have much to lose if I'm wrong, because this is probably all just a weird dream, anyway. But if what she says is true, and I don't help, I could be trapped here forever. With her. I get up from where I'm sitting, which is now the edge of the curb in front of the bus shelter. I dust off my butt. "Yeah, I guess. Not like there's anything else to do around here."

"Not that you know of, anyway," Deb smirks.

I can't think of anything easier than getting into a fight with her. *Now, how do we get to the mall so I can hurry up and get back to my normal life?*

Chapter 3
The Fountain of Sirin

So is there a bus? How do we get there?" I just want to get this over with and wake up.

"Bus? Nope. Not where we're going."

"Thought you said we were going to the mall." *Now what?*

"And who do you think is going to see us there? Nobody. We have to do something different, okay?" Deb starts walking down the sidewalk.

A tattoo of a scary fairy stares at me from just above the top of Deb's pants. Her wings are black and cobwebby, and her dress is purple and skimpy. Maybe it's just the way Deb's walking, but the fairy's wings appear to be fluttering. Weird. I don't even feel drunk anymore.

"So where are we going?" I ask, looking up at the back of her head instead of that creepy tramp stamp. Did she have that before she died, or was it something she got here?

"Sitnalta. That's where we'll meet our, guess you could call it, case worker. Okay?"

"Case worker? You're kidding, right?"

Deb keeps walking. "Case worker is close enough. It's –"

"I know. Complicated," I snap at her. I wish she'd stop talking to me like she thinks I'm stupid.

Just up ahead, a guy is painting a mural on the side of a building. I stop to watch. The picture has a fierce looking unicorn roaming through the remains of a burned out city. Light gleams off the pointy metallic horn. A saber toothed cat lurks in one of the ruined buildings. Strange vines twine around sign posts and up street lights.

"That's, uh, different," I say to the artist.

He turns to look at me. His brown hair is almost long enough to brush his shoulders and he has big, brown eyes. He seems very familiar to me, but I can't place where I might have seen him. He isn't from my school and he doesn't live in the neighborhood.

"You're new here, aren't you?" he asks.

Deb giggles. Somewhere nearby, a horse whinnies. I look around, but there's no horse to be found. Nothing but a painted unicorn.

I look at the painter again. "Yeah. What of it?" I say.

"You just look a little lost, is all." His eyes are kind, and I suddenly feel like a jerk.

"Deb and I," I nod my head towards her, "are going to Sit-something or other."

"Sitnalta?" the painter asks.

"Mimi, come here." Deb scowls at me.

"What?" I ask when I get close to her.

"Not everybody here is what you think they are. You might want to keep your big fat mouth shut, okay?" Deb hisses at me.

"Don't talk to me like that, you freaky little cow," I snarl back.

"You know, I was thinking of going there, just to see what it's like," Artistboy says. "How 'bout if I tag along?"

"How 'bout if you don't?" Deb gives him a sarcastic smile.

I don't really care one way or the other – I just want to piss Deb off. "That would be so cool if you came with. What did you say your name was?"

"Brent," he says.

"Mimi, you don't know anything about this dude, okay? Didn't the 'rents ever give you the Stranger Danger talk? It goes double for here."

My dad is the General Director of the opera and my mom works in the office there. The only talks they ever gave me were about operas. That's where they are tonight. At the opera. Opening night of the new production of Carmen. And of course, they wouldn't want me hanging around to spoil it for them. Although, personally, I'm not sure which is worse – this crazy dream about being dead, or being at the opera.

"Oh, come on. Don't be such a buzz kill. Besides, he knows where we're going, now, anyway," I say.

"Fine, whatever. We don't have all day. I hope we don't regret this, okay?" Deb stands a little way from us, her arms crossed over her chest.

"Let's go, then," Brent says.

We start walking, following Deb. After a while, the city changes to suburbs and the suburbs change to countryside. Big trees, possibly redwoods, shade many of the houses, and an occasional pine cone the size of my head lies on the road. As we leave the city in the distance, I look back at it – it almost looks like it's made of gold from where I'm standing.

There are a lot of animals – birds and squirrels and cows and horses and so on. Sometimes, though, I catch glimpses of something I don't quite recognize. Something almost familiar, but not. These things, whatever they are, don't stay still long enough for me to get a good look at them. It's almost seems they know I'm trying to see them and they don't want me to. That's alright. Brent's not too hard to look at, so I'll focus on him. He's got to be better than Deb, anyway.

The lane slopes gradually uphill. We see clumps of people on the road here and there, but they mostly ignore us. A few smile or wave. Once, I thought one of the men had an eye in the middle of his forehead. Must have been a trick of the light, because when I looked again, it was gone. I'll be glad to get out of this crazy place. It's almost like the time I stayed awake for forty-eight hours. By hour forty, I was seeing all kinds of weird stuff. Kaya and I had a contest to see who could stay up the longest. I think she cheated, but I still won. I wish she hadn't moved away.

Ahead of us is a meadow filled with wildflowers. At the far end, a fountain shoots water into the air and then it falls into a pool. Beyond that, foothills sprout up, then give way to blue-grey mountains. In this meadow, though, there doesn't seem to be any grass, just flowers. I try to smell them, but that only makes me cough – they all smell like chlorine. I have this mad, crazy desire to just run through them to the fountain.

So I do.

I put my arms out, airplane-style, and run, leaving Deb and Brent behind. I suppose they'll catch up sooner or later. In no time, I'm all the way up the hill and at the fountain. I should be puffing and panting, but it seems I don't have to breathe at all.

The fountain is bigger than I thought, and made of some kind of stone. We have granite countertops, and it's definitely not granite. Maybe marble? It's very pale pink, almost white. There are some vines and flowers, but mostly birds, carved into the outside. Some fat koi fish swim in the water. Bright yellow water lilies float on big leaves at the edges of the pool, just out of the fountain's spray.

"Ahem."

I look up. A woman is standing about a third of the way around the fountain from me. She has pale sage green skin and pointed ears. And wings. Big aqua and purple butterfly wings. I feel my mouth fall open as I stare at her. She walks toward me, her gauzy dress impossibly sparkling in the half-light.

"Do you know where you are?" she asks me.

"Limbo?"

"Limbo. That word is not known to me," she says, shaking her head. "This is the Fountain of Sirin. It is not for you."

"What? Why not?" I ask, too stunned to be angry.

"You are yet among the living. You do not belong to this place." She points to my middle, and I can see a glowing silver cord that runs around behind me and stretches off down the hill. I hadn't noticed it before – has it been there this whole time? As I turn to follow it, I almost bump into Deb and Brent.

"Who are you talking to?" Deb asks.

"Her!" I turn to look at the fairy, but she is gone. "You had to have seen her. Glowing lady with red hair and wings?"

Brent shakes his head.

"You are, like, so losing it," Deb says. Her eyes narrow, and she shakes her head.

She sits on the edge of the fountain and splashes a little water on her face. I touch the silver cord and close my eyes. I can feel my heartbeat, and I feel peaceful and floaty.

"What are you doing?" Deb barks at me. "Let's go."

She marches us past the fountain and back onto the path. The road gets steeper. I would guess we had walked a mile, but distance here doesn't seem to be the same as distance at home. We come to a pass, which is blocked by a huge iron gate.

Deb knocks on it, as if it's someone's front door.

Soon, a creature that appears to be the result of an unholy union between a human and a frog ambles up to the gate and slides it open just a little.

"Deborah," it says in a croaky voice, putting the accent on the 'bor' of her name.

"Hey, Darjon. Three of us," she says. "Please."

"Is that one authorized?" asks Darjon, nodding to Brent.

"Don't know. He just tagged along," she says.

"Then we shall see." The frogman grabs Brent's wrist and then reads something on a little screen that he pulls out of a pouch in his stomach. "You may pass," he says.

Darjon pulls the gate open wide enough for us to get through. We hurry past him and he closes it with a clang.

"Where are we?" Brent asks.

"The Fourth Plane. Sitnalta," Deb says.

"I thought that was the name of the city," I said.

"It is. It's like a city-state kind of thing. Zariel can explain it better, if you ask him."

"Who is Zariel?" I ask, scowling at her.

"He's the agent — I mean case worker - we're going to meet." She starts walking up the path.

"Whoa, whoa, whoa. Agent? What do you mean 'agent?'" I ask. "A spy?"

"Do you mean an agent of the Lords of Karma?" Brent asks, ignoring my question.

"Yes," Deb says.

"Cool," Brent replies.

"Alright. Would someone please tell me what, exactly, that means? This is starting to sound like some computer game or something," I say.

"The Lords of Karma rule this place," Brent says. "But they don't actually come here. They send their agents to do stuff. The agents are a kind of angel."

"How do you know all this?" I ask.

Brent shrugs. "Library."

I'll have to visit this library when we get back. Maybe they've got some manga.

We walk up a path that snakes around the side of a small mountain. As we get to the other side, Brent and I stop dead. A city rises out of the plain, surrounded by three layers of moats in concentric rings – moat, ring of land, moat, ring of land, moat, central island city. A crystal bridge that spans all three moats arches toward the grey sky. The central buildings seem to be made out of gemstones. Some are translucent and some are not, but they are all lit from within, shimmering and glowing, even in this pitiful excuse for light.

"That is Sitnalta City," Deb tells us.

Chapter 4
The Fourth City

The city only gets more spectacular as we get closer. I feel I'm in one of those movies where people get shrunk down to the size of ants. Set in a jewelry store. If I listen carefully, it sounds as if the crystals are singing. Not in words, but like bells at a Christmas concert, just very far away. There is a structure to the light and sound, a rhythm. I feel for the silver cord near my navel and find it matches the buildings' pulse.

The crystal bridge looks beautiful from a distance, but walking over it is scary. Looking down through the clear floor, I see large, dark shapes moving in the waters of the moats, but I can't tell what they are. I would just as soon not find out by swimming with them.

Deb leads us to a place that could be a hotel, or perhaps a high rise apartment building. It doesn't just look like gemstones – it is gemstones. Even the twilight glitters on them. Flawless green emerald and pure purple amethyst tower far above the street. I sometimes catch a glimpse of movement inside, but can't tell what is happening.

A doorman lets us in. He has on a red uniform with gold braid on the shoulders and on the matching red hat. He also has a long furry lemur tail that coils behind him on the polished tile floor.

We walk into an atrium, where an enormous tree stretches up toward the ceiling. A pond with large fish lies near its roots. Long and thin, they are similar to the arowanas in the giant fish tank at Chen's Seafood and Noodle restaurant. Except instead of silver, they're amethyst, emerald, sapphire and ruby.

"What is this place?" Brent asks, looking at bright birds flying high above us.

"Do they give out umbrellas?" I ask, also looking up at the birds. The ones perched in the branches make the tree look like it's on fire, with large blobs of moving red and orange.

"Ha. Ha. Aren't you the funny one?" Deb sneers at me. "Those birds are spirit birds. They don't eat." Then she looks at Brent. "This is called The Tower, okay? It is where you go when you have to talk to the agents."

We follow Deb up a grand marble staircase. I lose track of how many flights. Good thing I don't need to breathe. Finally, we go down a hallway. Deb stops and knocks on the door numbered seven hundred twenty nine.

It only takes a moment for it to open.

The room reminds me of my dad's office. The green and cream couches look dyed to match the pale green walls. A gold floor lamp stands next to each couch.

"Welcome," the agent says, looking at each of us. Then "I am Zariel," to Brent and I. I can't tell if Zariel is male or female. 'It' somehow seems wrong, so I'll choose 'he.' His eyes are not just golden, but seem to be made of sunlight. Or something brighter. He has high cheekbones and long hair, but is wearing a tunic and baggy pants. I was expecting wings, but I don't see any.

Zariel notices me staring. "Teleportation is much quicker than flying. But I can put on wings, if it would make you feel more at ease."

"No. It's cool." I say, a little embarrassed that he can read my mind.

"Brent, I am aware that you have some interest in the outcome of this adventure. But I'm not sure this is the right assignment for you. If you choose to stay in this room and listen, you become bound to this mission," Zariel says.

"It's got nothing to do with him. He should go." Deb pouts.

"That's harsh, Deb. Might be fun to have a guy along. Besides, I could use the company," I say.

Deb glares at me. Brent looks only at Zariel.

"I want to go. I need to help," Brent says.

"Understood," Zariel shoots him a quick smile.

Who says chivalry is dead? Brent barely even knows us and he wants to help. But that's how things often work in dreams.

"Deborah, the choices that you made are what brought us all here. You have no right to complain."

"Yeah. I didn't know, okay?" she growls. She crosses her arms tight across her chest and gives Zariel a hard look.

"You should have waited for an exit point, that's all," Zariel says.

"An exit point?" I ask.

"Yes. Every life has exit points built in. You are at an exit point now. Whether or not this mission succeeds determines whether you live or die in the Earth Realm," Zariel says.

"Oh." *Fantastic.* Now it is not just about inspiring someone to maybe start a foundation so a girl maybe gets a scholarship and maybe becomes president and maybe averts a nuclear holocaust. Now it is about life or death. My very own personal life or death.

I look around. Deb is scowling at Zariel, arms still crossed, feet wide apart. Brent has his back to us, staring out the window. I feel a little queasy. I never was any good with tests of any kind. Saving the world? No pressure there.

"Now, what you're going to have to do is to find someone named Laura Samuels. When you have found her, you must enter her dream and have the altercation that you should have had at the food court at the mall next Saturday."

Next Saturday. I hadn't planned to be at the mall next Saturday. Then again, I hadn't planned to be dead this Saturday. *Why am I going to the mall? Do I have a date? A girls' day out? Will I live to find out? Or just wake up?*

"There is an art to entering dreams and being remembered," Zariel tells us. "Sometimes a dream is nothing more than a person's brain trying to sort out the information from the day. Sometimes, they visit up here. It is certainly much easier if they can be intercepted while traveling astrally. Arrangements will be made for this training. You will be summoned when all is prepared."

"I guess we'll be going, then," I say.

Deb moves toward the door. Brent is still staring out the window, so I go tap him on the shoulder.

"We're having a break," I tell him.

"Thanks," he says. He looks into my eyes for a moment before walking towards the door. I feel fluffy.

"Mimi?" Zariel says. "Would you stay here, please. There is something you need to see."

Ordinarily, that kind of request would have made me bolt for the door. I'm not entirely sure I'm making the right choice, but I stop. I wonder if I'm going to regret this.

"Fine," I say.

Zariel holds out his hand and I take it. He hesitates for just a moment, as if he is making a decision. Then an ultra-bright light blossoms and we are in a different place.

"Why is it so dark?" I ask.

"Smoke. All the major cities of the world are burning, have been for three months," Zariel says.

"What are you, the Ghost of Christmas Future?" I knew I would regret this.

"This is why most refuse the gift of future sight," Zariel says.

We are standing in the remains of a neighborhood. Maybe half the houses are heaps of bricks and wood. Those still standing have had all the windows boarded up. There are no street lights – the one pole that isn't uprooted is dark.

"No electricity," Zariel says, seeming to follow my thoughts.

A woman creeps out from one of the houses. She is filthy and her clothes are torn. One side of her face is badly burned and looks infected. On the other side, tears have washed almost clean streaks down her hollow cheek. She is carrying a bundle of rags. Another, much older, much more ragged, woman crawls out of the partially boarded up door, dragging a shovel behind her. She looks similar to my mom, but different. Finding a bare spot amid the fallen trees and ruined landscaping, she sets to work. She seems more than tired as she starts to dig. It is hard work for her and from time to time, she stops to cough up blood.

The first woman puts the bundle of rags on the ground and starts to unwrap it.

"Deborah, don't. It will just make it worse," the older woman says.

The younger woman ignores her, and soon a skeletal baby is revealed. It is wearing a blue shirt, so maybe it's a boy. Large patches of his head are bald and the hair that remains is like dead grass. The woman gently shakes his arms, as if she is trying to wake him, but he is long gone.

"Why are you showing me this, Zariel? Who are these people?" I ask, although I am afraid I already know the answers.

"Don't you know?" he replies.

I wish I could cry. "The older woman. She's me, right?"

"Yes," Zariel answers.

"Deborah is my daughter? And we're burying my grandson?" I ask, hoping that I'm wrong, but knowing that I'm not.

"Yes," Zariel says.

"I've seen enough," I say.

"Perhaps," he answers.

I close my eyes. "At least I had a sense of humor, naming my daughter Deborah."

"Perhaps," Zariels says.

Even though I refuse to look, I can feel the brilliant white light flood over me. I open my eyes, hoping we are back in room seven twenty nine. We aren't.

Instead, we are in the kitchen of a small and run-down house. A girl about my age, with slightly curly hair and dark eyes, sits at the table with a woman who must be her mother. The mother is going through the mail, and the girl is doing what looks like homework.

"Look, Terry. It's your SAT results," the woman says, handing over the large envelope.

Terry takes it, looking nervous. She pulls in a deep breath and very carefully unseals the packet. Her scores are impressive, almost perfect. I'm briefly jealous. I will probably be lucky to make the minimum acceptable score to get into college.

"That is excellent, baby," the mother says. "Let's fill in your score on the grant application and get to the post office. We still have almost half an hour before it closes."

Zariel squeezes my hand and the scenery blurs by. When it slows down, Theresa is making her college valedictory address. Zariel squeezes my hand again, and we flash forward through her career: public defender, state representative, state senator, and finally, her inaugural speech in the snow in front of the Capitiol building. Something is different about the people in the crowd. They don't seem at all ordinary. They seem…lighter. At least most of them. A few are heavy and dark, filled with anger and fear.

One last squeeze of Zariel's hand and the light washes away the scenery. As it fades, I open my eyes. This time, we're back in room seven twenty nine.

"That was a dirty trick, Zariel. Not fair," I complain at him. There was something about helping my daughter bury my grandson that left me feeling old and sad inside. "There's a good chance that my future really sucks."

"These are the likely futures based on current events. Even if you do succeed (or not), things may still turn out differently than you expect," Zariel says. "If you hurry, you can still join them."

I frown at the door. That can't be. I'm certain this spy excursion couldn't have taken any less than half an hour. Still, when I look out, Deb and Brent aren't even at the end of the hall.

"How did you do that?"

Zariel shrugs. "Go."

I run down the corridor and catch them up.

"What was that about?" Brent asks.

"Zariel showed me what the future is if I don't help versus if I do," I say.

"Yeah, he did that with me, too," Deb says, and sadness drifts across her face. She shakes it off and we go outside. For a big fancy city, there doesn't seem to be anyone around.

"Why doesn't anyone live here?" I ask.

"They do. There's tons of people. Well, not all of them are people, okay? But there's a bunch of them. We just can't see them. They're, like, on a different wavelength from us," Deb says.

"Deb? Why is this your fault?" Brent asks.

"Why is what my fault?" she snaps.

"Zariel said that it was choices you made that caused this situation. What choices did you make?" Brent wrinkles his forehead as if he was trying to solve a hard puzzle.

"That is none of your damn business." Deb storms off.

"Well, this is going to be fun," I say. I'm still seeing the skeletal baby in my mind.

"Try not to think about it," Brent says. "We may as well have a look around, since we're waiting."

We make a point of going in the opposite direction from Deb. She has some serious issues and I'll be glad when I don't have to be around her anymore.

This city is so different from any other city I've ever been in.

"Where are all the shops?" I ask Brent, since he seems to know so much. Surely people in this city want all the best stores to buy their things from.

"There aren't any shops or restaurants," Brent says. "People here don't need any food or stuff. If they want something, they just make it out of thin air. You know – thought-forms."

I don't know, but I try to imagine all the hordes of invisible people Deb and Brent say are here, creating invisible stuff. What brands to they like? I glance down at my shirt. It is top quality silk, and the pool water probably didn't do it any favors. But it drapes against my skin, the perfect color and shape. The right designers make all the difference.

I look around as we walk. They seem to be very big on artwork here. There are parks on every other block. Each park has at least one statue or fountain. I look really closely at one statue as we walk by. It is made of white stone, but I see it breathe. I touch it, just to be sure I didn't imagine it, and feel a pulse. Now, I'm afraid to sit on the stone benches that are all over the place in the parks. I see a building that could be a library or museum. It is large and has Roman columns in the front. Stone Chinese lions guard the entrance.

Just as I start to tell Brent I want to go there, someone in a grey robe comes for us. I'm sure I hear seagulls. I notice that the hand that comes out of the sleeve is more of a flipper and it makes me think of dolphins. I wish I could see his face.

A vision of being a dolphin, racing under the water and then shooting out into the air, then splashing down and doing it again flashes into my mind. I don't know if seconds or minutes pass, but then I feel someone touch my elbow. Brent looks at me, a question in his eyes. I pretend I don't see it.

We go back to Zariel's office in The Tower. Deb's already there, waiting for us. Zariel is not around. We sit down on a couch that is warm and soft – it almost feels alive, like a sleeping cat – and wait. In the uncomfortable silence, I just look out the window.

The door opens and Zariel comes in, herding a girl in a long nightgown. Her long brown hair is in a braid and she looks about ten. She stares straight in front of her, expressionless.

"Anna has agreed to help in your training," Zariel says.

"What have you done to her?" Deb asks, suspicious.

"I have done nothing. The child is merely asleep," Zariel says. He guides the girl to the over-sized armchair near the couch.

She sits down and her eyelids sag closed.

"Many people, probably most people, visit the Astral Realm while they slumber. Some just sleepwalk around and others actively explore," Zariel says. "The sleepwalkers almost never remember. You need to talk to her and make her remember."

"Why do we have to start with something hard?" Deb whines.

"If you can manage the thing that is hard, you can surely do the thing that is easy," Zariel says. "You do not know what the state of Laura Samuels will be when you find her, and you, most of all, know that time is of the essence."

"I thought there was no time on this plane," Brent says.

"Time in the sense of minutes and hours does not exist. But in the sense that it does exist on the Earth Realm and things on the Earth Realm must take place in a certain order and within a certain range of time, and that all things are connected between here and there, we are partly bound by it."

"I have no idea what that means," I say.

Zariel frowns and closes his eyes. "Imagine you download your favorite movie. On your hard drive, don't the beginning, middle and end exist all at once?"

"I suppose so," I say.

"But if you want to watch the movie, to experience it, you have to open your media player and start at the beginning, and go through to the end. Is that not so?" Zariel says.

"I guess," I say.

"When you play the movie, it is always two hours and six minutes long. And yet, in the file, it exists out of time, beginning, middle, end, all together. The player bridges the two states of the movie. It shows each frame, each scene in just the right order at just the right time. You see only the scenes on the screen, and yet all of them, prior and yet to come, still exist, just as they always did."

"If you say so," I say.

"Are you saying that the beginning, middle and end are already written before we even start?" Brent asks.

"Ah, my poor analogy," Zariel says. "That is a difference between reality and movies. In the movies, the ending is always the same. In reality, it all depends on the choices one makes. It is sometimes the seemingly smallest of choices which change our lives. Like choosing to call one girl instead of a different one."

Brent looks at the floor.

"I've had enough of this mumbo jumbo. What do we have to do for Sleeping Beauty here to see us?" I ask.

"Anna. Her name is Anna," Deb says.

"Fine. Anna. What do we have to do?" I ask, trying to clench my teeth and finding that I can't.

Zariel's shoulders sag and his head cocks slightly to one side. "Try talking to her and see what happens."

Deb, Brent and I all approach Anna. Her eyes are still closed.

"Anna, hey! Anybody in there?" Deb asks.

"Hello?" I say and I try to poke her. It's like she is wrapped in greased plastic because my hand just slides off of her arm.

"Anna? Anna?" Brent says, right in her face.

No response to anything.

"It is as I feared," Zariel says. "The three of you are on a different wavelength from her. I thought that since Mimi is still connected to the Earth Realm, she would be at a similar vibration, but it is not so. Think of a rainbow. Red, orange, yellow, green, blue, indigo and violet are the colors that you can see. But before red is light you cannot see – infrared. After violet comes another range of light you cannot see – ultra violet. Try to imagine that you have moved into the ultraviolet range. You can still see all the way down to red. Anna, however, cannot see past violet.

"That sucks, okay?" Deb says. "How are we going to fix it?"

"There are ways," Zariel says. "All things that exist on the Earth Realm have reflections and shadows in the Astral Realm. There is a certain jewel that exists only on this plane, but it casts a shadow in the Earth Realm. It is called the Twilight Crystal. It has the ability to synchronize your vibrations with those of a different level. Perhaps I can arrange for you to borrow it, although it will likely take a good bit of arranging."

There wasn't much else to do, Deb, Brent and I went downstairs. Deb seems to have forgotten that she had been such a cow earlier. She takes us around on a park tour.

It seems a very long time before the short grey-robed figure comes to get us. When he does, his head is bowed and his shoulders slump. When we get up to the office, even Zariel looks dejected.

"No crystal?" Deb asks.

"I have located a crystal," Zariel tells us. "The one you need is in the Eighth Plane."

Chapter 5
Bad News

N o crystal would have been better," Deb says.

"So we're screwed, right?" Brent asks.

"Why?" I say.

"The Eighth Plane is a SuperMax," Brent replies.

"The Eighth Plane is sealed from the other seven. The Seventh is bad enough," Zariel says. "But the Eighth is where those rare and terrible individuals who have given themselves wholly to evil are kept. They were so wicked in life that they created a schism – the divine soul split from the malevolent personality, which persists for some time, but eventually disintegrates. These are the Lost Ones, the ones for whom there is no redemption."

"So you're saying that we have to break *in* to a maximum security prison and steal the crystal and then try to get out? I've seen that movie. That didn't work out so well for most of the characters," Deb says.

"You don't have to steal the crystal. Hades will give it to you. You just have to get to his citadel," Zariel says.

"Hades?" I ask. "The Greek god-dude?"

"Yes. He's a very advanced being who has sacrificed himself for the care of those who cannot be helped," Zariel says.

"So if he's so super nice, why can't he just meet us at the door with the crystal?" Deb asks.

"I never said he was nice. He is as he must be to do what he must do," Zariel says. "But he is reasonable."

"So what about his three-headed dog? Is that real, too?" I ask.

"There are no animals on the Eighth Plane. But there are three gates. The first gate is the Gate of Tears, because here you part from your guide. The second gate is the Gate of Truth, for here you must make sure you are cleansed and pure before you enter the Eighth Plane. The third gate is the Gate of Terror, because that is where you first look upon the Eighth Plane and all its horrors," Zariel says.

"Why is it we have to go to the Eighth Plane? Can't some big strong advanced being go and get it for us? Wouldn't that be eaiser?" I ask.

"Perhaps, but you are the ones who need the crystal and the crystal is on the Eighth Plane," Zariel says. "Should you succeed, consider it time off for good behavior. The Lords of Karma have decided it so."

"What is that supposed to mean?" Brent asks.

"Nothing. It means nothing," Deb growls.

"So, here is another question," I say. "How long do the things on the Eighth Plane live?"

"They are not immortal. Eventually, they all disintegrate. Some do persist longer than others," Zariel says. "Now, there is some training you must receive before you set off."

"Like Tae Kwon Do?" I ask.

"Not exactly," Zariel says.

"You must learn to see," says an unfamiliar voice.

We turn and discover yet another hooded figure. *What is it with all the hooded guys around here? How he got into the room?* I have no idea. Instead of grey, his robe is vermilion, the color of red bricks.

"We can already see," Deb says.

"Deborah," he says, accenting the 'bor'. "As you should know, the Seventh Plane is a tricky place. There are entities which are almost good and ones that are very bad, ones that will try to trick you. You must learn to see the difference between the almost good ones and the tricksters," says the robed man.

"Is this going to take long?" I ask.

"That depends on you," the man in the red robe says.

I scowl. I feel very impatient, like I haven't got much time. I want something to happen, and happen now. I feel a little light-headed for a moment, as if I'm going to float away, and I grab the edge of the chair.

"You may call me 'Master James,'" the red cloaked man tells us. He pulls his hood back. His features are kind of Asian and kind of something else. Maybe reptilian – he doesn't have scales, but his pupils are vertical slits and he doesn't blink.

"Is that really your name?" Brent asks.

"I don't think you could say my true name. Master James is sufficient," he replies.

Brent gives him a little karate school bow. I notice that Zariel is gone.

"Have any of you ever seen a ghost, down in the Earth Realm?" Master James asks.

Deb and Brent shrug and shake their heads. I'm not sure, so I shrug.

"The reason most people," and here he looks straight at me, "don't see ghosts is that they vibrate at a different wavelength, so they are simply unaware of them. To people in the Earth Realm and most on the Seventh Plane, you are now ghosts. They just don't see you. However, those who have burned off almost enough karmic debt to rise to the Sixth Plane might catch a glimpse of you, might even see you clearly. The living who are traveling here can see you. A few of those living are black magic operators. These are the ones who would seek to harm you for their own benefit."

"Yeah," I say, "it's not like we've got any money or anything. What are they going to do to us?"

"They steal your energy. Suck your blood. Pretty vampires in stories can be quite charming, but real ones are best avoided," Master James says.

"You can tell because vamps look solid, and the others are transparent," Brent says.

"What are you, some kind of vampire hunter?" I ask. "Is that why you're tagging along?"

"Me? No. I –"

Master James cuts him off. "There isn't time for tangential discussions at this moment. Be on your guard, always – a hungry vampire is a tricky vampire. It might use a shell, or it might shapeshift."

"A shell?" I ask. I can only picture a pie shell. Or maybe a conch shell.

"A shell is the empty remains of someone, like an etheric skin. It can be controlled by somebody else," Brent says.

"Good," says Master James. "If you look very carefully, you will be able to see a black aura around a vampire. Once you know how to do it, it is easy, but it might take some time for you to master."

My confidence that this is just some odd dream starts to crack. What if this is real, and I am dead or dying, somewhere in the Earth Realm? For the first time, fear starts playing down my spine with icy fingers.

"I'm not sure I have much time," I say.

"Then master it quickly," Master James replies.

The thing that bothers me here is that Deb and I are supposed to be saving the world from a nuclear apocalypse. No one seems to care. I close my eyes and touch the silver cord. I can feel the dull throb of my heart beating, but slower. I am still floating.

"Let us adjourn to the training room. There is not time for a proper course, but we will do what we can with what we have." Master James turns and opens the door. We follow him through the hall and down the stairs, past the jewel fish and the fire birds.

Outside, we walk along until we come to a house with a kitchen garden. Or at least that's how it looks. When Master James and Brent get close to them, the 'plants' bloom big beautiful flowers. As Deb and I get near, the plants start to change color. Instead of pretty flower colors, they are shades of deep red, grey and black. Then they twist crazily into different contorted shapes.

"What's wrong with them?" I ask.

"Those are elementals," Master James replies. "They react to passing thoughts."

"You're telling me that this garden is reflecting my thoughts? Our thoughts? Am I torturing it, just by standing near it?"

"They possess a very limited consciousness. They do not feel pain. But I would suggest you govern your mind better."

We hurry along the immaculate street until the little garden is out of sight.

I can't stand the silence. I catch up with Brent. "So. What about you? Are you dead or alive?" Kind of a personal question, I suppose.

"Dead. I got hit by a bus," Brent says. He doesn't ask about me, but he does smile.

Too bad there's no fresh air or sunshine. Being with a guy who's not constantly trying to get in my pants is nice. I make wishes that can not possibly come true. I wish we could go out on a date, and I could be with someone who would like me, just because I am me, and treat me like a person, instead of a piece of meat. We pass by a park and I see some mutant six legged, two-headed squirrels hurrying up and down the trees. I'm suddenly drowsy. I close my eyes and I feel that strange floaty feeling. But now I'm cold. I hug myself and rub my arms, trying to shake it off. My top is starting to cling a little, as if it is damp.

On the other side of the park is a large dome. It is smooth, white, and opaque, but sparkly, maybe a kind of quartz. Master James opens the bright orange door and we step inside. There's no furniture, just a soft, spongy floor. It reminds me of the planetarium show where we all had to lay down on the floor and watch the stars and planets go by on the ceiling.

"Mimi." Master James calls my name.

"Yes?"

"Let us start with you. I'm going to generate some thought forms and you decide which are safe and which are dangerous. Okay?"

I shrug.

Immediately, a person appears in front of me, maybe four feet away. I'd swear it's Steven, my neighbor from three doors down who wrapped his Mustang around an oak tree a couple months back. He's shimmery and ghostly looking.

"Not vamp," I say.

"Wrong," whispers Steve, whose face is being peeled off like a mask by something horrible underneath. It vanishes.

"You've got to learn to soft-focus your perception. If you see anything, even a flicker, that looks remotely black, get away," Master James says. "Brent, you try."

A wispy old man appears. Brent stares at him for a moment. "Gramps."

The old man smiles, then disappears.

Master James tests each of us three times. Deb's gotten them all right and Brent's missed one. I have missed all three. They are allowed to be excused. Deb leaves and Brent stays. Master James and I practice again and again and again. On the seventeenth try, I finally get one right. By the twenty third try I get another one.

"Well, we will have Deb with us," I say, disappointed. But I have a plan. Whatever I think it is, I will do the opposite.

"Perhaps," says Master James. "Time has run out for your practice. We are leaving soon. The journey will be difficult. Take a short break to refresh yourselves up before we leave." He nods towards a covered picnic basket sitting on the coffee table. Suddenly, Brent and I are out in the lush meadow with the fountain we passed through on the way here.

"What do you suppose he meant by that crack about 'time off for good behavior'?" I ask.

"My guess? It will be subtracted from our karmic debt," Brent answers.

Deb appears out of thin air. "What the…?"

Then she sees us. "Oh. It's you." She narrows her eyes and cocks her head. "What's that you've got?"

Deb pulls the basket cover back. There is nothing inside. I don't care. I lie back in the flowers and look up at the grey sky. Then I get up and run, run to burn off the fear and the anger. Run because as long as I am moving, I am alive. As I get near the edge of the forest, I hear a noise. Something big is crashing through the bushes just ahead.

Chapter 6
Picnic at the Fountain

A large deer bounds past me and runs up the hill. It gets a drink at the fountain, then turns to look at me with huge amber eyes. It crops a few wildflowers, which grow back instantly, before it shakes golden antlers and trots back into the trees.

"Did you see that?" I shout.

"I didn't see anything," Deb says.

I can tell by the way she's got her head tilted and her arms crossed that she is probably just about to accuse me of making stuff up.

"I saw it," Brent says.

Brent and Deb both stare at something over my shoulder. I turn to look.

There is a chariot behind me, rolling over the flowers, and driven by a woman in a loose green dress. But there aren't horses pulling it along. Four deer, identical to the one I saw a moment ago, are harnessed to it.

"Excuse me," she says. "Have you seen a Cerynitis?"

"A who?" I ask.

"A deer, like these," she points to the four hitched to her chariot.

"One of them got a drink and went that way," I point to the trees.

"Thanks," she says. She flips me a coin as the deer trot toward the woods.

I hold the silver coin in the palm of my hand. It looks brand new. On one side, it has the profile head of someone with pouffy hair wearing a headband. Four dolphins swim in a circle around the head. On the other side, a person leans into the scene, waving a stick at two horses. An angel or fairy thing is flying above them.

"Thanks, Deer Lady," I call after her. I don't think she heard me. Or maybe she thought I said "Dear Lady," and just wanted to get away without a scene.

Brent comes over to where I'm standing. I hold my hand out to him, with the coin still shining in my palm.

"Looks wrong - it should be really old, not all shiny and new," he says.

"Lemme see," says Deb, jerking my hand towards her and almost making me drop the coin into the flowers. "Maybe it's lucky," she says.

I hope so. We're going to need all the luck we can get. I put the coin in my pocket.

I notice an odd shadow on the ground. I know it can't be an airplane. When I look at the dull sky, something large and green is flapping bat-like wings high above us.

"That can't be," I say.

"But it is," adds Brent.

"Indeed, it is a dragon," says another voice.

A centaur is standing not too far from us, maybe ten yards away. I want to go and pet the horsey part of him. The human part of him is kind of old and hairy, though.

"Hello? Shouldn't we, like, run?" Deb asks. She's edging toward the woods.

"Why?" asks the centaur.

"Oh, I don't know, the whole fire spitting, people eating thing, maybe?" Deb says.

Suddenly, an image of a bumper sticker I have seen flashes into my mind. There is a short, pudgy dragon with smoke coming out of its nostrils, standing on its hind legs and picking its teeth. 'Do not argue with dragons, for you are crunchy and taste good with ketchup.' I remember thinking how lame it was at the time, probably belonged to some gamer. But now, it seems to be good advice.

"Dragons usually only eat people who really annoy them. And that one, she's a water dragon. She brings rain," the centaur says.

"Guess that means you better keep your mouth shut, Deb. You don't want to annoy the dragon," I say.

"Guess you better keep your legs shut, Mimi. You don't want to bore the centaur," Deb says.

"Would you two just stop already?" Brent shouts. "I'm sick of this. Why do you always have to pick at each other? Isn't there enough other stuff going on?"

I look down at the ground. What's he going to do? Ground us? And why does he think his opinion matters, anyway? He's just a tag along. Deb doesn't say anything, either. Bet she's thinking the same as me.

"Our father, Chiron, has heard that the three of you will be travelling to the Eighth Plane, and he sends a gift. When all seems lost, use this as a last resort," the centaur says, handing a small box to Brent. It's made of very dark wood, and the lid is inlaid with mother-of-pearl.

"What's in it?" Deb and I both ask.

"Don't open it until it's needed," the centaur says, holding up his hand in warning.

Deb sags to the ground and starts picking flowers. Doesn't seem to be her day.

The flowers near the edge of the forest start to wave and ripple. Something is moving underneath them. And it is heading straight towards Deb.

"Deb, get up!" I shout as I back away from her.

Brent takes a step in her direction, but before he reaches her, something brown and tan explodes out of the wildflowers.

"Yap! Yap!" a dust mop-sized dog jumps on Deb, licking her face.

"Sammie?" she says, holding the dog out a little bit and looking at her. The dog barks again and her whole body wags, not just the tail.

"I missed you, girl," Deb tells the dog, hugging the puppy, while the dog desperately tries to lick her face. "I'm so sorry," she says.

I feel something cool on my head and face, and I look up. Drops of water are glistening diamonds falling from the sky. "Rain?"

"Dragon's tears," says the centaur. He looks thoughtful. Then he turns and gallops away.

I look up, but the dragon is a green speck disappearing into the height of the sky. Turning around, I almost trip over Zariel's messenger. It's time for us to go back to the city, I suppose. Deb puts Sammie in the empty picnic basket, and I can't help but think of Dorothy and Toto.

Back at Room seven twenty nine, Zariel says, "I trust your picnic was enjoyable." He paces in front of the window. "We need to travel to the city of Airumel on the Seventh Plane to acquire some provisions. Master James will be accompanying us."

"Provisions?" Brent asks. "What kind of provisions?"

"Particles. Gross particles, that is. You vibrate at too high a frequency to be able to function on the Seventh and Eighth Planes. Normally, these particles burn off, enabling you move up to the next level."

"What, exactly do you mean by 'gross particles?' Is it like slime or something?" I ask.

"Not exactly. What I mean by gross is large or coarse. But these particles might feel slimy or disgusting because they no longer suit your state of development."

Does this adventure ever get better, or at least, stop getting worse?

Chapter 7
The Seventh City

W e make our way out of Sitnalta, through the gate, and down the mountain. I want to run through the wildflowers to the fountain again, but I can't. I have to stick with the group and we have a job to do. A weird, scary job in a weird, scary place. Bet Dad would think this was great material for an opera.

We pass beings on the road from time to time, some of them human, some not. Deb carries Sammie-dog in her picnic basket, treating her as if she's made of glass or something. Brent has his hand in his jacket pocket. I'm pretty sure it's the one with the box in it. I pull the coin out of my own pocket.

"Where did you get that?" Master James asks.

"The Deer Lady gave it to me. She had a funky chariot pulled by deer. She said she was looking for a sarah-night something," I say.

"A Cerynitis?" Master James replies.

"Yeah, I guess." I say.

"Interesting," he says.

"But I didn't get a centaur. One came out of the woods and gave Brent a little box. Said it was from Chiron, and to use it as a last resort," I say. I still feel slighted. The hanger-on got a nifty mystery box and all I got was a new ancient coin.

"A Last Resort Box? Indeed. That can not be bad," Master James says.

"Well, at least Deb seems more tolerable since she got her dog," I say. I never had a dog, or any other pets. My mom didn't want any 'filthy animals' messing up her fancy things in her fancy house.

"Pets can be very healing," Master James says.

We march along in silence after that. As the foothills get smaller, the flowers thin out and are replaced by grass. It is longish, and seems to be waving in the breeze. Except there isn't any. I half expect Julie Andrews to come running over the top of the hill, singing. My parents are obsessed with old movies almost as much as they're obsessed with opera, and they've inflicted both of them on me for as long as I can remember.

"We're almost to Alobic," Zariel announces, to no one in particular.

"What's that?" I ask.

"The Fifth City," Brent answers

I can see the edges of the suburbs in the distance, little pastel yellow and beige houses squatting between the ankles of giant trees.

"I believe this is where you came in, Mimi," Zariel says.

I flash back to sitting in the nothingness, talking to Deb.

Everything still looks mostly earth-like (only better) and it is very pretty, it just doesn't seem as 'lofty' as Sitnalta. I don't think it's just the mountains, or the pale colors of these buildings, versus the rich jewel hues of the ones in Sitnalta. There is something different about it. It feels denser, thicker, slower. Or maybe it's just that I can see the people.

I shiver. I'm still cold. As I hug myself, my hand brushes the silver cord. My heartbeat is barely there. *Is it about to stop?* "Could we hurry this along?" I ask.

Zariel takes my hand and Deb's. Master James closes his fingers around Brent's wrist. Suddenly we're at a gate. Behind me is the city of Alobic. A human-sized orange tabby opens the gate for us and we pass through. He winks an enormous green eye at me as I stare at him. I've never seen a cat with an iron helmet and a spear before.

Outside the gates, Zariel puts his left hand on top of Deb's head and frowns.

"The vial, then," says Master James.

"I suppose it cannot be helped," Zariel replies.

He removes a small bottle of what appears to be gold glitter from a pouch tied around his waist. Funny, I hadn't noticed it before. He removes the lid and hands it to Deb, who gulps it down.

"What are you giving her?" I ask. Just seems a bit weird to me.

"Consider it an energy drink," Master James says. "Deborah is...tired."

"Next stop, the gate of Udanax, city of the Sixth Plane."

This so-called Twilight Crystal better be worth all this. I don't like the way Master James said 'tired.' They know something they aren't telling us, and it makes me nervous. Before I have time to think about it, we are standing inside the outer wall of a large fortified city. The solid wood gate, topped with parapets and protected by a portcullis, reminds me of that time we went to Edinburgh Castle in Scotland over summer vacay. The other Astral cities had guards and gates, but this one seemed darker, more ominous. The city behind us looks really, really old – the buildings are made of stone blocks and topped with what looks like bamboo roofs.

"You might find the occasional trickster on this plane, but most of the beings here are reasonably good," Zariel says. "It is the Seventh Plane where things become difficult. It is separated from the other six, but not sealed as is the Eighth Plane. Those on the Seventh Plane still have a lot of work to do, a lot of bad karma to expiate. In Airumel, many of those on the Seventh Plane won't see you, or if they do, you'll appear to be ghosts. But to some of them, you will be visible as a bright, shining light. They will see your energy as something to be consumed."

"Consumed?" I ask. "You mean they want to eat us?"

"Yes," Zariel replies. "But on the way out of Airumel, burdened with your coarser particles, you will appear to belong on that plane and they will likely take no notice of you."

"Those on the Seventh Plane can be quite dangerous," Master James adds.

"Some of them are, like, vampires," Deb says. She's holding Sammie as if she's a baby. Or a security blanket. "Or pervs." Her lip curls and she shakes her head.

"Mimi," Master James says. "Are you familiar with the idea of repercussion?"

"You mean consequences?" I ask.

"Not exactly. Repercussion is the principal that if the astral body is injured, that same injury will show up on the physical body. Something you might want to keep in mind," Master James tells me.

I move my hand to my mid-section, feeling for the silver cord. I close my eyes and I can feel my heartbeat. It's very weak and slow, but it is there. That's something, anyway.

The road between Udanax and Airumel slopes down more steeply than any of the others. *Guess it's all downhill from here.* The further we get from Udanax, the darker it becomes. On the other planes, there is no sunshine, but it feels the same as any overcast day, where you know the sun is burning hot on the other side of the clouds. Here, there is only the ominous sky of a brewing storm, with towering black thunderheads and what I would expect to be a chilly wind. We are sandwiched between Master James, who leads the way, and Zariel.

"Why can't we just hyper jump, like we did between the other two cities?" Brent asks.

"Teleportation is not without risk. The denser the plane, the more risks. It is not safe for you at this level."

So we hike.

At last, a fortress comes into view. Airumel is different from the other cities already. The others only have a gate between themselves and the lower level. This one has a gate into the city from the higher level. I feel even colder and more shivery.

The guards at the gate of the Seventh Plane look as if someone pumped some Komodo dragons up with steroids, stood them on their hind legs, and dressed them in leather armor. They have got to be at least seven feet tall. Their eyes could be glass beads – cold and unflinching.

"Greetingssss, Zariel," says one of the lizard guards. "Infrequent it isss that the gate openssss thisss way."

"Long may it be so," says Zariel, bowing slightly.

We pass through not one but two of the immense wrought iron gates and into the Seventh Plane. We are contained by this big freaking room made of black rocks. They are all climbing up the walls toward the ceiling like a group of black beetles. It gives me the creeps, especially since they appear to be moving when I see them from the corner of my eye.

We shuffle down a long stone corridor and come to a thick wooden door. Zariel swings it open and we get our first look at Airumel. And it isn't pretty. It feels like a bad part of a not so great town. A thin mist drifts through the streets and alley ways. Decay is everywhere. Layers of graffiti gang tags obscure a traffic sign. The jagged teeth of broken bulbs hang from street lights. The corpse of an oak tree casts mean shadows in the half light. I catch glimpses of shapes twisting in the fog, but I can see nothing I recognize. The city appears to be deserted, but I can feel an undercurrent of something conscious and aware, just below the surface.

We walk closely together, tripping over each other's feet. I notice that Deb keeps her dog basket toward the center of the group and sticks as close to Zariel as she can without him carrying her.

As we continue down the street, the city gets worse and worse. Vacant buildings with yawning broken windows and abandoned warehouses take up most of the blocks. There is one grimy one story building up ahead that surprises me. Dingy yellow light shines from an inexplicably unbroken bare bulb that dangles above the door.

"See that light? That's where we're going," Zariel says.

We're half a block closer when a human-shaped figure steps out of the mist. "Hello, Deb," it says.

"Leave me alone, Lucas!" she snarls at him.

Master James steps up next to Zariel, between Deb and Lucas. "Don't interfere," he says calmly.

"Interfere? I'm just saying 'hello' to one of my friends. Right, Deb?" Lucas says.

"I'm not your friend," Deb replies.

"Awww. Now you have gone and gotten all goody-goody on me. But that's okay. You'll be back. I know you," Lucas says. Then he fades into the shadows.

"Who was that?" I ask Deb.

"Nobody," she says.

"No one with whom you wish to associate," Zariel adds. "Lucas Crowley is not dead. He chooses to travel here, especially to this plane, for dark and dangerous purposes. You would do well to remember that he is but a hair's breadth away from the Eighth Plane, and act accordingly, should you encounter him again on this plane or any other."

That makes me all the more interested in knowing how he knows Deb.

We reach the pathetic little building and Master James opens the rusty and dented door with a loud screech. A short bald man sits at a card table. He looks up at us and pushes his wire-frame glasses back up the bridge of his nose.

"She's in the conference room," he says, then looks down at his papers. The glasses slither toward the end of his nose again.

We follow the filthy carpet to a half open door that does not quite fit in the frame. Master James pushes the door open and we all go in. A dirty woman in ragged clothes sits on a rickety chair next to the table. She could be the homeless lady I sometimes see near the grocery store.

"Greetings, Maya," Master James says, bowing his head towards her.

"Hello, ronin," she says, smiling at him. Four of her teeth are missing and the rest look doomed.

"So, let us have a look, Zariel. What have you brought me?" She gets up and shambles towards us.

I'm glad I can't smell anything. I try not to cringe as she touches my hair. This seems to amuse her, because I can see she is trying not to smile. She inspects each of us, touching my hair, caressing Brent's cheek and gazing into Deb's eyes.

"Yes," Maya says, I suppose to herself, as she shuffles over to a shopping cart near where she was sitting. Odd that I didn't notice it earlier.

She pulls a bag out of her cart, then fishes out something that looks like a pile of cobwebs.

"This one is for you," she tells Deb, handing her an item that a whole generation of dust bunnies must have died to make.

"And for you," she hands another cobweb coat to Brent.

She rummages in her bag, pulling out one, then another of these awful things. Finally, she finds one she likes and holds it up to me. "This is a Cloak of Shadows. It will allow you to move in the lower planes and disguise you as one of them. Like so," Maya says, pulling something up over her head. Suddenly, she's a beautiful, dark haired woman with luminous hazel eyes and cinnamon colored skin. "You do not wish to attract their attention," she adds.

I gingerly pull the cloak over my head and pull up the hood. Brent and Deb do the same. Brent is now a zombie and Deb looks is a filthy old hag.

"Thou art most ugglesome to behold," Deb says, snickering.

"Oh, I don't know. Yours might be an improvement," I snipe.

"Ouch!" Brent says.

Deb's face falls. I shouldn't have said that. I'm not sure why I did. I wish I could take it back, but what's done is done. "Sorry," I mutter as I take off the cloak and leave the conference room.

I don't want to go outside, not here, not by myself, but I suddenly feel raw and awkward near the others. I just need some space. I take myself out to the lobby.

I stare at a yellowed newspaper clipping hanging on the wall in a cheap plastic frame. A group of people look seriously into the camera.

"I am sure it was just the cloak." Brent's voice comes from behind my left shoulder.

"I don't know why I said that to Deb. She didn't deserve it. Maybe it's the cloak. But maybe it's me," I say.

That is the end of the pep talk. The others file out of the conference room. Maya is wearing her Cloak of Shadows again, and she pushes the wobbly cart in front of her. She does not look at me and says nothing to me as she passes. The door skreeks open and she's gone.

Brent has his back to me. "Master James," he says. "Is it true? Are you a ronin?"

Master James smiles. "I am my own master – I have no other," he says. "I use my skills as I see fit, and do the bidding of no one."

"Are you coming to the Eighth Plane with us?" Deb asks.

"No," Master James replies.

"Why not?" I ask. "Don't you think we'll need you?"

"Perhaps. But it is not my task. The Lords of Karma are very strict and they allow no one to cross them," Master James says. "A debt is owed. It must be paid. It is not up to me. Nor Zariel."

"Neither of you is going with us?" Brent asks, incredulous.

"Okay, so we're supposed to just hike on down to the Ninth Circle of Hell all on our own and pick up some stupid crystal?" Deb says.

"You need not go that far. You only need go as far as the citadel," Master James says.

I don't know if he's kidding or not.

I walk along with the others, following Zariel. The dilapidated city gives way to something more…rural. At least there are not any buildings. There are large things, and I don't know if they're plants or animals, that stand up maybe eight feet tall. They make me think of corals or sea anemones. Then a gust of wind rattles them. Instantly, they start changing shapes, flashing from one to another, almost too fast for me to see. All the time, they are quivering and moaning.

"What's wrong with them, Zariel?" I ask.

"Wrong with them? There is not really anything wrong with them. They are doing what they are meant to do. They respond to waves of human thought, changing their shapes in response to fleeting ideas."

Like the flowers back in Sitnalta.

"Does it hurt them?" I ask, wondering if they are any different from the smaller ones.

"I don't suppose that it hurts them. Some thoughts might be unpleasant for them. But I don't believe they are physically hurt. These, too are elementals. As in earth, water, air and fire," Zariel says.

I walk to the one closest to me and touch it. Instantly, it shifts into an imitation of me, but it's deformed and ugly. I'm sure it snarled at me while it was changing. I step away from the elemental and it resumes what I guess is its natural shape.

"Are they evil?" Brent asks.

"No, but they are dense," Zariel replies.

"They're stupid?" Deb asks.

Zariel blinks. He does not understand. "No, they are not stupid. They have a very limited consciousness, but they are not particularly unintelligent for their consciousness level. By dense, I mean they contain heavy particles."

It hurts me to hear them moan and groan every time there's a breeze, although some of the shapes they slip into are…fascinating. Still, I am glad when we get past the field where they're growing.

Some dark, bare mountains rise ahead of us. There isn't a single tree or blade of grass in sight. Foreboding almost overwhelms me and it is all I can do to not to turn and run. Compared to the fear steaming off those peaks, the elementals we just passed are charming.

"The mountains are warded," Master James tells us.

"And that means what?" Deb asks.

"Protected. Guarded. There is a strong fear magic that makes most turn away," Master James says.

"Why aren't we turning away?" she asks.

"Zariel is an agent of the Lords of Karma. He is immune. As long as we stay in his presence, we can get through," Master James tells her.

"What if people coming in up here don't turn away?" she presses him.

"That summons the guardians," Master James replies.

"Sounds bad," Deb replies sullenly.

The grade gets steeper and the fear gets stronger. But still, we climb up the narrow dirt track that winds into the mountains. I am terrible at making guesses at heights, but I think we are about the height of a ten story building. There is a small cabin there, sticking off the side of the mountain at the edge of the trail. The wood and stones that form its shell are weathered black and grey.

"Make sure you are on your best behavior and use your best manners," Zariel says. "This guide is easily offended, and you truly do not wish to offend her."

Zariel knocks forcefully on the cabin door three times. It seems like minutes before we hear a shuffling sound approaching the door. It swings silently open. On the other side is a tall person in a dark robe. I wonder if this is a reverse Halloween. Sammie yaps twice and hides in her basket. Deb reaches in to comfort her.

"Enter Zariel, and your party," a female voice says. She sounds as if several people are all talking at once, saying the same thing, but slightly out of sync.

Chapter 8
The Gorgon's Pet

T hank you, Sthenno," Zariel says. "You are a gracious host."
Sthenno nods. Then she turns around and seems to glide into
the dimly lit cabin. What appears to be a small cabin snuggled
against the mountain from the outside is actually a small cabin that
is covering up the entrance to a very big, very dark cave. And I'm
sure that very dark cave is where we will end up going.

When she faces us again, something sticks out of her
hood, just for a second. As impossible as I know it is, I'm sure it's a
snake. A little black one with yellow eyes. I start to open my mouth
to say something. If there was a snake crawling around in my
clothes, I would want to know about it. Zariel catches my eye and
shakes his head. Guess she already knows. Eww.

Neither Brent nor Deb seems to have noticed this. Either
that, or they're really good at hiding it.

Sthenno gestures toward the uncomfortable looking
furniture. "Please have a seat," she says. We all sit. There is an
advantage to having an astral body over a solid one. When you
have to sit on furniture that's made out of cave rocks, it's still pretty
comfortable.

Zariel stands up. "By your leave," he says to Sthenno.
She nods.

"Sthenno has consented to be your guide to the Eighth
Plane. Its location is both secret and protected. You will not be
able to find or access it without Sthenno's assistance. Pray listen to
her and give her no cause to think you are undeserving of her
help," Zariel says.

Zariel is yapping on about something. I'm not listening.
The top of my head really hurts. I reach up to rub it and find a big
lump. What is that about? I scan the place for mirrors. There is not
so much as a framed picture.

Strange. What are the odds she has a restroom? It is a long shot but I'll ask.

"Excuse me, but do you have a bathroom?" I ask. I try to sound extra polite.

"A bathroom?" Sthenno asks. I can see her craning her head to one side. I try not to look at the squirming going on under her hood.

"Yes. Powder room? Toilet? Lavatory? I just need a mirror," I say. I even smile afterwards.

"You need a what?" Sthenno growls. She strides towards me, closing the distance in three long steps.

The hood is not just squirming now; it is twisting and writhing. Six snake heads poke out from under the edge of it. They all hiss at me. I can see the lower part of her face, but not her eyes. Light glints off some serious fangs. I take a step back, as far as I can, without falling over. From the corner of my eye, I see Deb cover her mouth with her hand.

"I am sorry," I stammer. "I just wanted to freshen up."

"Sthenno, may I have a word with you?" Zariel asks.

They retreat into the corner. She waves her hands when she talks to him. He makes smoothing gestures. They are speaking quietly to each other. I catch snatches of the conversation, but I don't understand the language. All I know is that I am in big trouble and I have no idea why. I decide if the lump on my head was too obvious, Deb at least would have said something rude, so it probably isn't anything to worry about. Probably.

After a while, Zariel manages to calm Sthenno down. She stays in the corner while he approaches me. I glance at Deb and Brent, but they avoid eye contact and shift uncomfortably in their stone chairs.

"Come with me," Zariel says. It is my turn to go into a different corner with him.

"What were you thinking?" he asks me, as if I'd just poured hot coffee on her.

"All I wanted to do was look at this bump on the top of my head. Does she have a phobia about bathrooms or something? How was I supposed to know?" I say.

"Not bathrooms. Mirrors. Why would you ask a gorgon for a mirror?" he says. I still hear the 'you idiot' that he doesn't say.

"Okay. So, never ask a gorgon for a mirror. Got it. Why not?" I ask.

"You don't know what a gorgon is, do you?" he asks shaking his head.

"Don't they make fish sticks? Oh, wait. That is Gorton. With a 't.' Tell me, please, who or what a gorgon is," I say. I try not to be too sarcastic.

"Not so loud. Have you ever heard of Medusa?" Zariel asks.

"The chick with the snakes for hair?" I ask. *Just like Sthenno.*

"Good. And do you remember what happened to her?" Zariel asks.

"No," I say.

"The gorgon has a lethal gaze. Looking her in the eye turns people to stone. It is a very long and complicated story, but a young man named Perseus was sent on a fool's errand to kill Medusa. But he tricked her by using a reflective shield and when she looked at it, she turned herself to stone and he lopped off her head," Zariel says.

"How was he able to cut her head off if she was made of stone?" I ask.

"Perhaps his sword was very sharp," Zariel says.

"Or maybe that Percy guy used a statue head and she is not really dead. Or maybe he helped her fake her own death –"

"Enough." Zariel cuts me off. He obviously doesn't watch the soaps.

"The point is," he continues, "that gorgons are very sensitive about reflective objects in general and mirrors in particular. So you need to go over there and apologize to Sthenno for insulting her."

"But that's not fair. I didn't know," I say.

"Are you aware of the adage, 'What you don't know can't hurt you.'?" He asks.

"Yes," I say, hopefully.

"It is incorrect. What you do not know can kill you. Besides, life is not fair. Go apologize. And it would not hurt to grovel a little," Zariel says.

"And what if I don't?" I ask.

"You will make a lovely statue out by the fountain," Zariel says.

"You're kidding me, right?" I ask.

"No." He looks very serious. Deadly serious.

"Oh, all right. Fine," I say.

I walk over to Sthenno. "Your gorgonship? I am really, really, really sorry. I didn't know about the whole mirror thing, with your sister and all. I would never, ever have asked for one if I had realized." I resist the urge to suggest that her sister might be alive and well and living in South America. Even though it might make her feel better. "I apologize for any inconvenience and ask you to please forgive me."

"I will consider it," she says.

She considers it for a very long time. Zariel talks with her some more. I probe the knot on my head, trying to figure out exactly how big it is. Finally, Sthenno comes over and says, "I will escort you."

"Thank you, your gorgonship," I say.

"Mimi?" she says. "Don't call me 'your gorgonship.'"

"Yes, ma'am," I reply.

"We shall wait here for you," Zariel says. "Deb, perhaps you should leave Sammie here with us. For safekeeping."

She hugs the little dog and scratches her ears. "You stay here and be good, okay? I'll be back soon." The little dog whines, but stays in her basket.

We put on our Cloaks of Shadows and we're good to go. Sthenno gestures for us to get behind her. Zariel and Master James wave goodbye. We don't need lights. I can see in the pitch blackness. I suppose Deb and Brent can as well.

We seem to have stepped into a badly lit black and white photo. Stalactites (they have to hold on tight so they don't fall down) drip chilly lime water on us. Stalagmites (eventually, they might grow all the way to the ceiling) form a hazardous maze. I think of repercussion. What if I end up with a huge, ugly scar on my face?

We seem to be walking into the middle of the Earth. We just keep going deeper and deeper. Occasionally, I see little creatures moving out of the way as we near. I don't recognize them, but maybe it is just because it's dark. I don't really want to get a closer look at them. The tunnel we are walking in gets shorter and narrower as we get farther into it. By the end, I'm stooping. We have to get down on our hands and knees to crawl through an opening at the end.

When we come out, I don't know whether to be scared or amazed. Or both. Enormous stalactites and stalagmites are colossal fangs surrounding a waterfall that plunges perhaps fifty feet in to a deep black pool, and flows away through a narrow gorge. The really creepy, scary thing is that it should be deafeningly loud. But it is not. Water spills, crashes and flows in total silence. Like it is all on a big flat screen TV, with the sound turned down, stuck on the cavern wall.

"This is the gate I am charged with guarding," Sthenno says in her odd multi-voice.

"Gate?" Deb asks.

"Yes. We are at the boundary of the Seventh Plane. You must go through the waterfall to reach the Eighth Plane. This is the Gate of Tears," Sthenno says.

"How do we get there?" Brent asks.

"As you approach, a path may appear to you. If you are allowed to enter, do so. If not, there is nothing you can do but turn back. Either way, take care not to fall into the water," Sthenno says. Then she whistles.

A massive head slowly rises from the water. Sharp teeth, the size of railroad spikes, stick out from top and bottom jaws, and interlock outside its lumpy, scaly mouth. Orange eyes glimmer in the darkness. Something tawny, that might be fur, disappears into the black water. The creature makes a deep booming sound that makes me think of someone pounding on a heavy door, then slides back under the chaotic water.

"Was it laughing at us?" Deb asks.

"Laughing? Perhaps, although Ahemait is not known for her sense of humor," Sthenno says.

"You've named that thing?" I ask. "Is it your pet or something?"

"Pet? Ahemait is, was, and always will be. She is not of the collective souls." Sthenno's voice rises dangerously and something, or many somethings, squirm violently under her hood. I remember the snake heads I saw earlier, and shudder.

"Sorry," I say. "I wasn't trying to make you mad." I step back.

"What do you mean by collective souls?" Brent asks

Sthenno frowns, and one eyebrow arches.

"It is, perhaps, an over-soul."

He bites his lip, seeming to want her to clarify, but afraid to ask.

The corner of her mouth twitches dangerously close to a smile. "For example, there is only one horse soul, but each physical horse contains a fragment of that one soul, and when the body of the horse dies on the Earth Realm, that piece of soul returns to the collective, bringing with it all the experience and knowledge gained in the life the individual horse lived."

He nods, and the squirming under Sthenno's hood dies down some.

"Here is where we part company," she says. "When you return from the Eighth Plane, do not leave this cavern. I will return to collect you. You will not be able to pass through the maze of caves without my protection and guidance," Sthenno says.

"Thank you," Brent says, bowing his head slightly.

"Yes, thanks," I add, trying to imitate Brent.

Deb says nothing. Brent and I both glare at her. She bows deeply from the waist, with a flourish, and says, "A thousand thanks, your most excellent gorgon-ness."

The hood things start to squirm again.

"I am so sorry. She doesn't know how to act," I say. I am hoping that Sthenno does not just get really pissed and push us in the pool with the monster crocodile thing.

Another head nod, although there is still movement under the hood this time.

"Okay, well, we'll be seeing you, then," I say. I start walking toward the silent waterfall, carefully avoiding looking at the pool. I assume Brent and DeBORah are behind me.

Chapter 9
The Gate of Tears

A path does appear. It is a skinny, slippery trail scratched into the side of the rock face. It isn't easy, but we scrabble up the side. Going up the mountain to Sitnalta was no problem, but this is hard work. I feel thick and heavy. Must be the Cloak of Shadows effect. Wonder what would happen if I took it off?

I finally make it to the top and stop to rest on an outcropping. I stand beside the waterfall and look down. Ahemait floats lazily below, an immense mythic crocodile. She is beautiful, in a lethal sort of way. Leopard spots dapple her armored hide and I have a sense of her ancient and inexorable power. I know if one of us slips, one of us falls, she waits and will not be denied.

Deb scrambles up behind me, then moves over to make room for Brent. The three of us stand clumped together on the ledge. I feel certain that Ahemait knows we are there, three potential hors d'oeuvres.

I hear a noise and see a pebble caroming off the rocks. I whip my head around and see that part of the ledge is giving way and Brent is losing his balance.

"Brent!" I shout as I twist in his direction.

He reaches out and Deb grabs for him with her right hand. His hand passes through hers, as if she were a hologram. She gasps, but freezes.

I see the panic on his face as I lunge for him. Somehow, time seems to slow, and I grab his arm, then pull back as hard as I can. The three of us collapse in a heap in the gateway.

"Damn. Brent, are you okay?" I ask.

"Yeah. Thanks," he replies.

"Deb, what happened? What is wrong with you?" I ask. I didn't mean it to come out quite like that.

Deb sits up. Even with Cloak of Shadows adding density, her hand has become transparent.

"It has started," she says. "My astral body has started to decay. We have to hurry. If we don't get into Laura Samuels' dream before I fall apart, I'll be nothing but a revenant, trapped between two planes, and I may be stuck here forever."

She looks so desperate. I'm not fond of her, but I don't want her to suffer, either.

We all hoist ourselves up to our feet and face the gateway.

"Let's do this thing," says Brent.

The gate looks flimsy, actually. Thin, wooden bars stretch across the passage into the mountain and thatched watchtowers flank either side of it. There doesn't seem to be anyone around. I walk up to it and shake the bars. I feel there is someone watching us, but I can't see anybody.

"Hello?" I say.

"Who has sent you to this place?" a gruff, hoarse voice asks.

"Zariel," I reply.

"We just want to run in, pick up something from Hades and run out, no big deal, okay?" Deb adds.

"Coming here is always a big deal," the voice replies. "Karma Agent Zariel knows this, and I expect you do, as well."

"He did mention it," Brent says.

"Is it your wish to enter this gate? Few who do ever return," the voice says.

"None of us wish to enter, but there is no other way for us to do what we need to do," Brent says.

"Well spoken, Brent Mitchell," the voice replies.

Mitchell. Mitchell. Where have I heard that name recently?

"You are still free to change your minds, to turn back, until you pass through the second gate, the Gate of Truth. That is the point of no return," the voice says.

"We have to go in," Brent says.

Why does he suddenly think he can speak for us? It isn't even his mission.

"There are many dangerous things on the Eighth Plane, some that will absorb your energy and leave only a shell," Invisi-voice says.

I suddenly feel like a boa constrictor is coiling itself around my body, squeezing out my life force and drinking it down. I can't even cry out. It is gone as quickly as it came. Now I know the real reason it is called the Gate of Tears. It is the preview of the Eighth Plane, not the parting of the ways. I can tell by their faces that Brent and Deb had the same thing happen to them.

"Do you still wish to continue, Mimi Sepulveda and Deborah MacDonald?" Invisi-Voice asks.

I wonder if Brent could go on his own, since he's basically taken over this adventure, anyway. There's probably some rule or something against that. I'm at least half dead, anyway, right? So, what the hay?

"Yes," I say.

"Like, I don't 'wish' to, but I have to, okay?" Deb answers.

She sounds more surly than usual. Hope the 'tude doesn't screw this whole thing up.

Invisi-Voice doesn't say anything, but the gate slides open enough for us to step through it. Then it snaps shut behind us, the sound echoing off the stone walls of the mountain.

For the first time since I came here, I feel really, truly afraid. Invisi-Voice remains silent, and we start to walk down the passage.

"Do you think the second gate is very far?" I ask.

"Probably not," Brent replies. His voice quivers, just a little.

Deb is quiet. I look at her and see she's staring at her right hand. The decay has spread to her wrist, now. I hope, for her sake, that Brent is right.

We haven't gotten to the point where we are holding hands like little kids, but we stay close together as we walk. Torches light the passageway, and the light flickers and plays funny tricks. We come to a bridge and I look over the railing as we cross it. Something dark and shaggy darts out of sight in the ravine below. I wonder if it is a troll.

The light starts to get brighter and there is less flickering. It is different from daylight – there is a lavender tint to it. I can see a structure now. This looks more prison-like – grey brick or metal with something that could be razor wire on top of the wall. Again, there are watch towers at either end. The closer we get, the brighter the light. It's almost too bright, now – a spotlight, shining in our faces. I hold my hand up to shade my eyes. Yay, Cloak of Shadows.

There are two human-looking shapes on top of the wall. They're silhouetted against the blinding light. I give up and just close my eyes. It helps, but the rays still seep through my eyelids.

"Welcome to the Gate of Truth," one of the people says in a man's voice.

"In the Eighth Plane, secrets can and will be used against you. To pass this gate, you must leave your secrets here," the other person says. A woman. "There is only one way for a secret to cease being a secret," she adds.

I was afraid of that. This could be really awkward.

An anti-spotlight, a cone of darkness covers Deb. She tries to step out of it, but it follows her every move, sticking to her tighter than her own shadow.

"Your turn," says the man.

"Do I have to be first?" Deb looks like she would cry if she could.

"Yes," he answers.

Deb closes her eyes and bows her head. "I have been on the Seventh Plane since I arrived here."

The cone of darkness fades a little. Deb remains still and quiet.

"Is there more?" the woman asks.

"Yes," Deb answers, but she doesn't continue.

"How did you die, Deb?" the woman asks. Her voice is kind, but detached, as if she is asking a little kid how her day at preschool was.

"You know the answer to that," Deb says.

"You must speak it," the man replies.

Deb shifts her weight from foot to foot. Her lips purse and relax. "I washed down a whole bottle of Valium with half a bottle of vodka, okay?"

I get it now. That's why Zariel was ragging on her about exit points. She took matters into her own hands. Now this whole

Astral adventure thing is pretty much her fault. And she has to fix it before she fades into nothing. Glad I'm not her.

The dark cone has dimmed a lot, but not gone away.

"That was the same day your father killed your little dog, was it not?" the woman asks.

Deb nods her head.

"What did you do before you took the pills?" the woman asks.

Deb raises her head, defiant. "I turned his worthless ass in to the cops. I knew he had been knocking over liquor stores lately. Mama knew, too. She also knew what else he was doing. I hate her. I hate her for not stopping him."

"But she did try to stop him, once," the woman says. "Do you remember? She had to have her jaw wired shut because he broke it in three places?"

"Why couldn't she just leave?" Deb asks. She shakes her head.

I have never heard so much despair in a person's voice. I wanted to go over and hug her, but my feet wouldn't move. I don't know if it was my own fear of her pain, or if I was in some control of the gatekeepers.

The cone of dark was gone and Deb seems to sparkle in the light. There was something changed about her, as if something broken had been fixed, or at least stuck back together. It just lasts for a moment. Then her Cloak of Shadows hag look returns. I notice that the transparency has spread a little further up her arm.

Now Brent is in shadow. He stands with his feet apart and his arms straight down by his sides, hands balled into fists.

"I lied," Brent says. "I told Jenny that I didn't love her, that I didn't care about the baby."

"Why did you say that?" the man asks.

"I don't know. I was scared. I was tired. The baby, she just needs so much, you know? Jenny was right, I knew she was. She said we ought to get married. But how was that going to work? We are, were, both still in high school. I wasn't ready for that."

"You were still arguing with her, and not paying attention to where you were going. How do you think that made her feel?"

"What, when I stepped off the curb and got flattened by the bus? She was so pissed at me, she was probably glad," Brent says. Misery makes his zombie look even more haunting.

"She loved you. She never gave up hoping you would do the right thing by her and your child. What is your daughter's name?" the woman asks.

"We call her Terry. But her name is Theresa," Brent answers.

Brent Mitchell. Daughter Theresa. Theresa Mitchell. OMG. It wasn't really Deb and I he was so interested in helping, after all.

The cone of dark is gone and now Brent is also shiny and new, just for a moment, under his Cloak of Shadows. I guess it is my turn now. We may be here a while.

Chapter 10
The Gate of Truth

Is it just me, or is my cone of dark darker than Brent's or Deb's? At least I can open my eyes now.

"It is your turn, Mimi," the woman says.

"I know," I reply. *Where to start?*

"We were just having fun. We weren't hurting anything by sneaking into the pool area at night," I say.

"Except when Josh insisted on breaking the lights," the man says.

"Yeah, well, I'm not his mother," I say. "We had to bring him along. His dad is the president of the Home Owner's Association. He had the keys. Believe me, that was the only reason," I tell them.

"Were you there every Friday?" the woman asks.

"Most. The 'rents have season tickets to the opera. They go just about every Friday in summer," I say.

"And you never go with them?" the woman asks.

"Are you kidding? Even if, in some weird, parallel universe, I wanted to go see the fat lady sing, I would not be welcome. Opera is the one thing they both love and having to deal with me would be too tiresome," I say. "They even named me after a character from an opera. La Boheme."

"Mimi dies in the end, does she not?" the man asks.

"Doesn't someone always die in the end of an opera?" *My hands are much warmer and I'll sleep now.*

"Not all," the woman says.

"What do you bring to the Friday night parties, Mimi?" the man asks.

"A brand new bottle of tequila," I say.

"And how do you always happen to have a brand new bottle of tequila on most Friday nights?" the man asks.

"I know things. Things that people don't want other people to know," I say.

"What sorts of things?" the woman asks.

"I have to tell other people's secrets, too?" I ask. Hardly seems fair.

"Secrets can be weapons, can't they?" the woman asks. "Tell all the secrets."

My cone of darkness does not seem to be any lighter. "Fine. Evan Cooper, Josh's dad, president of the Home Owners Association, is having an affair. With a man. I saw them kissing. That is why he leaves the keys where Josh can find them and doesn't come looking for him at night."

"Does he buy you the tequila?" the man asks.

"No. That would be my brother. He has his own place, but he came in and stole some expensive earrings from Mom's jewelry box to buy pot. She thinks she lost them at a party." I say.

"Were they your mother's favorite earrings?" the woman asks.

"No, not really. But if our parents knew he was smoking, they would check his butt into rehab so fast. He's already been to a dry-out camp. Didn't like it much," I say.

I check the cone. Still there, but maybe it's not quite as dark.

"You are still holding something back," the woman says.

"Why do you need to know? What harm can come of keeping this secret?" I ask. I don't want to share this one. I know it shouldn't, but it makes me feel tainted somehow.

"Because you are resisting. That means it has great power over you," the man says.

"Who is going to tell? Deborah and Brent are dead," the woman says.

She does have a point. I still don't want to say, though. I catch a glimpse of Deb. The fingers on her left hand are starting to go transparent.

"My mother. She used to be a stripper. Wanted to be a ballet dancer, but she wasn't quite good enough. Not too many jobs for Theater Arts majors. I'm not sure, but I think she turned tricks on the side. She had to feed my brother," I say.

"Does your father know?" the woman asks.

"I think so. She obviously had a kid when he met her. But none of her stuck-up opera friends know. That would kill her if they found out," I say.

"How did you find out?" the woman's voice asks.

"We were out shopping. We ran into someone she used to work with. Mom tried to pretend she didn't know this lady. Lady made a scene. Mom called the cops. Lady had a warrant for bad checks. But she said a lot of things before the police hauled her off. I asked Mom a lot of questions on the way home, but mostly, why didn't my brother look much like Dad? He was about a year old when my folks got hitched, so there were always pictures of my dad with him when he was little, just not as a baby. I'd never thought to ask about it before."

"But you used this information as blackmail against your mother to get things you wanted," the man said.

I take a deep breath and cough. "Yes."

The cone of dark melts away. I feel clean, as if I have just stepped out of the shower. I touch my hair, half expecting it to be wet. It feels good, better than I thought it might, to be free.

The gate grates along the floor of the stone passage as it opens.

"Once you have passed this gate, there is no turning back," the woman says.

Brent, Deb and I step through the gateway. I don't let myself look back as I hear the gate scraping closed – I might try to make a break for it.

"On to the next," says Brent.

"On to the next," Deb and I say together. I'm trying to sound braver than I feel.

My good cheer and happiness quickly evaporate. The tunnel to the third gate gets dark rapidly. The bright lavender light of the second gate is soon swallowed up in the gloom. Sometimes, I see little flickers of motion in the darkness – black on black – but I can't see what it is that's moving. Up ahead, we can hear sounds –

people crying and shouting, and the occasional scream. The scent of rotten eggs is faint, but unavoidable. The Eighth Plane was just an idea, a very unpleasant idea, until now. Now it is real and right in front of me, and I am going to have to go into it. I can't think of anything I would care to do less. I fight the urge to run, but I am barely winning.

"Brent?" I ask.

"Yeah?"

"Why didn't you just say that you were Theresa Mitchell's father?"

"If you knew that I abandoned my girlfriend and baby, would you have let me come?"

"He's got a point," Deb said.

"And you," I say, rounding on her, "you just said you died. You completely failed to mention that you had everything to do with that." *Big, fat jerk.*

"I can't imagine what kind of pain you must have been in to make that decision, Deb," Brent says.

Now who's the big fat jerk? "Look," I say. "We all screwed up pretty badly. Why don't we just start over, and act like none of this ever happened?"

"Fine with me," Deb says. But there's an edge to her voice.

"Okay," Brent says.

Back to torches again. They barely illuminate a wall that looks like it came straight from a medieval castle. A solid iron gate blocks our way. The crying and screaming is much louder now. Two over-sized guards patrol the top of the wall between the two watch towers. Light glints off of something behind one of the tiny windows in the wall. Are there archers there, waiting to shoot us full of arrows if we do the wrong thing?

"Ho there, travelers," one of the men calls out to us.

"Ho, yourself," Deb answers.

"Do you wish to enter the Gate of Terror?" the other man asks.

A particularly loud and anguished scream sounds behind him.

"I don't suppose you could get Hades to come to the door and just give us the item?" I ask.

The man laughs. "There is no art that can summon or constrain Hades," he says.

"I don't see what choice we have," Brent says.

"You always have a choice. You can choose to pass through these gates or not."

"Like, I thought they said that we couldn't go back through the second gate without going through this one," Deb says.

"That is true," the second man says.

"So we would just be trapped between here and there, forever?" I ask.

"Yes," says the first man. "Some have made that choice."

"And what happened to them?" Brent asks.

"They become shadows," the second man says.

"Still not much of a choice. Open the gate," Brent replies.

"Please," I add.

"As you wish," The first man says.

The iron gate rattles and clacks as, at the top of the wall, the chain wraps around the spool and jerks the gate haltingly upward. I notice iron spikes sticking out from the bottom of the gate as it rises. At the top, it hangs, a row of iron shark's teeth, waiting to crush us. We hurry past it. It slams down behind us with an echoing thud. A drawbridge clunks down in front of us. As we cross it, a dark tentacle comes out of the moat and probes around on the bridge. We run the rest of the way. The wood and iron gate creaks open in front of us as the drawbridge is drawn up.

We step out into the Eighth Plane and the heavy gate groans shut behind us. I expect everything to be pitch dark, but a lurid red light shines on the scene nearby. It reminds me of a Halloween haunted house and I half expect people in latex masks to jump out of the shadows.

"Excuse me," I call up to the gate guards. "How do we get to Hades' citadel?"

"Follow the road. It will give you some protection. Straight ahead. You cannot miss it," says the second man.

"Thanks," I say.

"Looks like we have already got Dorothy, minus Toto. Are you the Scarecrow, the Tinman or the Cowardly Lion?" I ask Brent.

"My mom loved that movie, too. I'll be the Lion, you be the Tinman," he says.

"What are you talking about?" Deb asks.

"Doesn't matter," I say. She was never terrorized by flying monkeys as a child? I would rather try to imagine singing munchkins and a yellow brick road than wonder who or what is screaming in the dark not far away.

I'm not sure how I came to be holding hands with Brent and Deb. But it keeps me from turning around and running back to the gate, begging to be let out.

I wonder. What would happen if I took off the Cloak of Shadows? Would I just not see or hear the horribleness around me? Would that make the awful things in here not be able to see me? Dread pulls at my feet, and with each step, they are harder to lift. I study Brent and Deb. Their disguises make their faces impossible to read. I wonder if they feel the same rising panic that I do. Perhaps being all dead (instead of partly dead, like me) makes things easier. Or maybe they are just braver people than me.

As we crest the small hill we have been climbing, a fortress looms ahead of us. My mind wants to hurry up and get there so we can leave this cursed place, but the rest of me wants to run as fast, and as far away as possible. I find it hard to force myself forward. Almost half of Deb's left hand is transparent now, and it feels to me that her fingers are missing.

I can't stand it. I have to know. I let go of my friends' hands and pull my hood down off of my head. I see nothing, hear nothing, feel nothing. It's as if I am in a sensory deprivation chamber. Sierra and I did that once. I had nightmares for three nights afterward.

I feel jostled, and someone pulls my hood back up.

"Mimi, are you crazy?" Brent shouts at me. "Do you really want to attract attention from them?" He gestures out to the red-tinged landscape.

"No. Don't shout at me, Brent," I snap. "I just thought it might make them go away, or maybe make me invisible to them."

"Well, it didn't, okay?" Deb says. "Listen."

The distant shouts and screaming have stopped. I hear something snuffling nearby. It could be a very large and drooly dog.

"When you took off your hood, it was like someone turning on a light. Don't do that again. You'll just attract them." Brent says.

We start walking again. Brent is holding tightly to my left hand. Deb is doing the best she can with the stump of her left arm.

I see a movement to my right. A man falls in step with us. He is dressed as a doctor, with scrubs and a stethoscope. His hair is dark, and he's got a gap between his front teeth. Cruel eyes frame his narrow nose and dominate his thin-lipped mouth. I want to scream and run away from him.

"Hello," he says to us. He puts a hand into his pocket. "Would you children care for some sweets?"

"No. No thanks, Pervo," Deb snaps at him.

He only smiles. Then he takes one big fast stride and gets in front of us. We stop to avoid crashing in to him, avoid touching him. He peers at Brent's face, then mine, then Deb's, saying "No," after each.

"You don't fit the criteria, but I still wish to examine you," he says, as if he is offering us a treat.

A deep booming laugh shocks the crimson twilight around us. It sounds like a boulder might sound if it could laugh. The doctor looks over his shoulder, scowling.

"Another time," he says. He flees into the rocks.

This doesn't make me feel any better. Just because it chased away the bad guy does not mean it's a good guy. It could be something much worse. If I wasn't trapped between Deb and Brent, I would be out of here.

Feet crunch in gravel, getting closer. A human shape approaches us. As it gets nearer, I can see it is a very tall, very built man. He brushes his thick dark hair out of his eyes, revealing a curved silver barbell in his right eyebrow. He reminds me of a manga character – improbably good looking and sad and heroic. And dangerous.

"Now," he says. "You will come with me."

Chapter 11
Break Up

Brent tries to put himself between the man and Deb and I. Very brave, but very futile. What is one teenage zombie against … someone with the body of a Greek God?

"You're Hades, aren't you?" I ask.

"Indeed," the man says.

I could tell by the way Brent squeezes my hand that he isn't convinced. But I know I'm right.

Hades starts up the road. "I don't carry the Twilight Crystal around in my pocket. If you want it, you had best come along." He takes a few steps, then turns his head. "By the way, there has been a werewolf that is particularly active in this area lately. You might not want to stand around in plain view." He starts walking again.

This time, we hurry to follow him.

When we arrive at the citadel, the heavy door slides open as Hades approaches it. The inside is dimly lit by torch light and some other light I cannot identify. It seems to seep from the bricks near the low ceiling, like track lighting, but with no tracks or lights. We are in a wide hall, with no furniture, but there is a barred window at the far end.

"How did you know to come and look for us?" Deb asks. Suspicion tints her voice.

"The guards at the third gate told me you had passed through," Hades says. "It was only a matter of time before the inmates smelled fresh meat. Turning on the homing beacon the way you did was incredibly stupid."

I look at the floor. Nice tile. Very dirt colored. Must make the housework easier.

"The Twilight Crystal is on loan to Zariel's boss. Do not damage it. Do not give it to anyone but Zariel when you have finished with it. Am I understood?" Hades says.

His tone is pleasant enough, but there is an underlying threat. I wonder what he would do to us if we did lose the crystal. I don't want to go there.

"Oh, there you are!" A beautiful young woman comes into the hall. She's wearing a long white dress and a thick dark braid flops over her shoulder, almost to her nearly naked breast. "We've been expecting you. Please come along and sit down," she says.

"Seph, they don't have a lot of time," Hades says.

"Don't be silly. They can rest while you go and get the crystal," the woman says. Her voice is fresh and sunny. It makes me think of spring.

Hades tries to glare at her, but even I can see it is only pretend. She kisses him on the cheek as he walks by.

"Come along, come along now. You may call me Seph. Most people do." She gestures to a door at the end of the hall. I hadn't noticed it earlier.

We follow her down a corridor and finally through the green door. The room on the other side is filled with tropical plants. Birds flit through the leaves and call to each other. A white wicker couch, loveseat, and glass-topped coffee table sit in the middle of the room. Something that appears to be sunlight filters through the vegetation from the glass ceiling and walls.

"I do so love the conservatory," Seph tells us. "Reminds me of home, you see."

Deb looks stunned when a quetzal bird lands on her shoulder, its long green feather hanging down her back.

"Oh, dear," Seph says.

I see she is staring at Deb. Her right arm is mostly transparent all the way up to her elbow and her left hand has become completely clear.

"I have an elixir for that. It can't stop what is happening, but it will slow it down somewhat," she says.

"Yeah. Yes, ma'am. That would be fabulous," Deb says.

'Fabulous?' I can't believe Deb would use that word. Seph leaves.

"Makes me think of the Tropical Bird house at the zoo," I say.

"Yeah, a little bit," Deb says.

"You okay?" I ask her.

"Been better." She turns to examine the tree fern next to her.

"What do you think, Brent?" I ask. "You haven't said a word since we got here."

Before he can answer, Seph comes back in, holding a vial with a golden liquid in it. "Drink this," she tells Deb. It reminds me of the glitter drink Zariel gave her outside the gate at Alobic.

Deb looks at us and shrugs, then up-ends the container in her mouth. "Whoa! What is that stuff?"

Seph laughs. "Do you like it? It is mead and a few plant extracts."

Deb knits her eyebrows. "Mead?"

"Yes, honey wine," Seph says. Then she takes a little pouch from the folds of her dress. "Sprinkle this on the person whose dream you visit. It will make him or her remember." She hands the pouch to Deb.

"Why does it matter to you?" Brent asks.

"My mother spends most of her time in the Earth Realm. I wouldn't wish her to be injured," Seph says. She looks a little sad. Perhaps she's keeping her own secrets.

Hades comes into the room. "I was hoping I would find you here," he says to Seph. He appears to have forgotten that the three of us are also here, just for a moment.

"Here." He hands me a necklace. The chain looks pewter. It is attached to a polished iridescent sphere. The crystal is a greyish-tan color, with lots of darker veins running through it, and it shines blue and green as it moves. I put the chain around my neck and tuck the sphere into my shirt. I start to say 'thanks,' but Hades and Seph are in a heavy lip lock. I don't think he would hear me.

"Come on," I say. It would probably be frowned upon to tell the God of the Underworld to get a room in his own house.

"Wait," Hades says. "Anubis will walk you to the third gate. That crystal could be very dangerous if any of the inmates got hold of it." He turns back to his wife.

We leave the conservatory and walk back down the corridor. In the main hall, a man with a sleek, black dog's head waits for us.

"Greetings," he says. "I am Anubis."

I can't help but stare. The dog head seems to belong there – if it's a mask, it's a really good one. Even the mouth movement looks real.

We follow Anubis out of the citadel and down the path to the third gate. It looked so scary and forbidding, coming from the other side. Now that it is part of the way home. It looks beautiful.

There is a large, dead bush next to the road that suddenly starts shaking and quivering. Deb and I both jump, but Brent only watches it and Anubis ignores it altogether.

"Mew! Mew!" something in the bush says.

"Oh! It's a kitten!" I run towards it.

Anubis makes a grab for my arm, but I twist away from him.

"Mimi! Stop!" Brent yells at me.

"I'm not going to leave an innocent little animal in this hellhole!" I snarl back at him. I reach the grey tabby kitten and pluck it from the bush.

"But it isn't –" Brent's words are cut short by a low growl from the innocent little kitten.

Instead of a small purring fluff ball, I find that I am holding something that is getting larger and less fluffy by the second. Scales replace fur and long fangs replace tiny kitten teeth. I try to drop it, but I am trapped in its talons. A large frill around its head opens up, umbrella-like and it hisses at me, mouth wide open.

"Farge, let go!" shouts Anubis as he whacks the thing on the back with his staff. It takes several whacks before Farge lets go of me and slinks off.

"Are you crazy? What were you thinking?" Deb asks. "Don't you remember anything Master James said about the Eighth Plane?"

The last thing I need is her reminding me about how crap I was at all of the exercises we had to do. I open my mouth to respond, but Anubis puts his hand on my shoulder and gently shakes his head.

"What is done is done. No harm came of it, but be more careful next time. There are far worse things that Fage in this place," Anubis says.

"Thanks, Anubis. That was stupid, I know," I say, looking at the ground.

"You are most welcome, Mimi," he says.

I look up into his yellow wolf eyes. Even in the gloom, his black fur is glossy. He reminds me so much or Sierra's black German Shepherd , Major, that I half expect him to lick my face. I don't suppose Gods of the Dead do that much. Bad for their image.

We continue up the road until we get to the Gate of Terror.

The guards on top of the wall wave to us and the gate slides open. We run through it.

"Thank you, Anubis," I say.

"You are most welcome," he replies. Then he turns and starts back down the road.

After we thank the gatekeepers, we practically run down the passage to the second gate. After the murky half-light of the Eighth Plane, the brightness of the second gate is almost unbearable.

"They are back!" the woman says.

"I knew they would make it," the man says.

This gate slides open and we dash through. We thank the gatekeepers at the second gate and run toward the first. As we pound over the bridge, I see a furry hand reach up from underneath and feel around on the bridge.

"Troll!" I shout.

Brent jumps over it easily, but Deb barely makes it. Even though she has not gotten any more transparent, she isn't looking so good. I have enough space to just run around the hairy hand.

The troll, if that is what it is, roars, but we are already past it. Too bad for him. We keep running. The bamboo gate comes into view.

"Open! Open!" I yell.

The gate slides open.

"Congratulations. You made it," Invisi-voice says as we run through.

I have to stop before we get to the waterfall. I can't breathe. Funny, I hadn't thought I was breathing here before, but now I am gasping and coming up with nothing. I drop to my knees and find I am clutching the Twilight Crystal that is still hanging around my neck. I see a flurry of movement, Brent and Deb, doing something. I can hear voices, but I don't understand them. I feel as if I'm looking at them through those big glass bricks. Or water. I close my eyes. I don't have the energy to keep them open.

I feel floaty again. *Am I dreaming about flying?* I am free and happy. Then I notice Zariel is here. *Is he asking me for the time?* I look at my wrist. I don't have a watch.

"Mimi, it is not yet time," he says. "Go back."

I am suddenly pulled back, as if I'm nothing more than a piece of popcorn up a vacuum cleaner hose. I open my eyes and I see Sthenno above me. Little snake heads, lots of them, sway in the dark of her hood. She's holding a Cloak of Shadows. I suppose it is mine.

"Welcome back," she says.

"Where did I go?" I ask. I'm not thinking clearly right now.

"It doesn't matter. You will go there again, sooner or later. Just not right now," Sthenno says.

I wish I could go back now. I sit up and look around. I think we are in the cave behind the waterfall. I wonder how I will get down without falling into Ahemait's waiting jaws in the state I am in. Then I realize that I am in Sthenno's cottage. Zariel is standing not far away.

"How did you get here?" I ask.

"Here and there are relative, not absolute," he answers.

"I knew you were going to say something like that," I reply. "Where are Deb and Brent?"

"They are going back to the city. Sitnalta. Persephone's elixir has stabilized Deb, but it won't last much longer," Zariel says. "The disintegration cannot be stopped, but it can be delayed."

"What will happen to her?" I ask.

"She will move up a level. That is how it works. As the grosser particles deteriorate, the soul is freed of them and moves to a higher plane," Zariel says.

"That's good, right?" I ask.

"Yes and no. It is good for Deb, but if Laura Samuels sees her as she is on a higher level, there is nothing to inspire her to start the Rhiannon Foundation to help troubled girls," Zariel says.

"Couldn't she just wear her Cloak of Shadows?" I ask.

"She would only appear as a monster," Sthenno says.

There is a knock at the door. Zariel goes to answer it and steps outside. A short time later, he comes back in, flanked by a man in green tights with a bow slung across his back.

"We have a problem," Zariel says. "Lucas has taken Deborah. Robin," he gestures to the archer, "has been unable to find Brent."

Chapter 12
66.67 Percent

Why would anyone want to take Deb?" I don't mean it as in 'why would they want *her*,' but '*why* would they want her.' "And what about Brent? Could they have taken him, too? Or is he just hiding?" I remember the slimy guy that approached us in the Seventh Plane.

"I don't know about Brent. But I know why Lucas covets Deborah. Lucas is what you might think of as a vampire. He was not an especially nice person when he had a motorcycle accident over a year ago. In the Earth Realm, he has been in a persistent vegetative state since that time. His astral body is stuck on the Seventh Plane because the connection to his physical body keeps replenishing the heavier particles as they burn off. He has become addicted to the negative emotions that are rife on the Seventh Plane. Because Deborah is oozing fear and pain and anger, she is irresistible to him. There are many others in a similar state, but Deborah was kind to him once, and that gave him a connection to her. He already had these tendencies, but they have been amplified on the Seventh Plane. If his body remains much longer on the respirator, he will be doomed to the Eighth Plane."

"Can't you just get someone to unplug the respirator?" I ask.

"It is not that simple," Zariel says. "We must get back to Sitnalta. You should be safe at the Depot until the other two can be located."

Sthenno has been sitting quietly all this time, listening. "I wish that I could go with you. I cannot. However, I can send for my sister Euryale and ask her to meet you in the Seventh City."

"Thank you, Sthenno. The gorgons have long been kind and helpful to the Agents."

"You are welcome. The Agents have long been kind and helpful to the gorgons."

Zariel, silent Robin, and I leave Sthenno's cabin and head back to the city. I have folded my Cloak of Shadows up as small as it will go (and that is pretty small) and put it in my pocket.

We head back to the city. As we pass the farm, the elementals flicking from form to form give me the creeps. They don't seem very happy to me, and I wonder if these waves of random thoughts hurt or bother them. But they have no way to do anything about it, like seaweed in the tide. Not unlike my house, where my mother does everything on a whim. Nothing sticks (except opera) and nothing else makes much sense.

Back at the Depot, that grimy building where we met Maya with her Cloaks of Shadows, I sit in an uneven folding chair by the front desk. *Where are Deb and Brent? Are they okay? If they aren't, how am I going to find Laura Samuels and inspire her all by myself? I've never inspired anyone to do anything.* I'm not doing myself any favors, here. *Of course they're okay. They just took the scenic route. That's what Mom always says, anyway.*

I'm not sure if the man behind the desk is a receptionist, a security guard, or a concierge. Or maybe all of the above. Zariel and Robin have been gone seemingly forever. I can't sit still any longer.

"So," I say, walking up to the desk. "What is there to do around here, uhh..." I look to see if there is a name tag on his shirt or a name plate on his desk.

"You may call me Stan," he says, looking up from his battered paperback.

"Stan. Does that make you Stanley the Angel?" I say. That could be the title of a book for little kids.

"No." He doesn't appear insulted or anything. "I am Stannonopholes, Agent of the Lords of Karma. Agents and angels are both of the Devic Kingdom, but are not the same."

Stan looks at me as if he is waiting for me to ask him something else.

"Oh I see. You're brothers and sisters or something," I say.

"It is more that we are cousins. But there is no male or female. We are neither, or perhaps both, depending on how one looks at it," Stan says.

I find it disturbing that I try to imagine that. "Right, okay. So what is there to do around here?"

"I recommend against all of the pastimes of the denizens of this plane," Stan says.

"I wish I could go for a walk or something," I say, hoping he will make some suggestions.

"That is not advisable without an escort," Stan tells me.

"Maybe you could be my escort?" I ask. I almost feel like I am making an illegal business transaction.

"Not at this time," he says. He looks back down at his book. Our conversation, such as it was, is ended.

I am bored mindless, so I walk around the Depot. There isn't much to it: the lobby, the conference room, a couple of shabby offices, and a storeroom, which is stacked with disintegrating boxes.

I hear the door creak open, and I poke my head around the corner to see who it is.

"Brent!" I shout. I run to him and throw my arms around his neck. I hadn't realized that I missed him so much. Without his Cloak of Shadows, he is kind of cute.

He gives me a cursory hug, then gently pushes me away from him. He looks a bit dirty and disheveled, but otherwise okay. He is carrying a picnic basket, and I can hear whimpering coming from inside of it. Poor Sammie.

"Hey, Mimi. Is Zariel here?" he asks.

"Nope. Just me and Stan," I say, nodding my head toward the man at the front desk.

"Damn. I know where Deb is. There are a bunch of them. I don't know what they're going to do to her, but they grabbed her while we were on the way back here, and she looks real scared," Brent pants. He carefully sets the basket down by the front desk.

"A bunch of who?" I ask.

"Zombies!" he replies, his fingers stretching out as if he's hurling the word with them.

"Where are they? I will alert Zariel. He has gone to meet Euryale, and should return here shortly," Stan says.

"I followed them, hiding behind old cars and stuff. There is a big abandoned shopping mall. Lucas has the big space on the second floor," Brent says.

"I know of that place," Stan says.

I feel Brent's hand slide around my wrist.

"Good," he says. "They can meet us there."

Brent pulls me along behind him as he rushes for the door. I follow him, not because I have to, but because I want to help Deb. None of this is her fault. Well, not most of it, anyway. It would have been a lot easier if she hadn't offed herself and we could have just had the fight in the food court of the mall.

It isn't difficult to keep to the shadows as we scurry through the degraded streets like lost mice. The decrepit mall isn't more than a dozen blocks from the Depot. It might have looked nice, back when it was new, but I'm not sure it was ever was. Perhaps things on the Seventh Plane are created run down and used up. It does make me think of a dystopian version of the Silverton Mall close to our house, though. Didn't Zariel say something about reflections and shadows? I wonder…

Brent and I scamper up the parking structure. It overlooks the collapsed roof in the middle of the mall. We can see down into the second floor, but not well and not everything. I can see Lucas, though. There is a pile of rags on the floor, and some ugly people mill around it. Brent had called them zombies, but I'm not sure about that. Some of them do seem to be decaying corpses, but others don't look especially human. More than a few of them have four, six, or eight legs. Lucas says something, but I cannot understand him. The goon squad crowds around him, as if listening for instructions. They laugh and moan and I feel disgusted.

The pile of rags moves. It isn't rags. It is Deb. She looks like hell.

Deb sits up, but she is very shaky. Lucas sees her and gets down on his hands and knees. He appears to be licking her face. She groans and tries to move away from him but she is too weak. She leans away and topples over.

"We have got to do something," I say. "We can't let him keep…doing that. He is going to kill her."

"Agreed. We need a plan," Brent says.

"A plan, is it?" a gravelly voice says from behind Brent.

We both look up and see three creatures standing around us. We are trapped against the wall by something that I cannot tell if it is a human-like frog or a frog-like human, a gaunt man with lank and greasy hair, and Humpty Dumpty's evil twin. The frog thing licks its lips with a fat tongue, revealing rotting teeth. It sniffs the air and smiles with half closed eyes.

Chapter 13
Bad Day at the Mall

I am frozen with disgust. Brent grabs both my hands and pulls me towards him. "Jump!" he whispers near my ear. I look over the railing. It's a long way down and I don't want to do it. I look at the Three Grossketeers, and I like that scenario even less. We scramble to the railing and hurl ourselves over.

I squeeze my eyes shut, expecting a bone crunching impact. But there is barely even a bump.

"Come on, Mimi! Get up!" Brent screams.

A horde of horror movie extras moves towards us. I half expect to hear them shouting, "Brains!" But they don't. They make laughing, groaning, gurgling sounds that are much more frightening. I don't know what they will do to us if they catch us, and I really don't want to find out.

Brent takes off running at top speed. Towards the mall. Panicking, I don't know where else to go, so I follow him.

The glass in the mall entry sliding door was broken out so long ago that there aren't even any slivers of it left scattered on the floor or clinging to the frame. We run through it and down a wide corridor. The corridor leads to the central area of the mall. Surprised monsters look up from whatever horrible things they are doing as we streak past them. We dodge around something pig-like and down a corridor marked "Employees Only."

Part of the external wall has collapsed and I can see what passes for daylight around here. But it gives me an idea.

"Brent, you still got your Cloak of Shadows?" I whisper.

"Sure," he says.

"Put it on. We'll pass as some of them," I say. I nod my head towards the hole. "They'll think we got out that way."

"Good plan," he says.

It only takes a moment to get our cloaks out and on, but it is not a moment too soon.

The horde is moving faster than a zombie shuffle, but they aren't going to break any land speed records.

Frogman is at the front of the pack. He sniffs the air and looks at us suspiciously. I try to look mournful and nod towards the hole. Some of the others climb out through it, but Froggy seems suspicious. He stares at us for a long time before he, too, leaves.

Brent and I try to look casual as we saunter back into the mall. We get our bearings and adjust our course to the big space on the second floor.

The Cloak of Shadows makes me feel heavy and sleepy. I find it hard to walk without gasping and groaning. I sound just like the locals.

It isn't long before we come to the area with the ruined roof. We climb up the stairs on the opposite side of the mall from Lucas. We find ourselves, ironically enough, in the vacated food court. Checking over our shoulders, we crouch behind one of the serving counters to stay out of sight.

"Okay, now what?" I whisper.

"I don't know. I'm thinking," Brent says.

"Do you think we can wait until Zariel and Euryale, get here?" I ask.

"*We* probably can, but I don't think Deb can," he says.

I'm sure he's right. I don't know what to do. In the movies, they usually have some kind of distraction at this point, and the heroes are able to swoop in and make the rescue. I peek around the edge of the counter to stare at the rubble. One end of a long girder rests on the railing near Lucas' hideout. The other sits on a pile of junk, only a couple of feet high on the bottom floor. It forms a big slide. A skinny slide, but still.

"Brent, does that look like a quick getaway slide to you?" I ask.

He moves over and looks over my shoulder. "Hmm," he says. "Maybe."

Brent looks at the rubble. Then he looks at the hideout. "Here is my idea," he says. "You walk past Lucas' group with your cloak on. Then take it off and get them to chase you. There's a fire stair at the end of this corridor."

I see the 'Exit' sign and a picture of stairs on the wall.

"Now, while they are after you, I will keep my cloak on and grab Deb. We'll get down to the first floor whichever way we can. There has got to be an exit downstairs. We'll make a run for it and meet up back at the Depot."

What was I thinking about a distraction earlier? I am not wild about this plan, but I don't have a better one.

An awful slurping sound comes from Lucas' hideout. I am glad I can't vomit just now.

"Let's go," Brent says.

I get up and stumble down the debris-strewn hall. A few of Lucas' minions glance at me as I pass, but don't really notice. When I think I have enough of a head start, I take off my cloak and shove it in my pocket.

"Whoo hoo!" I shout.

The minions look up this time. Lucas snarls, "Get her!"

One of them crawls up the wall, like a spider. I am so fascinated by its weirdness and speed that I almost forget to run. I sprint to the door on the far end, just ahead of the pack. There is a piece of pipe lying on the floor in the stairwell. I use it to jam the door as best I can. It works on TV, anyway. I pelt down the stairs and fly out onto the bottom floor.

I hear yelling and roaring. Someone is clearly not happy. I see a flash of movement and color – Deb's purple hair. There is a clatter and a crash in the stairwell. Guess the pipe didn't hold them for long. I race after Brent and Deb. The twisted frame of a side exit door hangs by a rusty thread and we power our way through it, to the outside. The Twilight Crystal under my shirt catches just a little on the metal, but not enough to slow me down, and I check the chain hasn't snapped without breaking stride.

We have come out on a different side of the mall from the one where we came in. I'm not sure which way will get us back to the Depot.

"Go, go, go!" growls Brent.

I just pick a direction and run. After a few blocks, we pause behind a shrub to take off Brent's Cloak of Shadows. It's slowing him down too much – he's already half carrying Deb.

Now I follow his lead as we weave in between buildings and run around houses. We're running out of city, now. We have somehow managed to miss the Depot. Lucas's goons seem to have stopped chasing us, at least for now.

The more we look for the Depot, the further away we seem to get from it. I clutch the Twilight Crystal in my left hand.

Then I see it. A little tea room with a magenta awning. At least I think it is a tea room because there is a big statue of a teapot and a cup on the roof. Inside the windows, magenta velvet curtains sport gold trim and tassels. It could have fallen right out of the 1800s. Except for the neon 'Open' sign.

"In there," I say.

Brent doesn't argue and I pull the door open. We trot inside. Brent helps Deb into one of the chairs.

"Hello?" he calls.

No one responds, but we can hear cheesy player piano music coming from the back. We follow the so-called music and end up in a little party room. The music stops. A woman in a long red dress carrying a stack of menus greets us. She keeps looking at us as if we're strange insects. Never mind that she has four arms instead of the usual two.

"Down there! Down there!" she says. That is just weird. Not only that, her voice is deep and distorted, a movie space alien voice. She hands us each a menu.

I think it is odd to find a restaurant on the Seventh Plane, but here it is. I look at the menu, but I can't read any of the words.

"Hmm?" I say.

Brent shrugs. Deb is too out of it to care.

"Could I get jasmine green tea?" I ask. Surely, any tea room would have that.

The woman looks at me like I asked for a cup of motor oil with hot sauce.

"Maybe we should just go. Deb, don't worry about Sammie. I left her in her basket at the Depot," Brent says.

I look at Deb. She looks really rough. Her skin has turned a greyish, almost corpse-like color and her hair is matted. A bald, bloody spot above her eye marks where a clump of it has been torn out. "Maybe we should rest a little longer," I say. Surely Lucas and his goonquad won't try to come in and grab us out of a restaurant.

Brent follows my gaze. "Yeah, maybe so."

Deb leans her head against the wall behind her.

"Is there anything we can do? I was afraid that Lucas was going to kill you." I ask her.

She shakes her head. "I'm already dead, remember? Thanks, though. Thanks for getting me out of there."

"Sure," I say. "No problem."

Deb absently rubs her left arm just above the elbow. There is a little dark bump there, possibly a bruise or maybe some dirt. I shake my head. I think I see it move. That can't be; must be a trick of the light.

I start to feel very light-headed and a little bit dizzy. I close my eyes and hold on to the edge of the table for balance. I suddenly feel as if I am falling up.

Chapter 14
The Busgirl

I open my eyes to see what is happening. Nothing looks different. Except now, there's a man in the room and he comes to the table. He has the same distorted voice as the woman in the red dress and the same number of arms.

"Blishtashl wite? Nee Nee? Reet!"

I shake my head. "I am sorry. I don't understand you," I say. I am uncomfortable. My chest hurts and for the first time since I came here, I can smell something other than water. And it smells like bad breath. The man shrugs and walks away.

"What was that about?" Brent asks.

"I don't know, Mimi. Was he trying to say your name? That's almost how it sounded," Deb says.

The woman in the red dress comes back. She is carrying a teapot in one hand, a cup and saucer in another and a box of sugar packets in a third. She sets it all down on the table and walks away, saying nothing.

I pour some tea into the cup. It is clear purple with little green things floating in it that appear to be bugs. Bugs in my tea is usually a pretty big turn off.

A young woman in an apron walks by with a tub full of dirty dishes. Which is odd, because we're the only ones here. As she gets level with me, her head doesn't turn, but her face rotates around to look at me.

"Don't drink the tea!" she whispers.

Then her face is where it belongs and she has already passed me.

"Yeah. Thanks, but I wasn't going to," I say.

"Who are you talking to?" Deb asks.

"Didn't you hear her?" I ask.

"No," she says.

"I didn't, either," Brent says.

"Deb, are you okay to move? I just want to get out of here. This place is freaking me out," I say.

"Never better," Deb says.

That Deb. Sarcastic to the end.

"I'm fine with that," Brent says. "Let's just make sure the coast is clear first."

We all stand up and look around.

I notice an *EXIT* sign just over a cave entrance. I'm sure that isn't where we came in. It seems wrong, but the sign does say *EXIT*, so we start towards it. The busgirl comes to wipe down our table.

"That is not the exit you want," she says. "You want that one." She points in the opposite direction from the cave exit.

"What difference does it make?" says Deb.

"A world of difference. A whole world," she says.

"Okay," I say, suddenly anxious to do something rather than sit around and talk.

We go through the exit pointed out by the busgirl. We're back to the front of the building. No one is around, so we look out the windows to see if anyone is on the street. I am guessing that Lucas won't be happy about losing his prize. The frog man and Humpty Evil are walking by on the other side of the street.

"Why don't we ask someone for directions to the Depot before we go outside?" I ask.

"Fine by me, but who are you going to ask?" says Brent.

"Stay here," I say.

I go back into the main room, and see the busgirl just finishing up our table.

"Excuse me?" I say.

"Yes?" she answers.

"How do we get to the Depot from here?" I ask.

"Perhaps you would like to go somewhere else?" she asks.

"No, not really," I say.

"It will be watched," she says.

I hadn't thought of that. "So where should we go?"

"Why not to the Sixth City? Most creatures from this level cannot survive there."

"And how do we get there?" I ask.

"Go to the end of the street and follow the road that goes up. You are already near the edge of this plane. You shouldn't have much trouble eluding capture," she says.

I'm not sure who or what she is, but she seems to be on our side. At least, I hope so. "Thank you," I say.

I go back to the front of the restaurant and I tell Brent and Deb what the busgirl said.

"Are you sure she can be trusted?" Brent says. "I think we should go back to the Depot."

"If you were the monster squad, where would you look for us?" I ask.

Brent crosses his arms. "You'd better be right."

Deb only nods. We start out the front door and find that the frog man and Humpty Evil have doubled back and are coming up the road the way we need to go. This time, they spot us.

"Run!" Brent yells.

We scatter, and I hope we will be able to find each other later. I run until I see scraggly, barely-alive trees. I throw myself down behind one. I wait, but there don't seem to be creatures of any kind about, good, bad or indifferent.

At least my chest has stopped hurting. For now. Felt like someone was hitting me, or shoving me against something hard.

I move into deeper shade.

I am just about to get up and go looking for Deb and Brent, when I see them. They are moving from bush to rock, keeping under as much cover as possible. I can see Froggy. He is a ways behind them and I don't believe he can see them, but I can't tell. If I shout at them, he'll know where all three of us are.

I flatten myself against the ground and try to blend into the shadow as much as I can. There is not much I can do now, except watch.

Froggy gets closer to Brent and Deb. He obviously doesn't see them, but I don't think they see him, either. They look like they are getting ready to move. Dammit. I look around and see a rock about the size of a tangerine. I was never any good at sports. Hope I don't bean Brent or Deb with it.

There is a pile of trash not too far from Froggy, in the opposite direction from Deb and Brent. I focus on that and lob the rock as hard as I can. It works. Froggy hop-shuffles over to investigate. Deb and Brent duck down. I know they can see him now.

"Pretty good throw, for a girl."

I roll over and see a barrel-chested bald guy standing near my feet. His ragged pants, and that is all he is wearing, are slung far too low on his hips (please don't turn around – I don't think I can handle dead guy plumber's crack) and he has more of a bundt cake than a muffin top.

"Dude! Who dressed you? The Damnation Army?" I ask.

He scowls at me.

"Seriously. I hope you have a shirt somewhere. That outfit is criminal," I say. I'm hoping that Brent and Deb can hear me and at least get away. With any luck, they will stop to rescue me on the way out.

He scowls even harder, which I didn't think was do-able. "Criminal, huh? I can show you criminal."

Then he happens to look up and see Deb and Brent crouching behind the pile of trash.

"Hey!" he shouts. The other two are over there!"

He grabs my arm and drags me to my feet. Then he wraps his meaty fingers around the back of my neck. I don't want him touching me, and it's very awkward trying to walk and be steered by him.

Froggy, and a man in a business suit, have yanked Brent to his feet. Deb gets up, very slowly, on her own. Froggy is squeezing the back of Brent's neck, too. I suppose Deb looks too weak and helpless for them to be worried about her running away.

They keep us separated as they herd us along the dismal forest of mostly lifeless trees. Dead grass sighs under our feet for a while, until it gives way to bare dirt. It isn't too far before we come to a ring of standing stones, maybe eight feet high or so. They're a mottled grey with worrisome red spots and streaks.

They take us inside the circle where a telephone pole-sized stake stands at the center. Froggy picks up a silver rope from behind one of the standing stones. It glows faintly, and the way it twists and shimmers as he carries it over to us almost makes it look alive. They tie my left hand to Brent's right hand, his left arm to Deb's remaining right arm and her left arm to my right, so that we are in a loose circle around the pole – we aren't tightly bound, but we cannot go anywhere, either. Henchmen start arriving in small clots. There may be as many as twenty hanging around now.

"How long do you think this will take?" asks the man in the business suit.

"Probably not long, once Lucas arrives," Froggy says with a wicked smirk.

Even as he says this, the crowd of minions begins to part. Lucas is striding up to us. He looks a little bent out of shape. I don't suppose he's planning to use that machete to trim the shrubbery.

I can feel Brent furiously trying to get something out of his pocket. Finally, he succeeds. It's the little ebony box that the centaur gave him. This certainly qualifies as a tight spot.

"You!" Lucas snarls. "I'm gonna enjoy drinking you." It feels like he's looking specifically at me, but he could mean 'you' in the plural.

"Help me open this," Brent whispers.

He holds the bottom of the box and I try to slide the lid open. It's locked. There must be a catch somewhere.

Lucas is almost to the standing stones.

I fumble the box right out of Brent's hand. But I slap it hard, trapping it against the pole. The rope is smooth and hard, digging into my wrist.

Lucas is coming through the standing stones, raising the long knife as he closes in. Red energy sizzles and crackles along the edges of it.

As my fingers scrabble to work the box up the stake, they find a tiny metal pin. I push it down and the lid slides open.

"What's inside?" Brent whispers.

Lucas grabs the machete handle with both hands now, and sweeps it high above his head.

I slide a small piece of paper out of the box. *Is that a ticket?*

In the blink of an eye, the three of us are on a beach. We're still tied together, but the sun is warm and the water is blue.

Chapter 15
The Last Resort

W here are we?" I ask the ocean waves.
"You're at the Last Resort, of course," A female voice says behind me. "Have a drink!"

"How about you untie us, okay?" Deb asks.

"As you wish," the voice answers.

I hear sawing, steel on fabric, and feel a little tugging from Brent and Deb. They are free from each other, but still tied to me. Next she cuts Deb and I apart, and finally Brent and I. We all rub our wrists and arms and thank her.

The woman is wearing a wide brimmed straw hat, white cotton shirt and white cropped pants. Just behind her is a Tiki bar with rows of hurricane glasses hanging from a rack on the low ceiling. The fronds on the thatched roof ripple in the sea breeze. The bitter laugh of white seagulls drifts down to us from the top of a large palm tree. I feel as though we've landed in the middle of a cruise ship commercial.

I could get used to this. I think. Guess it depends on what happened to the other resorts, though, if this is the last one. Or maybe it is just the newest. No, that would make it the Latest Resort.

"So, we just had a ticket, and that's all it took to get here?" Brent asks. "I know you said this is called the Last Resort, but what is this place? I don't really understand."

Deb is oddly quiet. She doesn't seem at all concerned or curious. She stands with her feet in the path of the incoming tide and leans over to pick up sea shells. I hope she's not about to disappear on us.

"The Last Resort is where you come when you have nowhere else to turn, no place else to go. It is where you come for a little rest when you are in trouble," the woman says. She smiles, and everything seems brighter, like sun breaking free of clouds. "How about that drink, now?"

"Sure, why not?" I say, even though I think it's very odd, since we are in the Astral Realm. Still, I'm happy to put Froggy and Lucas and all of the Seventh Plane behind us. "What drinks have you got?"

"I have a cup of good cheer in mango, pineapple or coconut flavors," she says.

"Mango, please," I say.

"Pineapple," Brent says suspiciously, as if he suspects this is all a trick.

Deb doesn't make a request, so the woman goes to the Tiki bar, and fills two of the hurricane glasses from an old-fashioned soda fountain. A glass in each hand, she returns to us.

"Mango," she says, handing one to me. "Pineapple," she says, handing the other glass to Brent. I'm glad she knows which is which, because they both look the same to me.

"Whoa! This is fantastic!" I say after my first sip. The drink is thick and cold, and tastes like summer.

"Cool," says Brent after he tries his.

"So, how are we able to drink this? I thought that in the Astral Realm, we didn't need anything to eat or drink," I say.

"Ah. Need and want are two different things. You don't need to eat or drink here. But you can, if you like. You can do most things here that you can do in the Earth Realm, and many that you can't," she says.

I think I hear someone singing, so I turn around. A head ducks under water so quickly I can only just tell it's a head.

"Ah, the mermaids. Enjoy their singing, but stay away from them. They're nothing but trouble, those girls," the woman tells us, shaking her head.

"How long can we stay?" I ask. I could easily just stay here, not worrying about getting into someone's dreams or saving the world.

"It says on your ticket," the woman replies.

"What happens when time is up?" Brent asks.

"You will be escorted to the gate," the woman says.

"What is on the other side of the gate?" I ask.

"That is not for me to say – it depends on you," the woman says. "Enjoy your time while you're here!" She then walks back toward the Tiki bar.

I go to Deb.

"Look at the pretty shells I found," she says. She sounds like a small child, showing treasures to her mother.

"Yes," I say. "Very nice." I watch her for a bit. She frolics in the surf and it seems that a lot of the hurt and pain has lifted from her. When she looks up at me, I notice that her eyebrow barbell is gone. I am not sure this is a good thing. What if she gets too purified and Laura Samuels doesn't feel inspired to help her when we finally get into her dream? Will this whole adventure be all for nothing? Does this make me a bad person?

"I can't find anything on the ticket that says how long we can stay," Brent says. He has wandered up to me and is now standing just a little too close.

May as well enjoy it while we're here. I suppose they'll come for us soon enough. I see a hammock underneath some palm trees a little further back from the beach. I go to it and set my drink down on the little end table. It takes a few tries, but I finally get in. I pick up my drink and relax into the bed.

Deb has waded almost knee deep into the surf. Maybe it is just the waves, but I think I see something dark in the water, just below the surface. I keep looking. There it is again. That really harshes my mellow.

"Deb?" I have to raise my voice above the waves. Even so, she doesn't hear me. "Deb!" I try again, louder.

Deb looks up at me, her face soft and dreamy.

"Deb, could you come out of the water?" I try to keep my voice even and non-panicky.

A dorsal fin breaks the surface of a wave.

"Brent! Get Deb out of the water!" I scream.

I try getting out of the hammock, but I get tripped up and crash into the sand. Brent has waded in after Deb.

"What's all the fuss about?" The woman in white has suddenly reappeared.

"There's a shark in the water!" I say.

"A shark? No, that's just a dolphin," she says. One side of her mouth twitches up into an almost-smile.

As if on cue, the dolphin breaches. Light sparkles off the water dripping from its fins as it arcs into the air, liquid gemstones scattering from its body. I wonder where his friends are. Don't dolphins usually travel in pods?

I give up on the hammock, and opt for a chaise lounge nearer to the Tiki bar. The warm air and the soughing of the sea make me feel sleepy. I close my eyes and just doze a little.

I sit up with a start. I am sure someone has just called my name. But Deb is playing in the water and Brent is scouring the beach. My chest hurts again, throbbing in a clear rhythm. I feel like the air is being pushed out of me. I get up and walk around to see if that helps. It does, so I walk over to where Deb is wading and looking for shells.

She is not quite waist deep. Is that her singing? Someone is. Deb doesn't see me, standing behind her in the sand.

"I don't know. I don't really like swimming," Deb says.

"Don't like swimming? Don't be so silly. It's fun. And besides, what could happen to you?" a voice says. I can't see who said that.

Deb takes a step further out into the water. "That's it. Come on. It'll be fun," the unseen voice says.

"Deb? Who are you talking to?" I ask.

She turns around. Behind her, I see a face glaring at me, just for a moment, before it slips under the water. Good thing looks can't kill.

"Oh," Deb says. "It was just a girl who lives in the sea. She wouldn't tell me her name. She wanted me to go swimming with her."

"Remember, the lady said the mermaids were dangerous? Why don't we go and build a sand castle or something?" I say.

Deb shrugs. "Okay," she says.

I take one last look at the water before I turn around. Nothing breaks the calm of the aquamarine sea.

"Come on, let's go up on the beach a little," I say.

I go up as far away from the water as I can get and still have wet enough sand to build a castle. We find some large scallop shells and start digging the moat. I work on the tunnel under the bridge to the island and Deb builds the castle. She has gotten a lot more done than I expected her to by the time I stop to take a look at what she is doing.

Her castle has walls and turrets and windows. There are even stairs inside. I don't know how she has done all that without sand molds. Even with plastic molds, mine never came out anywhere near that good.

"That is very fancy. How did you do that?" I ask.

"I'm not sure, okay? I imagined what I wanted, then as I shaped the sand, it just came out that way," Deb says.

"Hey, guys! Look at this!" Brent shouts.

He comes running toward us, holding a large shell in his hands. When he gets to Deb's castle, he stops. Carefully, he sets down a heavy, creamy white conch shell.

"It's a Yellow Helmet," Brent says. "Very rare."

A shadow falls over the superb shell. We all look up to find a soldier standing there. His face under his hat is stern, and appears human.

"It's time," he says.

"Oh, man!" Deb says, dusting sand off of her pants.

"Can I keep the shell?" Brent asks.

"I'm sorry, but no," says the soldier.

We follow him up the beach, towards the buildings and trees. The resort has many flagstone walking paths and sitting areas that are landscaped with lush tropical plants. Double red hibiscus flowers the size of dinner plates search for the sun. Large-leafed banana trees shade gingers which sport white and pink flowers. I think I could wander around in this place for hours. We pass a building – a hotel, perhaps – on the left. The guard stops at a large wrought iron gate.

"This way, please," he says, holding the gate open.

We shuffle through it glumly, and find ourselves on a barren plain. I turn to look longingly at the tropical paradise, but there is no sign of the gate, let alone the ocean.

"What the hell?" asks Brent.

I look closely at Deb. She looks a little softer, but maybe she will still inspire Laura.

A city rises in the near distance. We walk quickly towards it, well as quickly as we can walk with Deb. As we get closer, we see that it is the Sixth City, Udanax. Not much to recommend it, but still, better than being anywhere near the Seventh Plane.

"Do they have a Depot or something like it here? Maybe we can find Zariel," I ask.

Deb stumbles and nearly falls over. Brent catches her. Her arms are transparent, all the way up to her sleeves. She is not going to make it to Laura Samuels' dream if we don't get there soon.

"I think so. I believe there is one on every level," Brent says.

"I know where it is," Deb whispers.

We follow Deb to a reasonably clean building. It is about three times the size of the Depot on the Seventh Plane. There's no graffiti or rusty flashing on this building.

Something white falls out of the tree onto Deb. Then another and another.

"Get it off! Get it off!" Deb screams.

Brent and I both run to her and start grabbing at the squirming nasties that have attached themselves to Deb. I grab the tail of one and have to let go. It's a maggot the size of a large house cat. I start hitting it and punching it. Brent has a maggot tail in each hand and he is pulling as hard as he can. The door to the Depot swings open and a woman comes running out, carrying a metal container with a hose.

"Wretched larvae!" she says as she sprays Deb down with what looks like a fire extinguisher. "We have had a terrible problem with them lately."

The larvae let go of Deb as soon as the foam hits them and wriggle through the air, back up into the tree.

"Get her inside," the woman says.

She holds the door open for us. Brent and I help Deb up. With one arm on each of our shoulders, she hobbles into the building.

"Larvae. Gross. What are they?" I ask as soon as we set Deb down into a couch.

"Hold that thought," the woman says. "I need to take a look at your friend."

She carefully examines at Deb. Where the maggots have chewed on her, the woman paints on a white paste. It reminds me of Liquid Paper. Then she gives her something to drink.

"Lie down, sweetie, and have a little rest," the woman tells Deb.

Deb swings her feet up onto the couch and rests her head on one of the fancy orange satin pillows with beaded trim. The woman shoos Brent and I over to the front desk.

"I am Bethany, by the way," she tells us. She doesn't bother asking our names. "I have to tell you, your friend is not in real good shape. But I suppose you already knew that."

"Yes, we did," I say.

"Well, I can only do field hospital work. You really need to get back to the Fourth City, to Sitnalta, ASAP. I have dressed her wounds and given her an energy replenishment drink – that will get her on her feet – but she really needs to get to the Fourth level."

"What happens if she doesn't get there in time?" I ask.

"Well, that's the sad thing. She will become trapped between planes. She will not be ready mentally or spiritually to ascend to a higher plane, but physically, all of her grosser matter will have been removed. And how do you think she will go about trying to replace that gross matter? She'll steal it from others, that's how. Driven by need, she, too, will become a vampire."

"That sucks," says Brent.

"This is no time to be cracking jokes," I admonish him.

"What? I am just saying," he says.

"We have mostly been able to keep them down on the Seventh Plane, but there is one called Lucas who has made some forays out. That is what has the larvae all stirred up," said Bethany.

"We've met Lucas. Can't you just kill them, the larvae?" Brent asks.

Bethany cocks her head to one side, as if he just asked her if she could fly to the moon. "No. Even if they could die, it wouldn't be right. The larvae are part of the astral clean-up crew — they eat the discarded husks of those who have moved on to a higher plane. The problem is, when we have a vampire draining energy out of folks, they look like husks to the larvae. It is not their fault."

"Okay. Eww. And by the way?" I say. "Lucas just tried to eat us."

"Sad story, that. His GA says that the family is just about ready to take him off life support."

"GA?" Brent asks.

"Guardian Angel, boy," Bethany says.

Brent raises his eyebrows at being called 'boy,' but doesn't say anything.

"So what is with the secret pow-wow over here?" Deb is standing behind Bethany.

"Do you feel well enough to travel?" Bethany asks her.

"I guess so," Deb says, shrugging.

"Do you have a case worker Agent?" Bethany looks at me.

"Sure. Zariel," I say.

"Oh," Bethany says, nodding. "You must be the dream seekers, then. Does Zariel know where you are? Can he escort you?"

"He went to find Eurayale," Brent says. "We don't know if he's back yet. We had some complications."

"I'm not surprised," Bethany says. "I will contact him and let him know where you are. I don't think your companion can wait until his return."

Bethany sprays a rainbow colored mist on us. "Larvae repellent," she says.

"It smells exactly the same as the big pink flowers my grandma used to grow," Deb says, her voice is soft and sleepy.

I can smell nothing but a faint minty smell, like old gum that is all chewed up.

"I will escort you to the main road. Just follow it up to the Fifth City and pass on through to the Fourth. If Zariel is your Agent, I assume you've been there before," Bethany says.

"Does Zariel have an office in the Fifth City?" Brent asks.

"Not specifically," Bethany answers. "He operates primarily from the Fourth City."

"Yeah. The ghost town with all the crystal buildings," I say.

"Ghost town? It is bustling with folk of all sorts, human and non-human both. Because your vibrations don't match theirs, you can't see them. A few of them might be able to see you, though."

"Why can we see all the buildings, then?" Deb says in her too-soft voice. I kind of miss the old loud one.

"Buildings are different. The buildings on the Fourth Plane are different from the ones on the fifth, sixth and Seventh Planes. You can see the Fifth City because it matches your vibrations. All can see the bones of the Fourth City. But only those who live there can see the true splendor of the place."

We walk for a few more blocks before we reach the edge of the city. I see the mountains rising ahead of us and I think of the Fountain of Sirin.

"Stay on the road. As long as you don't wander off of it, you will be fine. There are precious few creatures above the Seventh Plane that would actively try to hurt you, and all of them are on the Sixth Plane."

I look at Deb. There is no small irony that she looks like death warmed over.

"Oh, and this is for you." Bethany hands a walking stick to Deb.

It's made of polished wood, but something about the twisted shape and the mottled color reminds me of a snake. Deb takes the silver-tipped stick and says thank you. It gives me the creeps.

"Safe journey. Zariel will meet you in Sitnalta. Don't leave the city without him."

"Thank you," Brent says.

"Thanks," I say.

Deb only waves.

We start up the familiar road. I walk ahead, Deb hobbles in the middle, and Brent brings up the rear.

"Sorry," Deb says.

"Sorry for what?" I ask. *Sorry for offing yourself? Sorry for being impossible?*

She looks at me like she thinks I'm an idiot. "Hello? That man I almost ran into?" She looks away from me. "You'll have to excuse her," she says.

Brent and I look at each other. He shrugs – he didn't see the man either. This does not look good for Deb.

Deb's head whips around to the left. "Do you hear that? A little animal is in trouble."

"No, Deb," Brent says. "We don't hear it."

She runs, as best she can, off the path (of course) to a rocky outcropping. She starts looking around in each crack and crevice. "It's okay. Come on out. I just want to help you," she says.

It makes me think of the homeless man that stands on the corner near my dad's office, arguing with people only he can see.

There is a narrow opening in some of the rocks. It leads downhill, but I don't think it's a trail, exactly. Even so, Deb scrambles down it.

"Wait! Deb, stop!" shouts Brent.

But she doesn't. Instead, she flounders down the rocky escarpment. Brent charges after her. I wait at the top, wondering if I'll be needed. After all, Deb is weak and hurt – how far can she get?

Deb uses her walking stick to climb up the other side, but it also dislodges some rocks, which tumble towards Brent. He dodges them, but they slow him down. Deb gets to the top of a ridge.

"Oh, there you are!" she says. The she topples over and disappears on the other side.

I start down the hill now. I catch up to Brent before he makes the ridge and we climb up together. We peer down the other side and see Deb sitting on the ground a couple of dozen yards from the bottom. She is holding something we can't see, and stroking it.

It is easy to see why Deb fell off. The top is very smooth and slants downward to a sheer drop off. If we both have to go down there to get Deb, I don't know how we'll get back up.

"Deb!" Brent calls to her. "Come back over here. We'll help you up."

She doesn't respond. Either she can't hear us or is ignoring us.

Brent tries to climb down the ridge, but he slides and tumbles to the ground. He works his way through the rock-strewn path over to Deb. I can see him trying to coax her to her feet. She does not want to get up, but he insists. She sets the invisible something down and gives it a pat before she struggles to her feet and follows Brent back to the cliff.

"Wish we had a rope," Brent says.

I'm not sure that would help, if he is expecting me to haul them up. I had thought that if we were all astral and whatever, we could just float around, but it doesn't seem to work quite that way. Maybe an astral rock is a lot lighter than a regular rock, but an astral body is a lot lighter than a regular body. And you still have the same level of strength you had before. The cliff is probably not taller than ten feet, which isn't so bad if you have to go down, but going up is awfully hard.

Brent tries climbing up several places, to no avail. It seems like a very long time before he sits down. Deb has been sitting on the rocks, petting something only she can see the whole time.

"What about Deb's walking stick? Maybe I can reach that and pull you up," I say.

"Good idea," Brent replies.

He picks up the stick and gets Deb to come over to the edge of the ridge with him. He hands her the cane.

"Deb, hold onto this. Mimi's going to pull you up."

She hesitates.

"C'mon, Deb. We've got to get you back to Sitnalta," I say.

"Fine."

She pushes the handle of the stick up to me. I can't reach it, so Brent lifts her up a little. It almost feels like the stick is twisting in my hands, but when I look at it, it isn't moving. I give a good tug, and my hands slip right over the top, causing me to flop straight onto my butt. The walking stick is just too slippery and inflexible to be useful. I frown.

"You're going to have to come down, Mimi," he says.

"Is that really necessary? Maybe I can go find a rope or something," I say, even though I realize just how unlikely it would be that I would find any useable length of rope lying around on the ground.

"We're going to have to try a different way. Come down here with us," Brent says.

"Little help?" I ask.

"Try coming off the edge backwards, near the wall. I'll try to help you," Brent says.

I am not graceful and Brent and I end up in a heap on the ground, but at least I'm down.

"Come on, Deb," I say to her.

She gets up, but she seems to be sleepwalking. Her eyes are open, but she stumbles along slowly, as if they were closed. I help guide her and Brent leads the way. We seem to only be able to go in the opposite direction of where we need to go. Surely we'll be able to turn and go up hill soon.

Brent stops dead and I almost crash into him. I've been paying more attention to Deb than to the scenery.

"Look at that!" he says, pointing down the path in front of us.

A turquoise and alabaster city sits at the bottom of the wide valley ahead.

"Do you suppose that's the Fourth City?" I ask. "Maybe we found a shortcut."

"I don't know. Maybe," Brent says. "It doesn't look the same though. Where are the moats and the crystal bridge?"

"That is not the Fourth City," Deb says. She has one eyebrow raised.

"Well, it is on the way," I say. "We may as well stop and ask for directions, because I have no idea where to go from here." *And Deb doesn't have time for us to wander around, lost.*

"May as well," says Brent.

Deb shrugs. "Why not?"

The city could easily have come straight out of the Arabian Nights, with its gleaming white minarets and columns inlaid with turquoise. I remember emerald and amethyst in the Sitnalta. But not turquoise. As we get closer, we see there are people milling around in the streets. Surely someone can help us there. We walk into town, not knowing quite what to expect. But I would never have believed we what we found, if I hadn't been there to see it for myself.

Chapter 16
The Collective

The place is crawling with people. Not human people, though. They have weak looking arms and legs and very skinny bodies that didn't appear that they were ever meant to support their enormous heads. Their faces are featureless, except for their huge almond-shaped black eyes. If they are wearing clothes, they are tight-fitting and the same color as their grey skin. There doesn't seem to be an easy way to tell which ones are girls and which ones are boys. Or if girls are even different from boys – perhaps they're all the same. We seem to have gone from a zombie movie to an alien movie. *What could possibly be next?*

"Excuse me," Brent says. "We need directions. We're in kind of a hurry."

They don't appear to understand.

"Maybe this was a bad idea," I say.

"Yep," says Brent.

We try to back out of the town square slowly, but too many of them have gathered around to look at us. I bump into one of them. It isn't wearing clothes, and its skin feels smooth and moist to the touch, like a stingray or a dolphin.

"Please, just let us go," I say.

I hear the answer in my mind. I can't tell which of them has provided it. Or if it was all of them. "No. You must be studied, assessed."

"We don't have time for that!" I shout. *We've got a whole world to save.*

I try to push past the grey people and run, but I find that I am floating, along with Brent and Deb, about three feet off the ground. I can flail my arms and legs and turn my body, but I can do nothing to change my forward motion. I open my mouth to ask Brent if he has any ideas, but no words come out. We are pulled along through town and up towards a huge pumpkin-shaped building. More grey people peer out their windows and stand in their doorways, watching us go past, an unwilling parade. All we need is confetti and a marching band.

The closer we get to the pumpkin building, the more of a sense of foreboding I have. I feel that terrible things happen to people in that building. I wonder how I know this. I can tell by Brent's face that he feels it, too. Deb is impassive. Almost as if she isn't even here. Perhaps she isn't, at least not mentally.

As we approach, a door in the pumpkin building slides open and we float inside. We are all put into a cell together. Suddenly, we are no longer floating and we fall in a heap onto the floor. The door to the cell must be some kind of force field. I can't see anything in the way, but I can't pass through it, either. Brent is helping Deb sit up. She is looking a lot worse for wear. We have got to get out of here and get to Sitnalta. I don't think we have much longer before it is too late.

A grey person stands in the doorway of our cell. I walk over to him or her. "Please. You have got to let us go. We don't have much time. Our friend is very sick."

"We shall examine her," the grey person says.

I don't know if I have done Deb a favor, or just destroyed the world.

Chapter 17
The Very Model

The grey person floats Deb out of the cell and Brent and I sit together, backs against the wall. I don't feel physically tired (although my chest hurts – feels as though someone has been hitting me again), but mentally, I'm drained. At the moment, I am just too tired to care if the world blows up at some point at least thirty five years from now. Unless they change the minimum president age, then it may be sooner.

I am out of ideas, maybe even out of time, and low on energy. I have no clue how to beat these guys that can levitate us at will and move us along as if we were human freight containers.

Brent's eyes are closed. I can't guess what he's thinking. He is very different from the guys I hang out with. I doubt that he got a red BMW for his birthday, like Josh did. No, Brent seems to be more the scrappy-hero-from-the-wrong-side-of-the-tracks character.

Something is digging into my leg.

I shift around and feel in my pocket. I find the coin that the Deer Lady gave me. Pretty, but what is it good for? I hold it in my hands so it doesn't gouge me. I really wish this whole story was a lot less Wagner and a lot more Gilbert and Sullivan.

I stand up and put the coin back in my pocket. I pace the semi-circular cell. Brent watches me absently.

"Maybe that could be our escape plan – you wear a hole in the floor," he says.

"Ha. Ha," I say. But I do look down, just in case. There is no worn-in foot path.

"Well, it's not like I have information animal, vegetable and mineral."

That's an odd thing for him so say.

A movement at the door catches my eye. Deb is floating back in. She doesn't look any worse than she did when she left, but that isn't saying much.

"There is little that can be done for her. She is preparing to ascend," the grey person says.

"So why not let us go? We have done nothing to you." I say.

"But you are research," the grey person says. "You are different from us and we desire to study you."

"Please, please, please let us go. We have to be somewhere, and the Agents will come looking for us," I say, hoping to cajole and threaten at the same time.

"They are unlikely to find you," he, she, or it says matter-of-factly. "This place is forbidden to all but the Foutharka. They will not come for you here. Since you wandered unbidden onto our territory, you are ours to do with as we wish."

I look to Brent, hoping for some back up.

"Don't look at me. I am the very model of a modern minor prisoner," he says, shrugging.

I am the very model... Had I not just held the Deer Lady's coin in my hand and wished this adventure was a little more Gilbert and Sullivan? This has to work.

"But you don't understand," I tell the grey person. "Deb is an orphan."

"An orphan, you say?" He cocks his head to the left as if he is considering something. "What of the other, the boy?"

"Yes, him too," I say.

"And yourself?" the grey person asks.

"My father is dead," I say, hoping that will be enough.

"I suppose that counts. Very well. You are free to go. You will be escorted to the border," the grey person says.

Brent and I have to help Deb, one of us on each side of her. Brent starts to say something but I shush him. I don't want any of us to say anything that might piss them off again and make them lock us up. We follow the guards along the rocky paths that led us to the forbidden city. They are kind enough to levitate us back up the ridge that Deb dove over and we couldn't get back up.

"Thank you," I say, waving.

"Farewell, orphans. Use care in this world," one of the guards says.

We scramble back up the almost trail to the road, where we pull Deb along as fast as we can. When he is sure the grey guards are out of earshot, Brent says, "Why did you tell them we were orphans?"

"Pirates of Penzance," I say.

"What makes you think they're pirates?" Brent asks.

"Do you remember that coin I got from the Deer Lady?" I ask.

"Sure," Brent answers.

"Well, I was holding it in my hand and I said, 'I wish this adventure was a little less Wagner and a little more Gilbert and Sullivan.' Then you started quoting the famous libretto from *Pirates of Penzance*. The pirates weren't very successful, and if any of their prisoners said they were orphans, the pirates always let them go."

"So, I was quoting an opera? Well, if it works." Brent shrugs. "Wonder how many wishes you get?"

"Don't you always get three in all the stories?" I ask.

"Sometimes you just get one. But sometimes you get as many as you want," Brent says.

"Look!" Deb says, voice ragged. "They are like, so beautiful."

Chapter 18
A Work of Art

We are almost to the Fountain of Sirin. I only see the wildflowers, but I am sure Deb is talking about something else, something she can see but we cannot. Reminds me of when my grandmother was dying and she kept talking about the butterflies in her hospital room.

"Yes," I say and we try to step up the pace. "Beautiful."

When we get to the border gate, it opens as we arrive, almost like the automatic door at the mall. I have a second of panic when I see Darjon, the frog-human combination. It reminds me of Froggy in the Seventh Plane, and I wonder if they are the same species. He just nods and waves us through.

Zariel and Master James are waiting for us at the entrance to the city. A person wearing a blue robe with the hood pulled up is standing next to them. I can see something writhing under her hood as we approach. I could swear it was Sthenno.

Master James scoops Deb up and carries her, rushing ahead of us over the crystal bridge.

"You are late," Zariel says. Then he turns to the blue-robed person. "Euryale, I present to you Mimi and Brent."

I don't know if I am meant to bow, curtsey, or what. I extend my right hand to shake. The writhing under the hood increases. I am sure I've done the wrong thing. But then, the hair-snake activity slows and she puts out her own hand.

"Pleased to meet you," I say.

Brent also shakes her hand.

"Sthenno sends her regards," Euryale says.

"Let us proceed to the Tower," Zariel says. "We only have a short window of opportunity left and we must not delay."

I'm not sure if that means we're in trouble. I look at Brent. He looks at me. We follow Zariel and Euryale back to the Tower.

When we arrive at room seven twenty nine, Deb is soaking in a tub filled with glowing golden gel. It smells nice, like outside right after a spring rain. How about that? I can smell things now. I wonder if that's good or bad.

"She is almost ready," Master James says, without looking up.

"What is that stuff?" Brent asks.

"It is a liquid energy, to replace that lost to the parasites," Master James says. "She is almost recharged. That is the good news. Now for the bad news. I don't know how much damage this has caused."

He holds up a sealed jar. A black eel looking thing with red streaks wriggles around inside. Six smooth spider legs stick out of its body just past the head. It hisses and butts its eyeless head against the glass. Its head is nothing but a big round mouth, filled with row after row of teeth.

"Gross!" Brent says.

I wonder if that is the dark thing I saw crawling under Deb's skin after we rescued her from Lucas.

"This is a lamprisect. It is an artificial life form that the dark ones sometimes use. They plant one inside the victim and it continues to draw energy from him or her and transmits it to its creator."

"Kind of like a wireless bloodsucker hotspot, then," Brent says.

"You could think of it that way," Master James says. "They start out small and get bigger and bigger until they consume nearly all of the victim's energy from the inside out. Very difficult problem to fix, if it gets all the way through."

"How is that?" Brent asks.

"Well, there is a giant lamprisect that has to be dealt with and the victim is stuck between two planes. The lamprisect can be destroyed and the soul can be at least partially retrieved, enough to get it through its own development, anyway," Master James says.

"So, is that it? You are just going to soak her in goo and she is good to go?" I ask.

"Not exactly. She will need to be sealed. Right now, her astral membrane is very porous," Master James says.

Zariel and Euryale are talking quietly together at the far end of the room and Brent is fascinated, watching the glowing goop seep into Deb. I stalk over to the window and look out. The usual overcast daylight coats the city. I remember the look of wonder on Deb's face as she looked towards Sitnalta. Part of me wants to see what she was seeing, and part of me is glad that I cannot.

"Euryale, I think she is ready," Master James' voice comes from behind me. "Mimi, stay where you are, and whatever you do, do not look into Euryale's face. Brent, would you step over here behind me?"

Brent moves behind Master James, but is he can still see over his shoulder. Eurayale comes forward. She pulls her hood back slightly and the squirming goes berserk. I can even hear hissing, now, too. Master James holds his hand over Deb's eyes. Euryale kneels and leans forward, picking up one of Deb's hands.

"What are you doing?" shouts Brent.

He rushes over to try to stop it from happening, but he is too late. One of the hair-snakes has sunk its teeth into Deb's wrist.

The gorgon's glare falls full on him and he freezes, then turns to stone.

"What just happened?" I ask, unable to comprehend.

"The bite from the gorgon's snake gives Deb enough solidity to be able to stay on the level she needs to, at least for a while. It is only temporary. But Brent tried to interfere and has incurred the wrath of the gorgon. That was very foolish," Zariel says.

I look at Brent closely, touch his face. "How long will he be frozen?" I ask.

Zariel shakes his head. "He has changed from something that is human to something that is yet to be human. Stone has its own evolutionary cycle. It could take a while. Or maybe not. He had already finished the elemental cycles."

Now I know why Brent looked so familiar to me. This frozen Brent is the statue that stands outside the Museum of

Contemporary Art. I pass it every day on my way to school. I struggle to think back to my life on the Earth Realm. There is even a picture from our last field trip there that Sierra took of me and Lexie kissing the statue of Brent, one of us on each side, one per cheek. It doesn't seem to be a big deal when it is a carved statue, but when it is someone you actually know, it's just weird.

"So, Zariel, if Brent has just been frozen now, how come this statue has been at the museum near my school for a long time?" I ask.

"Do you remember our discussion about how the past, present and future all exist at once?" he says.

"Sort of," I reply. I hadn't really gotten my head around it then.

"When you are in the Earth Realm, time appears to only flow one way. But when you are removed from the physical, it is easy to navigate in any direction you choose. Within limits, of course."

"Appears?" I ask.

"Yes," he says, smiling. But he doesn't go any further.

Deb seems to have fallen asleep in the golden goo. But she does look a bit better.

"Mimi?" Zariel asks. "It will take some time for Master James to complete the sealing process for Deb. Would you care to go with me to take Brent to the museum while you are waiting?"

"Sure," I say. "But the director might recognize me. He's good friends with my dad."

"I don't think that will be a problem," Zariel says. "Do you have any idea how long that statue has been at the museum?"

"No," I say. I probably would if I ever bothered reading any of the plaques.

"It was the first sculpture donated, back when the museum was just getting started. In 1953," Zariel says.

"My parents were not even born then," I say.

"That is true," says Zariel. "Your connection to me and the Twilight Crystal will enable you to pass through the barriers that normally only Agents can pass. Are you ready?"

"Ready as I will ever be," I say.

Zariel wraps his fingers around Brent's wrist and takes my hand in his other hand. There is a blinding flash of light.

Chapter 19
Time Stream

The light is so bright I can see it through my eyelids. When it goes away, I cautiously open my eyes. We are in what I know in the future as the Sculpture Garden. Right now, it is an uneven grassy area bordered by a manicured lawn, some trees, and a wild vacant lot.

Somehow, Brent has been placed onto a dolly and been covered with a big piece of cloth.

We walk towards the building. So, this is how the Museum of Contemporary Art looked when it was new. We go inside and have to leave Brent with the ticket-taker upstairs. Zariel steers us down the stairs and into the basement. You don't see too many basements here in Houston. They tend to become indoor swimming pools.

Zariel finds the business offices and then a white door with the name Dr. Jerimiah Kelley on it. He knocks loudly before opening it.

"Welcome, welcome, I have been expecting you," says a man's voice.

The high-backed leather chair turns around to reveal a man with a dark full beard and shaggy hair. He looks at me suspiciously. "Who is the girl you have brought today?"

"She is my niece," Zariel says.

"Ah. Well then, let us see this young man of yours," Dr. Kelley says. He pushes his chair back and locks the desk drawer before he gets up.

We say nothing as we climb the stairs, the clanging of our feet on metal steps echoing loudly in the close stairwell. Dr. Kelley sees the draped figure next to the ticket taker and hurries toward it. He looks around carefully at it, as if he is afraid it might bite him.

"Would you remove the drape?" he asks Zariel, eyes narrowed.

"As you wish," Zariel says. He pulls the cloth over Brent's head to reveal my petrified friend.

Dr. Kelley carefully examines Brent, touching his face and tugging on his arms. "Unusual choice of medium. Most of these things are marble or bronze. Is it granite, perhaps?"

"Basalt," Zariel says.

"I see. The detail work is amazing. This must have taken years." Dr. Kelley shakes his head. "My acquisitions budget is very small. I don't believe our tiny museum could afford a piece such as this."

"The artist, who wishes to remain anonymous, would like to donate it," Zariel says.

"Donate it? Are you sure this is not stolen?" Dr. Kelley asks.

"I understand your concerns, Dr. Kelley. But I represent someone who could become a target of persecution, should her identity be revealed."

Dr. Kelley nods his head slightly. "I understand."

He walks around Brent again, peering closely at his face and hair. Right arm crossed at his midsection, he strokes his own beard. "I will have the paperwork prepared."

"Thank you," Zariel says.

"No, thank you. This piece will be quite the attraction at our new little museum. Come inside. The secretary will prepare your receipt."

We follow Dr. Kelley back into the business office section of the museum. The secretary must have been away when we arrived. Now she sits at the enormous wooden desk that stands guard over the offices.

Her dishwater blonde hair is teased up into a beehive hairdo and cat-eye glasses with little rhinestones perch on her nose. My grandmother used to have those same glasses. Then I notice the name plate on the desk – 'Rebecca Fisher.'

OMG! She is my grandmother. But that can't be. My grandmother is old, and this lady is barely older than me. I have to remind myself that my parents haven't even been born, much less met each other yet.

"Miss Fisher, please prepare a donation receipt for Mr. Smith. The item is a basalt statue of a youth. Value $5,000."

Dr. Kelley turns to us and extends his right hand to Zariel. "If you will excuse me? I've much work to do."

When Dr. Kelley is gone, Miss Fisher gets up and goes to a filing cabinet. Her skirt is a little too tight and her top is a little too fitted. Grandmothers should not dress that way. It's embarrassing. Can't she just wear a moumou or something?

"My I have your first name, or your first two initials, Mr. Smith?" she asks.

"Of course. J Q," Zariel answers.

I look at him and mouth, "John?"

He shakes his head. "Joab."

Miss Fisher gets thee sheets of white paper and two sheets of black paper, then carefully stacks them white, black, white, black, white. She rolls them into a seriously antique – well, I suppose it was new back then – typewriter and starts to peck at the keys.

Finally, she's done. The typewriter clicks as she very carefully rolls the paper sandwich out of the machine. She brings it to the desk and sets it down. After retrieving a ball point pen from her desk drawer, she hands it to Zariel, her fingers brushing his.

"There, Mr. Smith. That is one of the new Bic pens. State of the art. Suppliers have only just started carrying them, you know," she says, proud of her disposable pen.

Is she flirting with him? That is outrageous. I start to say something, but Zariel has already signed his name and takes the top copy. "Thank you, Miss Fisher. We will just leave the sculpture were it is. Take good care of it for us, won't you?" He turns to me. "Come along, Mimi."

I hear a snicker. Miss Fisher is hiding her mouth with her hand.

"Is there something funny?" I ask. I'm a little hurt that she seems to think my name is ridiculous.

"I am so sorry," she says, looking up at me from behind her massive desk. "It's just that we had a standard white poodle named Mimi when I was a child. No offense. She was a very sweet dog."

I remembered some old pictures of Gran as a child, with a big frizzy dog. She always had little bows on her ears. She used to tell me stories about that dog, although in the stories, her name was Duchess, and she had canine super powers.

"It's okay," I say.

"We don't want to be late," Zariel says, prodding me.

I am suddenly sad to leave Rebecca Fisher. "No, can't be late," I say.

I slow down to brush my fingers across Brent's cheek as we walk out of the museum. "Take care," I whisper.

We hurry across the lumpy bumpy future sculpture garden and onto the sidewalk. No one is coming from either direction.

"Hold my hand," Zariel says.

It's just like before. As soon as I feel his fingers close on my hand, there is a blinding flash of light. When I open my eyes, we are back in room seven twenty nine.

"There is a problem," Master James says.

Chapter 20
Scar Tissue

W hat problem?" Zariel asks.
"That lamprisect has caused some damage – there are scars,"
Master James says.

"I see," Zariel says.

"What does this mean?" I ask.

"What it means is that Deb has been compromised. She
will probably be just fine, unless she comes into contact with
Lucas. The scars from the lamprisect are like a scab or sore that
acts as an entry point for his influence. He may be able to get to
her through them, the same way bacteria invades a cut," Zariel says.

"It is unlikely that he cares one way or the other about
what you are trying to accomplish. However, he will be very angry
that you helped Deb escape," Master James adds.

"Lucas' GA says that he was removed from life support.
As long as his body is alive, he has access to the lower four planes.
Once his body is relinquished, he will be confined to the Seventh
Plane. He might, even now, be trapped there," Zariel says.

"Or he might not. Don't you have some board or
something that shows where everyone is?" I ask.

"Not exactly," says Zariel.

"There seem to be a few flaws in the way this place is run,"
I say.

"Many things seem to be one thing, but turn out to be
another," Zariel says. "For example, do you remember seeing a
shadow right before you fell into the pool?"

I had to think hard to force my mind to return there. The
whole Friday Night Swim seems so long ago and far away, now.

"Maybe," I say.

"That was, in fact, your GA. She pushed you into the
pool," Zariel says.

"That makes no sense!" I say, fluttering my eyelids in disbelief and shaking my head. "Aren't Guardian Angels meant to 'guard?'As in keeping people from drowning?" I ask.

"GAs exist to help you with what you need, which is sometimes different from what you think you want," Zariel says. "Sometimes GAs pull you out of danger, sometimes they push you into it. It just depends on what you need at that time."

"If that's true, she's been making herself pretty scarce since she pushed me into the pool to drown," I say, clenching my jaw.

"Not true. Do you remember the busgirl in the restaurant? The woman in the hat at the Last Resort? She's been with you all along."

I cross my arms. Then I uncross them. "Well," I say. "Why didn't she just say who she was?"

"What would you have her say?" I can hear the smile in Zariel's voice. "'Good afternoon! I'm your personal Guardian Angel, and I'm here to try and keep you out of too much trouble, if you'll just bother to listen.'"

"Maybe they should have a different name, if they're not actually doing that much guarding," I say.

"Perhaps, but Guardian Angel sounds much better than, say, Life Coach Angel. Or Suggestion Angel, does it not?" Zariel says.

"So what you are saying then, is that we all have some pre-planned destiny, with hall-monitor angels trying to make us behave? Does that mean we have no choices about what we do?" It's probably a good thing I don't have a physical body right now, because I would probably start crying, I'm so mad.

"No, not at all. Angels just help to arrange the situations. You always have choices. You could have refused to participate in this adventure, still can if you wish," Zariel says, as if it does not matter to him.

"Maybe I will," I say, knowing it's a hollow threat. The burned face of my daughter and my dead grandson are seared into my mind. I have to try to stop this from happening.

"As you wish."

Deb sits up. She doesn't look great, but she does look better. Her skin has a greyish cast, as if she had a very thin layer of concrete brushed over her. It's darker on her arms and legs, where she had gone transparent before. The color makes the purple in her hair stand out. The little Sammie dog leaps into her arms and wiggles joyfully.

I don't see Master James or Euryale.

"Have you guys seen Brent?" Deb asks.

"She has no way of knowing, does she?" I ask.

"Know what?" Deb asks.

"Brent had an unfortunate encounter with the Gorgon. He was petrified," Zariel says.

"Yeah. I'm kind of scared of them, too," she says.

"No," I say. "He's turned to stone. He's a statue now."

"That sucks," Deb says. "He can be un-petrified, right?"

"Yes and no," says Zariel. "There is no immediate reversal, but he will become human again in time."

Deb starts twisting the little stud in the side of her nose. It grosses me out and I turn around to look out the window.

"Are you ready, then, to find the dreamer?" Zariel asks. "It is time."

Chapter 21
Dream Quest

There is a knock on the door. Zariel opens it and Anna, the little girl who helped us earlier, sleepwalks in.

"Anna will help you find the right dream. Because she is dreaming, she can see things you can't. Not all dreamers travel to the Astral Realm, but you are very lucky that she often does," Zariel says.

"What do we do when we find Laura Samuels?" I ask.

"Once you enter the dream, you have to get her attention. It may be easy, or it may be hard, depending on what she is dreaming about. The Twilight Crystal will make you visible to her, so Deb, make sure you stay near Mimi. If you are too far away, she will not be able to see you. Look around at what she is dreaming and try to integrate yourselves into that dream."

"And then what? Do we just talk to her?" I ask.

"No. It was the violence of the fight that originally got her attention. You should have a fight."

Zariel looks at Deb and she looks back at him, nodding almost imperceptibly. I have the distinct impression that they know something I don't, and I don't like it.

Anna beckons to us. Time to go.

"Good luck," Zariel says.

"Thanks," I say, only half sarcastic.

Deb only waves. She must not be good at good-byes.

We follow Anna out the door and down the hall to the stairs. She is thin and has an old-fashioned nightgown on, reminding me of Clara from The Nutcracker ballet. I half expect to hear the 'Waltz of the Sugar Plum Fairy' as we reach the marble tile of the lobby. My mother took me to see that ballet every year, from the time I was little. Last year, I said I didn't want to go, but she still bought tickets. We went, but I made it miserable for her, for both of us, actually. *Why was I such a jerk?*

Anna leads us through the lobby to the opposite door from our usual one. We get to the street through a side door, and I discover there is a small park, the size of a city block, right across the street from the building. I wonder if it is really as deserted as it looks to me, or if it is crowded with people I can't see.

"Do you see anything, Deb?" I ask, wondering how much of her is still on a higher plane.

"You mean other than the fountain, trees, benches and the flowers?" she asks.

"Yeah," I reply.

"Just a little cat, sitting in a sunny spot, cleaning itself," she says.

I look up. I don't see any sun. Just the usual overcast grey.

I lose sight of Anna for a moment, then I see her head bobbing between the trees in the middle of the park. When we catch up with her, she is on her hands and knees, looking into the reflecting pool at the center of the park. Trees rise above either side of it, darkening the water.

I see nothing but our vague reflections on the surface, but Anna appears to be watching a movie. After a short time, she gets up and looks around for us. Finding me, or maybe it is Deb, she smiles and beckons. I wish she would talk.

That gives me an idea. I put my hand in my pocket and find the Deer Lady's coin. I hold it between my fingers. I wish Anna would talk to us.

"Anna, have you found her?" I ask.

She nods her head and smiles. Oh, well. It's a pretty coin, anyway. I guess unlimited wishes might have been greedy. Three would have been nice, though.

We continue to a building that appears to be a train station. Apparently, we don't need tickets. I don't see any kiosks or booths. There is a map, however, and Anna studies it. She smiles and waves us over to Platform D. As soon as we arrive, a vehicle pulls up on the tracks. It looks more like a zucchini than a train. There is only one car, and as far as I can tell, no driver.

The top opens up and we climb in. The seating is very…organic. It seems to just grow out of the walls and floor, rather than being constructed. It is very soft to sit on, although, in retrospect, so were the rock chairs in Sthenno's cave. It makes me think of some kind of gel with a velvet covering. The windows aren't large, but we can see scenery passing by. We stop in the middle of nowhere, but I think it may be the Fifth City. If anyone gets on, I don't see them. We stop again in the Sixth City. We don't stop in Airumel, the Seventh City.

We go through a seriously dark tunnel. When we come out, we are somewhere that is still dark, but there are stars in the sky and city lights in the distance. On the outskirts of the city, the zucchini car stops. We get out.

"Now where are we?" I wonder out loud.

"Gimme a break. Don't you know?" Deb asks.

"If I knew, I wouldn't have asked," I say, irritated.

"Look up, then. What do you see?" Deb asks.

"Buildings," I say.

"What kind of buildings?" Deb asks.

I can tell she isn't going to drop it. "Tall buildings. Wait," I say as I read the sign 'M.D. Anderson Cancer Center.' "Hospitals! We're in the Medical Center."

"Bingo." Deb smirks at me.

"Where's Anna?" I ask.

"Crap!" Deb says.

We see her flitting like a little girl ghost behind the bus shelter toward the main doors of the big pink building. We run after her and catch her just before she goes in. The automatic sliding doors don't open for us, but we pass through the glass easily enough, even Deb, with her hair-snake veneer.

I'm surprised at first at how many ghosts and dreamers are here. If I look very carefully, I can see the very thin silver cords of the dreamers, tying them to their bodies. Just like mine. It's still there. Very faint, but still there. The place is wall to wall with both kinds of them. None of the awake and alive people seem to notice that they are there.

The wail of an ambulance from outside jostles me. I suddenly feel dizzy and have a hard time keeping my balance. I cough. There seems to be something in my throat that I can't swallow. I can't move my legs – they seem to be tied or strapped to something. I'm on the verge of panic.

"Mimi, what's wrong?" Deb has caught my hand and she is tugging me along behind the relentless Anna, who waits for no one.

My throat still feels a little full, but I shake it off. My feet are working fine now. "Nothing," I say. "I am fine, really."

At least Anna has slowed down. She is waiting for us at a fountain. We follow her to a bank of elevators marked F. A nurse is getting into one of the cars. She pushes the '9' button, and Anna smiles.

"So, you think Laura Samuels will be up here?" Deb asks.

Anna shrugs and holds her hands out, palms up.

Deb has an evil look on her face. She starts to make all kinds of faces at the nurse. She looks almost demonic and I feel a little scared, thinking about Master James' remarks about the lamprisect.

Deb laughs. "She has no idea what's going on."

She looks normal again. At least, normal for her.

"Hysterical," I say and roll my eyes.

The car slows down and the circle with the nine in it lights up. The doors open and the nurse strides out. We follow her out and down to the children's ward. We follow Anna through the closed wooden doors. She passes several rooms, until she finally stops. She inclines her head towards the room. But her smile looks forced.

We pass through the wooden door and go inside. A child lies in the bed. Maybe a girl, but the kid is bald, so I can't really tell. There are IVs in both arms and a tube going down her throat.

Deb points to Anna, then at the person in the bed. Anna nods. *Oh. I hadn't realized.* Why did that not occur to me – Anna was taking us to her dreaming body?

Anna ducks behind the chair. A woman comes in, a dreamer by the look of her. She stands and looks at Anna's form, lying in the bed, connected to so many machines. Anna comes out from behind the chair, arms out. The woman hugs her. Her back is to us and Anna points to the woman's head.

"She is your mother?" I ask.

Anna nods and keeps pointing.

"She is Laura Samuels," Deb guesses.

Anna nods vigorously. Deb and I both move around to get a look at her face. She looks like anyone's mom – much older than us, not ugly, not pretty. She has a flowery dress on – a print with lots of different colored pansies. Her bottle blonde hair is pulled back in a clip and it is obvious that she hasn't had her roots touched up in a while. Puffy dark circles, as if she has been doing too much crying and not enough sleeping, make her eyes stand out. Does she remember standing here with her daughter, as I am sure she's done night after night? Or does she think it is just a dream?

"Hello?" I say to her.

Deb waves a hand in front of her face.

She doesn't notice us. She is only paying attention to Anna. I try clapping my hands, but it makes no sound. I now can see why Zariel recruited Anna to help us. She is probably the only one who can get Laura's attention. I was terrible at this to begin with, anyway. Deb was pretty good, but if Laura only sees Deb arguing with nobody, she might be inspired to start the wrong kind of foundation.

I look at the clock. 1:03 AM. According to it, I have been at the pool one hour and three minutes. It seems a hundred years ago.

There is enough light to see the second hand jerking around the clock face, counting down the night, counting down my life, counting down to the end of the world. If I had breath, I would take a deep one.

Focus, Mimi, focus. I try hard to sync up with Laura's vibration, but I can't seem to find anything that works. I even pull the Twilight Crystal out of my shirt and wave it at her. Deb isn't able to get anything accomplished, either. Maybe it isn't us.

"Anna?" I ask.

The girl looks up and smiles. It makes me a little sad to see this well and healthy copy of a sick and maybe dying child. Both aspects of her should be well and healthy.

"Anna, could you try to get your mom to go to a different room, one where she isn't so focused on you? Maybe the cafeteria or somewhere like that?" I ask.

Anna nods her head. She pushes and pulls at Laura, who finally turns around. Anna takes her by the hand and leads her from the room. Almost immediately, we lose them in the crowd. We try to fight through a sea of living and dead people, and I may as well be a salmon swimming upstream. Some of them are aware of us and move out of the way to let us by. Others are not and we have to try to go around or push by.

"Let's try to catch them at the cafeteria!" I shout to Deb.

"Great idea! Where is that?" she answers.

"I don't know!" I reply.

"These things are usually on the first floor or in the basement," Deb says.

We squeeze onto the jam-packed elevator. The two nurses chit chat about the antics of the new residents, oblivious to all the people around them. I look carefully at each face. Anna and her mother are not there. Things are going well until the elevator stops on the fifth floor. The nurses get out and everyone else stands around, waiting for the elevator to be called. Deb and I look at each other, then at the door.

We both charge for the closed door. The steel is cold and more difficult to pass through than the glass or wood doors we went through earlier, but we get through it.

There is a small map on the wall by the elevator bank. I look at it for a moment. "Stairs that way," I say.

We find the fire exit and start down the stairs. After about three flights, I have an idea.

"Deb, do you think we could just pass through the floor the same way we did the doors?" I wonder.

"Don't know. Try it and see," she replies.

I start trying to push myself through the floor. It's filled with wires and cables and pipes. The electricity doesn't hurt me, but it is uncomfortable, and that is just on my feet. I don't want it going all the way through my body and face.

"I don't think that will work," I say. "Too much junk in there."

We start back down the stairs. When we reach the bottom, I look for signs on the walls to tell us which way the cafeteria is. Admissions. Radiology. Cashier. Cafeteria.

"This way, Deb," I call. The hallway is more crowded than ever. Her purple/blonde/black hair makes her easy to keep track of as we wade through the masses of humanity. Every so often, though, I catch a glimpse of something that doesn't look quite human. Whenever it sees me looking at it, it ducks into the crowd. I don't have time to wonder what it is, or if there are more than one of them.

We find the double doors and pass through them into the cafeteria. It's not at all crowded. In fact, we are the only ones here.

"Anna?" Deb calls.

"Laura?" I try.

No response. Where could they be? Dammit. Something moves in the darkest corner.

"Hello, Deborah," a wretchedly familiar voice says.

Chapter 22
Bad Penny

Lucas," I hiss.
Deb takes several steps back. Lucas is partially lit in the dim light. He does not glow or shine the way most astrals do. He is a dense black shadow.

"This is getting old, what is your name again?" Lucas says to me. "But maybe you'd like to make a trade, something old for something new?"

"What does that mean?" I ask, maneuvering myself between him and Deb, even they are a whole room apart.

"Simple. I trade you this," and here he steps aside to reveal Anna, "for that," he says, motioning towards Deb.

"Let her go, you creep!" Deb snarls at him. She takes a few steps forward. I grab her arm before she passes me.

"Or what?" he purrs.

I know that I cannot lose either Deb or Anna and have any hope of pulling this dream thing off. I just need some time to think. Unfortunately, that isn't my area of expertise.

Through the gauzy draperies, I see red and blue flashing lights outside the window. I can hear people talking, but the voices are muffled and I don't understand what they say. Did I catch the word 'drowning?' Must be the night for it. I need to focus on Lucas. But my mind does not want to cooperate. It keeps going back to the lights and voices, trying to understand what they're saying. Nosey Rosie.

Deb tries to pull away from me, but I hold on to her. "Wait," I say.

There is something I try to remember about Lucas, but my mind is fuzzy. I hold on to Deb more tightly. It isn't helping much. Then Anna starts to cry. I snap to attention. I am all focus.

"Leave her alone," I say as sternly as I can.

Lucas laughs.

Deb yanks her arm out of my grip and rushes at Lucas. He slides his arm around her waist and crushes her against him.

"Never mind," he says. "I'll just keep both of them."

I try to run to him, but it feels as though someone is standing behind me, holding onto my shirt. I don't get there fast, but I do get there in time to grab Anna's hand in one of mine and the top of Deb's oh so low pants in the other. I throw what little weight I have into it and lean back. I feel weak and all I really want to do is close my eyes and go to sleep. I shake my head. I shout, "No! No! No! No!" as loudly as I can manage. I don't know whether falling asleep means I will live or I will die, but either way, I can't do it now. I start rocking my body back and forth, yelling "Heave!" each time I go back, trying to encourage them to pull with me, pull away from Lucas.

Anna and Deb struggle with me, trying to free themselves. Lucas stands there, pretending he is bored, I suppose, but I can't see his shadow features clearly. He starts to lose his grip on Deb. I tug harder. Anna is also almost free.

"What the – ?" Lucas asks.

The girls pull free of his grasp and we all tumble together on the floor. Little flashes of color speckle Lucas' form. Reminds me of when the satellite TV loses the signal during a storm, and the picture goes all pixelated. The flashes of color get more frequent and numerous, until his whole shape is throbbing with light. What must be the image of the true Lucas flickers onto his face for a moment. Then he is gone.

That worked out well. "Deb? Anna? Are you okay?" I ask.

"Yep, fine," Deb says, getting up and dusting herself off. I notice that some of the hair-snake veneer on her skin is starting to crack.

Anna is still cowering next to me.

"It is okay. He is gone and he isn't coming back," I tell her. "But we have got to find your mom. Now." I get up and help Anna up, too.

Anna motions to us to follow her.

We slip through the closed doors into the crowded hallway. I am very light-headed as we push and shove our way through the throng. I feel that if I closed my eyes, I would just fly away like a piece of milkweed fluff.

When we get to the fountain in the hospital lobby, Laura is standing on the rim of it, scanning the crowd. "Anna! Anna!" she shouts, looking this way and that.

Anna runs to her, arms outstretched.

Laura sees her and leaps into the crowd. She pushes her way towards her daughter and grabs her, holding her tightly. I can barely keep my eyes open.

"I need some air," I say to Deb. I'm not sure why. It's not as though this astral body needs to breathe.

I pass through the glass picture window to the outside. There is no one out here and it is good to have room to move. Anna, Laura, and Deb all squeeze out of the window and join me on the patio.

"Thank you," Laura says. She looks from Deb to me.

She can see me.

"Thank you for saving my little girl." Her hands squeeze Anna's shoulders.

"No problem," says Deb.

I'm not sure I have the energy to speak. I nod my head. Wait. Is this where Deb and I are supposed to fight? I can't quite get things straight in my head.

"Do you have the remembering dust the lady from Hell gave you," I ask Deb.

"Oh, yes," she replies. She sounds far away. Still, there is something wrong about her voice. It sounds kind of like...Lucas.

"You have to remember," I turn to Laura, pleading. "Find Rhiannon, create the foundation, and help the girls."

Deb takes something out of her boot. Even without the snick of metal on metal, I know it is a switchblade knife. But it isn't an ordinary knife. This one glows red and shimmers as if it's made of pure energy. "Don't worry, this won't hurt." she says. "Much."

"Run, Laura!" I scream as Deb slices my arm from elbow to wrist with the knife. Deb is not concerned with Laura and Anna as they disappear back into the building. She is inhaling the cloud of astral particles that is pouring out of my arm.

Chapter 23
Cruel to Be Kind

Somewhere in my foggy brain, a little idea forms. Hit Deb with the Twilight Crystal. Crack the hair-snake patina. If Deb is suddenly all fine particles, maybe she will be saved from becoming a vampire. I am already incredibly sleepy and the energy loss is not helping. I grope for the crystal around my neck. I pull the leather thong over my head and wrap it around my fingers. I swing it in a circle, like a lasso.

"What do you think you are doing?" Deb snarls.

"Saving you," I say as I let the crystal fly.

It hits her on the shoulder. I can see a dent where it lands. She tries to grab it away from me, so I just hold it in my hand and try to punch her with it. She is a lot stronger than I am, and not half as groggy. Still, I manage to make a few cracks in the veneer. Just when I don't think I can move my arm another time, a large chunk of the patina falls off. White light shines through the gap and all the little cracks. I have to close my eyes.

The moment I do, I feel myself being pulled backwards. I don't want to watch. But I can't escape from the white light. Even with my eyes closed, it seeps into my head. I try turning my head from side to side, but it doesn't help. I suddenly feel as if I'm being squeezed into a cold, tight bag that's stiff and heavy. There is something in the way, and I can't move much. I try swallowing, but there's a big lump of something in my throat. It's uncomfortable, but I can breathe, so I don't worry about it too much.

"Be still, honey, be still," a voice says. It is a low, gravelly voice, but I think it's female.

I open one eye. I can't tell with the bright light above.

I close my eye and lie still. I can hear the voices and I listen for a little while.

"Why didn't EMS bandage that gash on her arm? It's going to need stitches."

"It's not in their report. Can't believe they didn't see that. Weird."

"Need a heater for the IV."

"Get these wet clothes off her."

"Got to get her to X-Ray and check out that neck."

"What is this in her hand? I am sure it wasn't there a minute ago. Some kind of rock. Put it with her stuff."

I get tired of listening and let myself sink into the darkness.

"Mimi?" A familiar voice calls my name.

"Zariel?"

"Yes," Zariel says.

"Am I dead?" I ask. It is very dark, and I can see the stars, billions and billions of them, burning in the inky sky above.

"No. You failed to convince Laura Samuels," he says. "You have to go back to the Earth Realm and try again."

"I get another chance?" I ask. I'm not sure if I should be happy or disappointed. I had gotten used to the Astral Realm. As long as I didn't go to the Seventh Plane or below, it was actually pretty nice up there. I'd liked the freedom of not having to deal with a body.

"That's one way to look at it. It will be harder this time," he says.

"Yeah. That dream invasion thing didn't work out so well. Speaking of invasion, where is Deb?" I say.

"She is contained," Zariel says. "She can't do harm to others. I think we can salvage her. That was good thinking, hitting her with the Twilight Crystal. By the way. Could I have that back so I can have it returned to Hades?"

"Sure," I say, reaching for my throat. It isn't there. I look at my hands. Then I remember. "Somebody in the hospital took it from my hand, said they were going to put it with my stuff."

"Mimi? Baby?" I hear another voice, coming from somewhere far away. I squint open my eyes in the bright light of the emergency room. Mom is standing over me, her sequined dress shimmering in the glaring lights. Dad is by the door, whispering with the doctor.

"Shhh," she says. "Don't try to talk." Her mascara has run all the way down to her cheekbones. She rubs my forehead and strokes my hair with the tips of her fingers, the way she used to do when I was little and had a hard time falling asleep. It still works. I fall back into the dark.

"I don't think Laura Samuels remembers what you told her. Anna does, though." Zariel says.

"She's dying, isn't she?" I ask.

"Yes," Zariel answers.

I hear music, and I pause to listen to it. It isn't music so much as it is a melody. A melody that someone is humming. It is so familiar to me. *All the Pretty Little Horses*. Mom always used to sing that song to me when I was little. I find myself drifting up to it.

I open my eyes. There is something covering up my nose and mouth. I go cross eyed trying to look at it.

"That's oxygen, baby," Mom tells me. "You're going to be just fine."

I nod my head. My eyelids are too heavy to hold open, so I let them close.

In the dark, I look up at the brilliant stars and just watch the universe go by. I have no sense of time passing.

Gradually, I am aware of squeaky rubber soles on the tile floor, then a rustling on the counter, and the clicking of electronics. I open one eye, just a little. The nurse is changing my IV bag. I see a big lump of clothes and blankets on the bizarre hybrid chair/fold out bed that they have in hospital rooms. Mom. I close my eye and pretend I'm sleeping, even as the automatic blood pressure cuff inflates and painfully squeezes my arm. No telling what the nurse will want to measure/poke/prod if she thinks I'm awake.

Chapter 24
Home Again

I got home from the hospital yesterday. Dad is barely speaking to me. His disappointment in me radiates off of him like light from the sun. I mostly try to avoid him. Mom being is nice, but maybe too formal. She is taking me to the doctor for a follow up tomorrow. I dread the hour and a half or so of alone time we will have in the car. I can tell she is working herself up to talk to me about not just the pool incident, but everything leading up to it.

Sierra and Lexie came by the hospital. They didn't have much to say and didn't stay long. They didn't ask how I was feeling or what it was like to almost die. Sierra is grounded (mostly), but Lexie's parents are out of town and the housekeeper doesn't much care what she does, as long as she doesn't get killed or arrested. They seemed to be under the impression that everybody being in trouble is somehow my fault. We were all charged with trespassing and malicious mischief. But Josh's dad is the president of the Homeowner's Association, so of course the charges were dropped.

Neither Tyler nor Steve has even bothered texting me. Jerks. Even my brother managed to come by for a few minutes during his lunch hour.

Zariel had said that Deb had been 'contained.' I hope they're able to fix her. I wonder if Brent is conscious and aware inside the statue, or if his mind is petrified, too. I scroll through the camera roll on my phone until I get to the picture of Lexie and me kissing him on the field trip to the museum. Does he remember that? I feel sudden heat in my cheeks.

I have been lounging in my pajamas all day, taking it easy. Not planning to go anywhere or see anybody, so why bother getting dressed? I haven't seen Zariel, or anyone else for that matter, since the hospital. I am starting to wonder if it was all a dream. Every time I think that, I touch the stitches running down the length of my forearm.

I sit upstairs in the game room, flipping through the channels yet again. How can nothing be on when there are over two hundred channels on the TV? I have to move the plate with the remains of my lunch over so that I can put my feet up.

The doorbell rings. It's followed by a loud knock, as if someone wants to make doubly sure we know they're standing there, demanding attention. I hear the door open, Mom's voice, then a male voice. The stairs creak.

Josh's head comes into view. Lovely.

"You knew. You knew about this. Why didn't you tell me?" he practically shouts at me.

"What are you talking about?" I ask, looking at his blotchy red skin and runny nose.

"My dad ran off with some dude. He left my mom, left us, for a guy." His voice is shaky and cracks.

And this, too, is my fault? "I am so sorry, Josh. That must be really hard."

"Why didn't you say something?" he pleads, his eyes moist.

"What would you want me to have said?" I ask.

"He said it was all going to come out anyway, and to ask you about it," Josh accuses me.

I have to set the clicker down so I don't throw it at him. "I don't see what this has to do with me."

"You know something. Were you blackmailing him?"

"Do you really think he just happened to leave his key ring lying around for you to find? You can act like Mr. Goody-Goody now, but you sure thought you were all that when you had his keys."

"At least I am not a scheming little whore," he snaps. "Besides, Tyler says you aren't much of a lay, anyway. Guess you get what you pay for."

I stand up. "Get out."

Josh's fists clench and unclench by his sides. Before he can say anything else, Mom comes up the stairs.

"Josh, honey, maybe you would like to go home so Mimi can get some rest now," she says in that way she has that sounds as if you have options, but it is clear that you really don't.

He stomps down the stairs and I hear the door open and close. The stairs are quiet under her weight as Mom comes back up.

"Are you okay, Mimi?" she asks.

"Yeah, I'm fine," I say. A big fat tear slides down my cheek.

Mom comes over and folds me in her arms. I start sobbing and I can't stop. I cry until there is no more liquid in my body that can be turned into tears. My mom guides me over to the couch and we sit down. I rest my head on her shoulder and she strokes my hair.

"I'm sorry," she says.

"You're sorry? For what?" I ask.

"Sorry for not being there when you needed me. You just kept pushing me away, and I let you. It was just easier to do my own thing. I should have tried harder," she says.

"I just wanted you to notice me. I didn't think you cared as much about me as you do about the opera," I said.

"The opera was not rolling its eyes at me and flying into histrionics every time I opened my mouth," she says.

"That's my job. Didn't you read the contract?" I say.

Mom laughs. It is a small little laugh, but it makes me feel I've won the lottery.

"All right, Mimi. If we're both being stupid, we may as well go out for ice cream," Mom says.

"I'll get dressed," I say.

I catch my reflection in the dresser mirror as I go in the door. I look like crap. My face is bruised and scraped from hitting the side of the pool. Nothing I can do about that. My eyes are puffy and my skin is blotchy from crying. Splashing cold water on my face might help a little. My hair is a disaster. Maybe I can squash it down with a headband.

The Twilight Crystal hangs off one corner of the mirror. When I touch it, if feels alive, and aware of me. The Deer Lady's coin stands on edge, leaning against the glass, in the bottom corner of the mirror. No one has asked about them – guess my parents so rarely come into my room they have no idea what's in here. I know if I tell anyone about my adventure, they will tell me it was all just a dream, same as Dorothy in the Wizard of Oz. It was real, and I have the scars to prove it.

I suppose Zariel will contact me when he's ready, but I wish he'd hurry up. I kind of liked all the adventure in the Astral Realm. I hadn't realized how…mundane my life has been so far. At least I hope Zariel is the one who comes for the crystal. I'm not sure I would want Hades to show up at my house. Maybe Seph could take it next time she is on furlough. But that still leaves the question of Laura Samuels. Did she remember? Zariel said I had another chance, so probably not. On the plus side, Terry Mitchell is only a baby. I have some time.

Why am I worrying about this when there is a waffle cone with my name on it? I strip off my pajamas and throw on some shorts and a tee shirt. I pull my hair back in a clip on my way down the stairs.

Mom and I talk about non-controversial subjects in the car on the way to the ice cream shop. It's better that way, to preserve the fragile peace we've made this afternoon. I watch the street we should have turned on go past.

"Mom, where are you going?" I ask. It is a reminder of my dad's betrayal with the Silverman Clinic, and I suddenly feel nervous.

"Oh! Sorry, sweetie. I wasn't paying attention. We'll have to take the scenic route," she says.

The 'scenic route' goes past the little museum where Brent stands watch over the sculpture garden. I rub my eyes. I am sure that his left hand was out in front of him, about waist high when we left him. Now it hangs straight down. I must just be misremembering. But I do remember something else.

"So where was it again that you said Grandma met Grandpa?" I ask.

"Well, there's a question from left field," she says, downshifting at the traffic light. "Your grandmother worked at that museum, the one we just passed, when she was young."

"I know." I say.

"She met some very unusual people there, that's for sure – she used to tell me stories. But she also met the love her life there, my dad. She first met him when he delivered a statue."

Chapter 25
Retail Therapy

He did what?" I ask. If it turns out that J.Q. Smith is my grandfather, I am just going to jump out the window.

"He was working his way through college, just doing odd jobs around town, until he started working at the museum full time. Went to school at night," Mom says.

I breathe a quiet sigh of relief. It would just be too weird if Zariel had gotten my grandmother pregnant. *Is that even possible?*

She pulls into the left turn lane and we sit at the light. When the green arrow flashes on, she says, "Well, you know what they say. Two wrongs don't make a right, but three lefts do."

"Mom," I say, shaking my head. But at least we're on the right street now.

There are some big ice cream chain stores closer to our house, but this shop is worth driving for. Everything is hand made. They even have a little farm out in the country where they raise their own cows and grow their own soy beans — they make tofu ice cream as well.

I can't decide what flavor to get. So I get two — butter brickle and pistachio coconut.

"Well, if you're having two, I'm having two," Mom says.

She gets mint chocolate swirl and fudge overboard. We take our cones and go sit out on the patio. Waiting for scraps, shiny black grackles sit in the heavy arms of the live oak trees that stretch across the wooden deck. It's warm, but not unbearable, especially not with ice cream.

Wood smoke from the restaurant next door drifts over. They have an actual wood burning pizza oven. I love that place.

"I don't suppose we could go next door and have pizza for supper?" I ask.

"It is a little early. It is just now five o'clock. Besides, your father would be sad to miss out," Mom says.

"I don't think he would miss being around me," I say.

"Give him time, baby. When they called to say Evan Cooper had pulled you out of the swimming pool and done CPR until the ambulance came, it broke your father's heart. He was so scared when we almost lost you, and now he feels he's done something horribly wrong as a parent, based on the poor choices you have been making lately," Mom says.

Did she say Evan Cooper pulled me out of the pool? Josh's Dad? He had every reason to let me drown. Wait. If he pulled me out of the pool, then he must have gone to round up Josh – he knew exactly where he was. It was 1:00 AM – it wasn't like he was calling Josh to come home for dinner. He had already decided to come out of the closet. It's not my fault.

Now, what was she saying about Dad? He blames himself for what I've done. I'll have to do something about that. Maybe they set up the situation, but I made the choices.

"Why don't you call him and ask him to meet us there when he gets off work?" I ask. Or maybe leave work at a decent hour to eat with us? Is the question I don't ask.

"I could do that," she says. "But let me eat my ice cream before it melts."

Mom still carries wipeys in her purse, just like she did when I was little. Most of the time, I think it's dorky, but when I'm sticky and the bathroom is far away, I'm glad she does. I bus the table while Mom gets out her cell and calls Dad.

The conversation I hear goes something along these lines:

"I understand that. I am not asking you to drop everything and leave this instant."

"Oh, how convenient for you."

"It's not like that. I am not taking sides."

"Walter, you're being ridiculous."

"Stop. Just stop. We will talk about this later. Hello? Hello?"

She flicks the screen back to the main menu and pretends that nothing is wrong. "Well, your father has a client dinner tonight. He won't be back until late, anyway, so we're free to do whatever we want."

My eyes feel hot and little tears threaten to escape from them. This, this is my fault. My parents never used to fight. They might not always have agreed, but they never argued. At least not in front of me. Fear, anger and sadness wrestle with each other in my stomach until there is no room for appetite.

"Do you still want to go next door for pizza?" Mom asks.

"I think you're right. It is kind of early," I say.

"Well, maybe we'll get takeout later. Or go to that Thai place you like," she says.

"Sure. That'd be good," I say, hoping later is a lot later. I can't imagine wanting to eat anything any time soon.

"So. Since we're out and about, is there anything you want to do? Go to the mall? The bead shop?" she asks.

"Sure, how about the mall?" I say.

The mall is busy, but not packed. I buy some citrus verbena body sorbet at L'Occitane and we look in the James Avery shop. The first display we come to has pendants.

"Look at the butterflies," Mom says.

"They're cool," I say.

"Do you want one?" she asks.

"Well, they're nice, but I don't know. Maybe they're a little too girly," I say.

Mom just keeps looking into the case. "Butterflies symbolize resurrection, you know."

No, I didn't know. "Really?" I say. She looks disappointed. "Why don't you buy it for yourself, then? I don't think it's really me," I say.

I can tell she is thinking about it by the way she is twisting her lips around. "Yes," she says. "I think I will."

"Then we can call you Madame Butterfly," I tease her.

"Or perhaps not," she says, suddenly looking very sad.

"Why?" I ask.

"Don't you remember the story?" she asks. "Poor Butterfly loses everything and she kills herself in the end. Do you remember when the high school put on Miss Saigon last year? You cried."

"That was Madame Butterfly?" I ask.

"Yes. Same story, different setting and the songs are a little different," she says.

Anyhoo, that put her off of buying the butterfly necklace. We end up watching the ice skaters for a little while and going for dinner at one the restaurants in the mall.

The turdmobile, Dad's custom painted Chestnut Brown (what was he thinking?) Porsche Cayenne, isn't in the garage when we get home. He is still not home when I got to bed at 10:30.

I don't know why I'm so tired – I have barely done anything all day long. I fall asleep almost as soon as my head hits the pillow.

I find myself in a meadow at the edge of a forest at night. I see a small bright light and I go towards it. It's a glowing silver butterfly, sitting on a flower. As if it has been waiting for me to arrive, it flutters is wings and flits down the path into the forest. I follow it.

Before long, we arrive at the Fountain of Sirin. I hear someone singing. When I look around, I see a transparent girl dancing through the wildflowers. I know she is Anna, just like I know Zariel is standing behind me.

Chapter 26
Anna

Hello, Mimi!" Anna smiles and waves at me.
"She can speak now," I say.

"Yes. She has transitioned," he says.

We watch her frolicking in the flowers for a little bit. I felt sorry for Laura Samuels. But if she knew how happy Anna was, she couldn't be too sad, could she?

"She arrived in the Fifth City. But she will soon pass through Fourth City into the Third," Zariel says.

"This is going somewhere. I can tell," I say.

"Once she has passed into the Third Plane, she will not be recognized by anyone on the lower planes. Even you will not be able to see her. The two of you must try to make contact with her mother before that happens. The dead often try to contact the living in dreams when they first cross over. But as they move up levels, they stop trying, stop being able to."

"So we should try tonight, then?" I ask. I have to say that I'm looking forward to the adventure.

"Yes. But you need the Twilight Crystal. Wake up," Zariel says.

As soon as he says 'Wake up,' I am instantly awake. I put the Twilight Crystal around my neck. Just for luck, I pick up the Deer Lady's coin. I don't have any pockets in my pajamas, so I tuck it into my sock. I lay back down on the bed. This time, it takes a few minutes for sleep to come.

Finally, I am back at the Fountain of Sirin. "Got it," I say.

"Excellent. By the way, Deb sent you a present," Zariel says, handing me a pouch. It is the Remembering Dust from Persephone.

"How is Deb?" I ask.

"She is much better. She is making good progress," Zariel gives me a small smile.

"I'm glad. What about Sammie Dog?" I say.

"Sammie is an integral part of Deb's recovery. If it were not for that little dog, I don't think she would make it," Zariel says.

I nod my head. I wonder if there is anything that I love so much that it could pull me back from the brink if I got infected with a lamprisect or attacked by vampires. Maybe my parents. Other than them, I'm drawing a blank.

"Okay, so what do we do now?" I ask.

"First, we shall talk to Anna and remind her why this is important. The timeline has changed, veering from peace towards war. There is still a small window of opportunity for Laura Samuels to be inspired. You and Anna will find her mother and give her the idea about the Rhiannon Foundation. Tell her to read the legend of Rhiannon. Sprinkle a little Remembering Dust on her, then come back," Zariel says.

"So, Zariel. I have a question," I say. "Laura Samuels appears to be a single mom with a really sick kid. Where does she get all the money to start a foundation?" I ask.

"She wins a lawsuit for wrongful death," Zariel says.

"Her husband's?" I ask.

"Yes," he says, but doesn't elaborate.

"Anna! Anna, would you come here, please?" Zariel calls.

She comes skipping up the hill towards us. Flowers are tucked in her hair and a sloppy daisy chain hangs off her wrist.

"Hey, Anna," I say.

She looks at me for a moment, leaning her head to the right then to the left, as if she is trying to get a different view. Then she smiles.

"I remember you now," she says. "We went to the hospital."

"Yep. That's me," I say.

"And you got rid of that awful man," she says.

"Well, I didn't do it all on my own," I say.

"Anna," Zariel says, "do you remember the other girl that was with Mimi? Her name is Deb."

"The scary one with the knife?" Anna asks, recoiling.

"Yes," Zariel says. "You know, Deb did not start out scary. She had a lot of bad things happen to her. Maybe if someone had been around to help her, she would have turned out differently."

"Does Laura, I mean your mom, like to help people, Anna?" I ask.

Anna nods her head. I can tell she is anxious to get back to the flowers.

"What about you, Anna?" Zariel asks. "Do you like to help people?"

"Yes. Always," she says, toying with the daisy chain.

"Good. Because you need to help Mimi find your mother and tell her about Deb," Zariel says.

"I know it doesn't sounds like much, but it could really help a lot of people," I say to her, smiling.

"Okay," she says.

"Go to the station and get transport. Anna will take it from there," Zariel says.

"Hang on. How do we know which zucchini thing to take? Last time it was Platform D. But how do we know where to go this time? Anna is in a different frame of mind now," I say.

"It is always Platform D. For Dreamers," Zariel says, smiling. "Go. It's getting late."

When we get to the park, Anna wants to stop and play. I'm not having much luck convincing her to come along.

"Anna, don't you want to see your mom?" I ask, using the one tactic I haven't tried.

"Mama?" Anna suddenly looks sad. She gets up, but her shoulders are slumped and her eyes are on the sidewalk.

I feel bad now, but I had to get her going somehow. It's a slow walk to the station, but once we get onto Platform D, the zucchini car zips right in to pick us up. Anna has cheered up a lot, but I'm not entirely sure that is a good thing. There are no stops before we barrel into the tunnel. Maybe we caught the express.

This time, the zucchini takes us to some kind of museum. It made me think of the Children's Museum, the Museum of Fine Arts and the Museum of Natural History all rolled into one weird mélange. Children are climbing on dinosaur bones. There is a pretend grocery store, but instead of plastic fruit and vegetables, it only has famous paintings. The place is packed with kids.

"Anna, hold my hand, okay?" I say.

She slips her hand into mine and we start looking around. Upstairs, a girl runs by who looks just like Anna, only five or six. We follow her and we see Laura. She looks tired and she is leaning against the wall.

"Mama?" Anna says.

The woman looks up and crinkles up her face. She is clearly unsure about her suddenly older daughter. "Anna?" she asks.

"Yes, Mama. It's me. The real me," Anna says.

I realize that the younger Anna is nothing more than a memory. I watch as the dreaming mother embraces her spirit daughter.

"I'm okay, Mama. You don't need to worry. It's beautiful here," Anna says, pulling back just a little. She is smiling and even to me, she is clearly an angel.

"Mama, do you remember Mimi?" Anna asks.

She looks at me, but my face doesn't seem to register. I hold out my arm with all the stitches.

"I think so, maybe. It's very fuzzy. Was it a wild girl who cut you? At the hospital?" Laura asks.

"Yes. That wild girl's name is Deb. She's not a bad person, deep down. She's had a lot of really bad things happen to her. If she had just had a little help, she would have made it," I say.

"What do you mean she would have made it?" Laura asks. She still holds Anna's hand.

"She killed herself. She had no hope for a future and couldn't live with the pain anymore. If someone had only been there for her," I say. I shake my head for emphasis. "But please, I am told if you study the legend of Rhiannon, you will understand."

Now is as good a time as any. I open the pouch and sprinkle Remembering Dust on Laura and myself. I try to sprinkle it on Anna, but it just falls through her and lands on the floor.

Anna looks around as if someone is calling her name. I hear nothing, other than the laughing children, younger versions of Anna.

"I have to go now, Mama. You'll be all right. I love you," Anna says.

Laura struggles to let her go. She stretches out her hands as Anna pulls away. I'm sure I have seen this scene in an opera somewhere. The weird hybrid museum, and Laura with it, pulls away from us and retreats beyond the horizon.

I turn around to see the zucchini car waiting for us. We both get in, but Anna has gotten so transparent that I can hardly see her. By the time we get back to the Fountain of Sirin, she is all but gone.

"Don't be sad for her," Zariel says. "She is moving up to the Third Plane. She is very happy."

"I am sure you're right. But it still seems sad to me," I say. A noise snags my attention.

Tap, tap.

"You have completed your project. At your next exit point, you will have a choice – either take on a new project or leave the Earth Realm," Zariel says.

"When will that be?" I ask, wondering if he will really tell me, and if I really want to know.

Squeak. Tap. Tap.

"Sooner than you might think," he says.

"If it is in the next six months, I need to stay. I think my mom really needs me," I say.

Tap. Tap, tap, tap.

"I thought you might say that," Zariel says.

"What is that noise?" I ask. It's very annoying.

"I don't know," Zariel says, but the edges of his mouth curl up, as if he's trying not to smile.

"You aren't a very good liar, Zariel," I say.

"I know," he says.

I find myself floating in the dark, drifting upwards. Then I open my eyes. I'm lying in my own bed. It's raining outside and a branch from the sweet gum tree outside my window scrapes the glass when the wind gusts. I smile as I touch the Twilight Crystal around my neck. There is a certain Lord of the Underworld who is going to be wanting this back soon.

ACT II

Chapter 27
Not So Happy Campers

Opera camp. That's my punishment for the whole underage drinking, nearly drowning in the subdivision pool fiasco.

I'm on a very short leash these days, and at least this gets me out of the house. The opera people are not crazy enough to let us sing. We build and paint sets, learn about staging and opera history. We even 'get' to be extras in a real opera production of *La Boheme* at the end of the two weeks. And my mother did make a point of mentioning to the camp director that I'm named after one of the characters. *Thanks, Mom.*

Although, speaking as someone who has actually been to Hell, this isn't so bad. We get lunch and a snack in the afternoon. And, as far as I can tell – no monsters.

It's a hot and muggy Monday morning. We wait backstage for Johan, the set designer to arrive. I sit next to a girl named Tara. She seems nice enough, even though I've only known her half an hour.

"Did you see the paper this morning?" Tara asks. She glances at the fresh red scar on my arm, but doesn't react.

The paper? Who reads the paper? "No. Why?" I ask. I'm pretty sure that no one has declared nuclear war. I rotate my hand so that the scar is facing downward. At least I got the stitches out before camp started.

"The statue at the Museum of Contemporary Art got stolen. You know, the one that has been there since they opened, the boy," she says.

I feel sick. *Not Brent. Who has taken him? Why would they do that? What if they smash him up?* "Do they have any leads? Why would anyone want that old thing, anyway?" I ask.

"Don't know. It isn't like it is made out of metal that they could melt down and sell," Tara says.

"Did they say anything else?" I ask. There could be something important that she doesn't realize is important.

I need to talk to Zariel, but I don't seem to be able to go to him whenever I want. He's in control, there. I know he'll be contacting me soon, because I still have the Twilight Crystal, and I expect Hades will want it back before too much longer.

I also need to find a newspaper. I've been almost entirely grounded from the internet. Wish Mom hadn't replaced my phone with a stripped-down loser-phone. I doubt that it will be a big story on the TV news. Who cares about an old statue when you can hear all about the latest suburban speed bump controversy?

Johan finally arrives and we paint unceasingly until lunch. I try sneaking out to get a paper then, but Ms. Krebbs is always watching. Especially me. I guess the whole swimming pool thing was in the paper, too. That, and my dad signs her paycheck.

We watch a short act from *La Triviata* after lunch. Then we get back to work. Camp seems to take hours more than it actually does.

When it's finally time to go, I'm the first one out the door. No driving for me without adult supervision for any time in the foreseeable future. "Mom, did you hear about the statue theft at the Museum of Contemporary Art?" I nearly shout at her when I get in the car.

"Yes, now that you mention it, I have read something about that. You know, that is one of the statues that Grandma Fisher took in during the early days." Mom says. "She used to tell stories about that one. Used to swear it was haunted – people heard voices around it when no one was there. In fact, the reason she left the museum was because she thought she started seeing a weird-looking girl near the statue."

A weird looking girl? "What did she look like? What made her weird?" I ask.

I can't tell her that the statue is my friend. I can't lay down in the car and fall asleep, to try to make contact with Zariel. It isn't recycling day, so the paper is probably still in the bin. I try to be calm, cool and collected.

"I don't really remember anything about the girl. Are you okay, sweetie?" Mom asks. "You're acting a little strange."

She's probably afraid I've been huffing paint or something. Sigh. "Oh, I'm fine. I just heard about the statue. It's almost an old friend. I see it every day on the way to school. On field trips, we always take our picture with it. You know," I say.

"I thought it was odd that you were so agitated about that statue when you got in the car. I'm sure it'll turn up − bound to be a prank," she says.

I hope so. When we get home, I rifle through the recycling like a raccoon through the garbage can. I find today's paper just below some junk mail and a frozen waffle box. The statue's disappearance isn't front page news, but it is on page three.

HOUSTON. The Museum of Contemporary Art suffered the loss of one of their oldest exhibits last night. The exhibit, the first sculpture in the museum's collection, is entitled "Basalt Boy" by an anonymous artist. It was removed from the sculpture garden, where it has been standing since 1953, sometime between two and three in the morning. The security guard discovered the theft while on his rounds.

"It seems to have vanished into thin air," Marvella Dragan, the museum's director, told investigators. "None of the equipment securing the sculpture was disturbed, and there were no footprints, even though the sprinkler head near the exhibit has been leaking and making a large area of the ground around it muddy." Police are still investigating. If you have any information about this crime, please call CrimeHalters at 1-800-555-HALT.

Vanished into thin air. *Could it be that Euryale's petrification has worn off? But where did Brent go?* Zariel will know. I suddenly realize that I'm starving, so I wolf down snack.

Page | 149

"Mom!" I shout. "I'm going upstairs!"

She says something, but I can't understand her. I'm already running up the stairs. I pull the drapes. It doesn't help much — they're too light and gauzy. I am kind of tired though, so maybe it won't matter. I kick off my shoes and lie down on top of my covers. My hair clip pokes me in the back of the head, so I take it out and put it on the nightstand. I stretch out and try to relax. It's hard. My mind will not settle down. I keep looking at the clock. It takes more than an hour before I finally drift off into sleep. I try to focus on Zariel. I don't know if that will let him know I'm looking for him, but it can't hurt.

I find myself in the wildflower field by the Fountain of Sirin. I pick a red flower and smell it. Last time I tried smelling the flowers, all I could smell was water. Now, I smell a sweet, almost spicy scent. It reminds me of snickerdoodle cookies.

"Zariel!" I call. I see a few butterflies, but not any people. "Zariel!" I try again.

"You don't have to shout," Zariel says from over my left shoulder.

I whip my head around to face him. "Brent is gone!" I shout.

"Gone? Is he really?" he asks.

This is a bad sign. "Yes. He disappeared from the museum last night. I thought he had melted and come back up here," I say.

"He has not returned here," Zariel says.

"What could have happened to him?" I ask.

"What, indeed," Zariel says.

Is he is mocking me? "Do you even care?" I ask. "'Cause it doesn't sound much like it. Brent could be in real trouble," I say.

"He could very well be. Perhaps you should go and look for him," Zariel says.

"Is this your way of giving me an assignment?" I ask.

Zariel smiles. "Guilty as charged," he says.

An assignment. All on my own. With no one to help me. It makes me think of Deb. "How is Deb, by the way," I ask.

"She is doing very well. She might even be able to come and see you next time you arrive," Zariel says. "Right now, I think the temptation of staying in the Seventh Plane is too strong for her," Zariel says.

"Oh. I see. What about Sammie? She still good?" I ask.

"The dog is also doing very well," Zariel says. "But about Brent."

"Mimi?"

Who is that? I feel someone touch my arm and I feel myself being pulled out of the field, away from the fountain, away from Zariel.

I awake with a start. Mom is standing over me. "Mimi? Baby, are you feeling alright?"

"Yes," I grouch. "I'm just tired."

"Dinner is ready. A nice, healthy meal will do you a world of good," she says.

I didn't want to wake up now. Zariel still had something to tell me. Why couldn't dinner have waited another five minutes?

"Okay," I say. The moment has passed. I can do nothing about it just now. I swing my legs off the bed and stand up.

My mother has recently subscribed to a cooking magazine. Now when she cooks, we have dishes like corn crespelle with mascarpone and capers, grilled squid skewers with anchovy butter, and grilled vegetable salad with Cuban mojo. Tonight there is something that appears to be a bowl of fresh blood and, and a plate of noodles with bits of grass and a bunch of clam shells.

"The specials for this evening," Mom says. "Are roasted root vegetable soup and spaghetti with clam sauce, with citrus glazed cheese cake for dessert."

Amazingly enough, Dad is home from work. But he doesn't seem to care that Mom went to all the trouble to make fancy restaurant-sounding food for him. Because she sure didn't make it for me. I think it usually looks very colorful, but doesn't taste very nice. Maybe somebody should invent fancy food that actually tastes good.

"That sounds very interesting, Mom." I say. I look at Dad. "You're home early. You didn't get laid off did you?"

"Mimi! Don't be so rude," Mom says.

"Well, I just hope we're not keeping Dad from anything important," I say.

"That is enough, young lady. You are skating on very thin ice as it is. Don't push your luck," Dad says.

"Sorry," I say, grudgingly.

We sit down for our meal. The blood soup obviously has beets in it. It tastes like dirt, with salt and butter.

I don't care for all the clamshells looking back at me from their bed of noodles in the main course. The pasta tastes good, but not restaurant good. It lacks something, but I don't know what. However, it is a big step up from her pumpkin raviolis, which were raw and slimy in the middle.

We have the usual dinner conversation:

How was your day at work, dear? Fine. How was your day at opera camp, baby? Fine. The end.

"That was nice, Mom. Thank you. May I please be excused?" I say.

"Who are you and what have you done with my child?" Mom asks.

"Ha. Ha. It just looks like you worked really hard. Thanks," I say and get up from the table.

I brush my teeth and get ready for bed. Sleep doesn't come for a while, so I read a book. I am at the part where a really hot pirate captain boards the heroine's ship. Sweat-glistening pecs and heaving bosoms just aren't working for me today. I put the book down. Rotten nap. It's several hours before I finally fall asleep. I dream about bats (the flying kind, not the baseball kind) and a tea party with Medusa, but I don't find Zariel. I wake up long before I need to, disappointed.

I actually get to opera camp on time today. That's a switch. I sit with Tara while we're waiting on our teacher. Once Johan arrives, we are sent into the depths of the storage room, in search of nature props – plastic plants, fake animals, silk flowers and so on.

The florescent lights are bright, but far away on the high ceiling. Everything is wrapped in plastic and the plastic is wrapped in dust. I am so glad they checked to see if we had any allergies before they sent us back here.

I had thought this was going to be easy. We would just go to the area marked 'Greenery,' pull out whatever was there and come back. The problem is that there is no area marked 'Greenery,' and all of the greenery is mixed in with the other sets and props.

I am trying to dislodge a potted ficus from the 'Inside House' section when I hear Tara's voice.

"Why are you here?" she asks.

I let go of the tree and look around. She is nowhere near me. I walk around and look for her. Finally, I spot her standing near the edge of a shelf. She is facing away from me, talking to someone on the other side of the storage unit. I think she looks a little nervous.

"Tara? You okay?" I ask.

She jumps at the sound of my voice. "Yeah, Mimi. I'm fine. Just fine."

"Well, I heard you talking to someone. I just wanted to make sure," I say.

"You heard me talking? No, I was…singing. I just sing to myself sometimes. I'm sure that's what you heard," Tara says.

"If you say so," I say.

I go back to extracting the tree. Eventually, Jessica comes to summon us for lunch. I pale at my pathetic pile of plants, but I pick it up and proceed. We leave our greenery backstage and head to the cantina.

Lunch isn't very exciting. The only thing noteworthy is that Tara keeps staring off into space and looking either bothered or guilty. She constantly looks around, as if she's expecting someone to jump out from behind something and get her.

"Are you sure you are okay?" I ask.

"Sure. I'm fine," she answers. "What makes you think I'm not?"

"For one thing, you're acting like you are in witness protection program or something," I say.

"I'm sorry," she says.

I wait for her to explain, but she doesn't. "Well, if you need something..." I say.

"Thanks," she replies.

She is worse on Wednesday. Several times I see her off by herself, whispering. I don't know if she is whispering to herself or someone only she can see. I wish I could help her, but I don't know what to do. Again, I ask her if everything is okay and again she says it is.

Tara looks still worse on Thursday, and I wonder if she will even show up on Friday.

"Is your friend is having a psychotic episode?" asks Jessica, snickering. She's one of the other students, and I don't like her much. She reminds me of Lexie and Sierra, who I thought were my friends, but they dropped me like a bad habit as soon as we got in trouble.

I don't know if Jessica is trying to make fun of both Tara and I, or if she wants me to make fun of Tara with her.

"Leave her alone. You don't know anything about it," I say. I hope she doesn't call my bluff and ask me what is going on because I don't know anything about it, either.

She rolls her eyes at me and struts away. Yay. I have found yet another place to be a social outcast.

I have tried every night this week to get in touch with Zariel. He seems to be on vacation or something.

On Friday, the circles under Tara's eyes are so dark, she looks like someone hit her. Just after lunch, I find her backstage, talking to a curtain.

"Please, just leave me alone," she says. She starts crying and runs away.

I follow her into the restroom, where she's splashing water on her face.

"Tara, please tell me what's wrong. I really want to help you," I say.

"I'm fine," she insists.

"No, you're not. Spill it," I say.

"You're going to think I am crazy."

"You might be surprised."

"I see…ghosts," she says, whispering and looking down at the concrete floor.

"Ghosts? You mean dead people?" I ask.

"Yes," she answers, still not looking up.

"Is that all? Some of my best friends are dead people," I say.

Tara looks at me warily. "What is that supposed to mean?" she asks.

"Last month, I drowned in a swimming pool. They revived me, but I had some, shall we say, experiences."

"Do you see them?" she asks.

"Not in the Earth Realm," I say. I hope I don't sound like a commercial for a psychic reader.

Tara sighs. "I do. All the time, ever since I was little. Most of the time, if I ask them to go away, they do, but not this one," she says. "He won't stop bothering me."

"Is it someone who used to perform here or something? It seems a lot of theatres have ghosts, usually someone who died there. Don't you ever watch those ghost hunter shows on TV?" I ask.

"No, I don't," she says. "But I don't think this guy is connected to the theatre."

"Why is that?" I ask.

"He keeps asking about you," she says.

Chapter 28
Sleepover

He what?" I ask. *Has Lucas, the vampire, escaped from the Seventh Plane and come after me?* "What does he look like?"

"He has kind of dark wavy hair and dark eyes, kind of cute," she says.

"Brent!" I say, probably too loudly. "He's one of my friends. I thought he was lost."

"Well, he's here," Tara says.

"Great! We can go out and find him, and —"

"He's here. Right beside you," Tara cuts me off.

I turn my head to the left. "Do you mind? This is the girls' restroom?" I say.

"This is probably the best place to talk to him. Fewer observers," Tara says.

"Maybe, but it's a little weird," I say.

"He says no one can see him, so what's the diff?" Tara says.

"It's the principle of the thing. Oh, never mind," I say. "Brent, what happened? Why did you disappear from the museum? Are you thawed?"

"Yes, the stone did finally melt and he was released. But he found that he was trapped in the Earth Realm. He can't reach the Astral Realm or contact any one there," Tara says.

"Yeah, Zariel has been shutting me out, too. Don't know what's up with that," I say. "Maybe what we need is that Twilight Crystal. Brent, can you find my house?" I say.

"He says he can," Tara says. "Who is Zariel?"

"Someone I know on the other side. He's sort of an angel," I reply. "What about you? Do you think you can come for a sleepover? I know it is short notice."

"I don't know. Maybe," Tara says.

"Let me call my mom first," I say. Since she is one of the few the approved numbers on my new cell phone. The one with no camera and that will only dial or accept numbers your parents program in. It's very humiliating. I hope they have gotten over this before school starts.

"I can't get a signal in here. I'm going to have to go outside," I say.

As we head for the door, Jessica comes barging in. She looks at us and almost makes a kissy face. "I am not interrupting anything, am I?" she says.

"Bite me," I say, pushing past her.

Tara pauses to look at her. Then a wicked smile spreads up her face. "At least I'm not knocked up," she says.

I did not know that color really could drain from someone's face. Jessica runs into a stall and closes the door with a bang. Maybe I'm not the only naughty girl sentenced to opera camp.

"How did you know that?" I ask Tara as we go out into the corridor.

She shrugs. "I don't know. I can just tell by looking," she says. "It is a boy."

"Jessica's baby?" I ask.

"Yeah. I wonder if I should tell her? It might make a difference," she says.

"You can try," I say.

A boy. It strikes me then that it is alive. I never once thought about what I would do if I got pregnant. Three choices, kill it, keep it, or give it away. Destroy its life, destroy my life, or something half way in between. There is a decision I never want to have to make. Guess it kind of sucks to be Jessica right now. Maybe that is why she is such a cow. Or maybe she's always that way. Who knows?

But enough of that.

"I think I should tell her," Tara says. She goes back into the bathroom.

I call my mom and ask if Tara can spend the night. She says it's fine. It will give her one more palate to tempt with ratatouille strata with lamb and olives. I should probably warn Tara.

She is gone for such a long time that I wonder if I need to go check to make sure Jessica hasn't done anything to her. While I am mulling this over, the door opens and Tara comes out.

"You okay?" I ask. "I was starting to worry she had drowned you in the toilet or something."

"No. We talked for a while. She said her dad was so mad that he had four girls but not a son that he named her youngest sister Douglas. If she has a boy, it might keep him from throwing her out on the street," Tara says.

"Wow," is all I can say. I'm sure that if I got pregnant, my parents would be hurt, angry and disappointed, but they would never throw me out of the house. I don't think. I would really rather not find out. Besides, after Josh runs his fat mouth, nobody worth looking at is going to want to be in the same room with me. Hey, but I have another seven weeks before I have to deal with that. I hope.

"I called Mom," I say. "She said it's fine if you sleep over tonight. We're having something with lamb and olives for supper. You might want to have a snack before you come over."

"How mad will your mom be if I don't eat with you?" Tara asks, chewing on her bottom lip.

"She'd probably get over it," I say. "Why?"

"Well, I'm a vegetarian, so the lamb thing is not going to work for me," Tara says.

"Oh. Yeah, Mom puts chicken or chicken broth in just about everything. We usually eat around seven. Why don't you just show up around seven thirty?" I say.

After a few calls back and forth, and exchanges of telephone numbers and email addresses, everything is arranged.

"We'd better get back or Johan is going to come looking for us himself," I say.

Tara laughs and we get back to our scheduled activity – listening to some of the songs from *Aida* as Johan explains the story. When we come in, Johan looks around the room. Guess he has just now missed us and Jessica. He motions to his helper girl (who is an actual understudy in the opera) and whispers something in her ear. She leaves the room. He is at the part where Aida and Radames are buried alive before Helper Girl and Jessica reappear. Jess looks like she has been crying. Can't say that I blame her.

Finally, we're released. Opera camp is officially half way over. I wave at Jessica and give her what I hope is an encouraging smile as she leaves.

"Okay," Tara says, pulling out her fancy phone. "What is your cell number again? I didn't get it all."

I tell her and watch her program it in, knowing full well it will reject her call unless my mom is so inclined to put it on the list.

I can tell by the way her thumbs fly over the keyboard that she does a lot of texting. I hope she doesn't try to text me. Mom has disabled texting. I don't know what kind of error message you get, probably 'Loser-phone can't receive text messages. Try and get some less lame friends.'

"Last thing. Give me your address so my navigator can find your house," Tara says.

I tell her where I live.

"I know where that is. You don't live all that far from me, actually," Tara says.

"Really? Where do you live," I ask.

"Riverbirch Place," she says.

Oh. One of those 'walled communities' where the cheapest house is about a million dollars.

My mom isn't here yet, so I walk out to the parking lot with Tara. I expect her to go to the black BMW Roadster. Instead, she goes to a very bland, very boxy blue vehicle.

"What do you think?" Tara asks. "It is all electric."

"Yeah. Cool," I say. I'm never going to figure this girl out. "See you at seven thirty."

Mom arrives just after Tara has left. As soon as I get in the car, Mom says, "I spoke with Dr. Berkman this afternoon."

I have no idea who this is. "You did?" I ask.

"Yes. Tara's mother. She seems very nice. She invited us over for dinner next Saturday," she says, tentatively.

"They live at Riverbirch Place," I say.

"Do they? I'm glad I accepted. So. How was your day?"

"Fine. We learned about *Aida* today." I can't tell her that I found my missing friend, or found out a girl was pregnant and may get thrown out on the street. I almost wish I could, just to confirm that she wouldn't do that to me.

Mom thinks for a few minutes. "Is that why she didn't want to come for dinner? She didn't think my cooking would be good enough?" Mom sometimes likes to find reasons to be offended.

"No, Mom. She's a vegetarian. You're serving lamb. And you put chicken in everything," I say.

"I see," she says. I can tell that she is still trying to find a way to be insulted.

Mom's something or another with lamb and olives is not the worst thing she has cooked recently. It is not quite good, but it is not horrible. I do feel bad that a lamb had to die for this dish, though.

At seven thirty five, the doorbell rings.

"Hey, Tara," I say, letting her in.

I bring her in to the kitchen and introduce her to my mom. Dad isn't home yet.

"Tara? It is so nice to meet you. It is so heartening to see young people interested in the opera," she says.

"Yes, ma'am. I suppose it goes well with the theater and ballet," Tara says.

"So, your mother is a doctor. What is she, a pediatrician? OB/GYN?" Mom asks.

"Actually, she is an organ transplant surgeon. My dad is a neurosurgeon," Tara says, finishing with a practiced smile. I bet she gets that a lot. In fact, I can see the little light go on above Mom's head – 'That is how they afford Riverbirch Place!' I know she will be trying to figure out ways to get herself invited to Tara's house, just so that she can tell her snooty frenemies that she has friends who live at Riverbirch Place.

Me, I don't care where she lives. I am fresh out of friends at the moment, and she seems like a keeper. Besides, how many people can actually see ghosts? Maybe I'll be able to tell her more about my near death adventure in the Astral Realm. Not yet, though. But I am sure she is going to wonder how I know Brent if he's dead and I can't see ghosts, if she stops to think about it.

We leave Mom in the kitchen and go to the living room. "So. It is kind of early to turn in. What do you want to do?" I ask.

"I don't know. What are the options?" Tara says.

"Well, we could stay down here and watch a movie or play a video game. Computer is down here, too. In my room we could listen to some tunes or something," I say. Usually when I have spent the night, especially a Friday night, with Lexie or Sierra, we went out to the clubs. We all have fake IDs and we know which places don't card very carefully and which ones don't card at all.

"What games do you have?" she asks.

"Let us see," I say, walking over to the TV armoire. I open the cabinet and start to flip through it and call out the titles of the games to her.

"How about the Cubes one?" Tara says.

That's my dad's game. I hate that one. "Sure," I say. I set the game up and hand her a controller.

I seem to suck worse than usual at this game tonight. Tara is kicking my butt. I can't get any of the creature thingies to stay on the cubes. All of hers do.

"You have this game at home, don't you?" I ask.

"Is it that obvious?" she asks.

"Hey, Mimi. Your mother said you had a friend over," Dad says from the living room doorway.

"Hi, Dad. This is Tara. Tara, Dad," I say.

"Nice to meet you, Tara," Dad says, shaking her hand. "I see you're playing one of my favorite games." He seems hopeful that we will invite him to join us. Maybe Mom's told him that Tara's parents live in Riverbirch Place, and he's networking for opera donors.

"Yeah, Dad. Why don't you take over for me? I have to go to the bathroom," I say.

I hand him the controller and go into the half bath under the stairs. When I come out, Dad and Tara seem to have a system down where they are flinging creatures like crazy. All of them stay on their little floating cubes. And of course, all the little creatures are helping each other. I think when I play, they push each other off. I feel a twinge of jealousy. It is almost seems Dad doesn't even know Tara, and he likes her better than me.

"Hey, honey. Do you want your controller back?" Dad asks.

"No, that's alright. I am a little tired, anyway," I say.

It takes for-flipping-ever for them to finish the game. I sit on the couch and read *People* magazine. Well, I look at the pictures, anyway.

"That was fun, Tara. Thank you," Dad says.

"Oh, you're welcome. I enjoyed it, too, Mr. Sepulveda," Tara says.

"You ready to head upstairs?" I ask her.

"Sure," Tara answers.

She picks up the backpack that she left by the front door and we climb the stairs.

"When you get to the top, go right," I say.

My bedroom is easy to find. The door is open and my queen-sized bed is unmade. Good. I only have two articles of clothing strewn on the floor, and neither of them are socks or underwear.

"I don't know if you want to sleep in here, with me, or in the guest room. Makes me no difference," I say.

"I have been told that I kick and sometimes snore, so it might be better for you if I slept in the guest room," Tara says.

Is she just saying that to be polite about not wanting to sleep in my room? If not, who has told her that she kicks and snores?

"Okay. Let me show you where it is and you can put your stuff down," I say.

I lead her to the end of the hall. "There you go. There is a private bathroom through that door," I say.

"Cool. Thanks," Tara says as she tosses her backpack on the bed.

We go back to my room. I close the door.

"Okay," I say getting the Twilight Crystal off my dresser. "This is the crystal that I was telling you about when we were talking to Brent. I wonder if he's here yet."

"He says he has been here all afternoon," Tara says.

"Oh. Okay. So now what do we do?" I say.

"What is it that you use the crystal for?" Tara says.

"I can visit people's dreams, and they can see me," I say.

"Cool. Can you use it to pull other people in, or does it only work for you?" Tara asks.

"If they're standing close enough, it works on them, too. Otherwise, just me," I say.

Tara thinks for a moment. "Okay. Why don't we try to do this? Let's both go sleep. Then you and Brent try to come into my dream. So we're all on the same page, let us try to meet at a familiar place," she says.

"Where do you have in mind?" I ask. What place is familiar to all of us?

"Brent suggests the Museum Contemporary Art," Tara says.

"Sure," I say. "How exactly do we do that?"

"Try to imagine yourself there as you are falling asleep. Try to focus on any details you can remember," Tara says.

Sounds like she's done this before. I wonder what other strange and mysterious information she has.

"Well, see you at the museum," Tara says, heading for the guest room.

"Yeah. See you there," I say.

I brush my teeth and get ready for bed. I am tired, but I'm having trouble getting comfortable. I think about the museum. I try to imagine details about it, but my mind wanders. Finally, I find myself in a park. It isn't a particular park, but a composite of parks I have been to. Children feed ducks and some people tool around in paddleboats on the pond.

"Psst!" someone hisses at me.

I look around, but I don't see anybody. "Who said that?" I ask.

"I did," says the red maple tree in front of me.

"What do you want?" I ask. In my dream, I don't think it's odd to be having a conversation with a tree.

"You're going the wrong way," the tree says. "What you want is back that way." A leafy branch rustles, pointing away from me.

"Thank you," I say and start down the path in the opposite direction.

This path leads through some dark woods. I follow it anyway. I don't feel frightened. After a while, I come out at the Museum of Contemporary Art. Brent and Tara are already there. I run to Brent and hug him.

"Glad you're unfrozen," I say.

"Me, too," he says. "Except for the part about being trapped in the Earth Realm."

"There has to be a way out of that," I say. "I wish Zariel would turn up."

"Yes. He's been making himself scarce lately," Brent says.

"I will help you whenever I can. But sometimes, you must find the answers for yourself," Zariel says as he comes into the sculpture garden.

"Zariel, where have you been?" I ask.

"I do have other cases to manage," he replies.

"I though you could be several places at once," I say.

Zariel smiles, but doesn't say anything else to me. "Brent, you are looking well. I see the gorgon's touch has not done you any long-term harm."

"Maybe, but I'm trapped here in the Earth Realm. I haven't been able to get back to the Astral," Brent says.

"Yes. There is a bit of a problem with that for you," Zariel says. "For something to become physical, it starts out as energy on the very highest plane. Then, as it gets more and more organized, it gets more solid and sinks through the levels to the Earth Realm. Once the physical form has completed its cycle, the soul moves to the etheric body, which often starts in the Sixth or Seventh Plane. As the second death, the separation from the etheric body, occurs, the soul moves into the astral body and onto a higher plane. This doesn't take long, and most people sleep through it. The problem,

Brent, is that you had already moved into the astral body. There is no longer a connection on the lower planes for you to move to from the Earth Realm."

"So, what do I do? Am I stuck here forever?" Brent asks. He looks upset. "And if you knew that, why did you bring me here?"

"I brought you to the Earth Realm because you would have sunk there anyway, since you had become something of the Earth Realm instead of something of the Astral. I thought it was better to put you in a safe place that we knew where and when you landed, than to let you fall in a random spot in space and time. There is a way to put things right. There is always a way," Zariel says.

"That makes it sound dangerous and/or difficult," Tara says. I can't tell by looking at her face it she thinks that is a good thing or a bad thing.

"When something has fallen outside the normal procedures, it is always difficult and sometimes dangerous," Zariel says.

"Okay, so what do we have to do?" I ask.

"One way is to find a sojourner, often called a shaman. Someone who often travels to the Astral Realm. He or she might be able to open a way for you," Zariel says.

"Might be able to?" Brent asks.

"Some are more skilled than others," Zariel says. "Some are charlatans."

"What are the other ways?" Tara asks.

"You could locate a vortex. They can be found in certain parts of the world, but the closest to you is in the Arizona desert," Zariel says.

"Anything else?" Brent asks.

"There is one other way. If you can approach the water fae, they have the ability to move easily between the realms. They will certainly be able to help you, but they are difficult to find and they are not fond of humans," Zariel says.

Brent's shoulders slump and I am sure that he would have let out a big sigh, if only he had lungs to breathe in air.

"Well, why don't we start with the easiest option?" Tara says.

"What would that be?" I ask.

"The shaman?" asks Brent.

"That's what I think," Tara says.

"Yes, that's probably the easiest, though the least reliable," says Zariel.

"Speaking of reliable," Brent says, "how is Deb?"

He doesn't know that Deb has been compromised and that she tried to kill me when we finally tracked down Laura Samuels.

"She is recovering. I think she can be saved," Zariel says.

"Saved from what?" Brent asks.

"Do you remember the lamprisect?" I ask.

"That creepy eel thing with all teeth and the bug legs?" Brent asks.

"Yes," I say. "After it infected her, she was okay until Lucas showed up. Then she went all rogue and tried to kill me."

Brent frowns. "Oh. Man, that's rough," he says.

I'm not sure if he means rough for Deb, rough for me, or both.

"I'm sorry about your friend," Tara says. "But back to the shaman?"

"Yeah. Good plan. We need to find one. What is a shaman, anyway?" I ask.

Tara looks as me as if I had just asked what a bra was for.

"A shaman is a medicine man," Brent says.

"Oh, like we are going to find someone like that in Houston," I say.

"There are plenty of them, if you know where to look," Tara says.

Why would a double doctors' daughter who lives in Riverbirch Place know where to find shamans in Houston? Do her parents know about this? There is a lot more to Tara than meets the eye.

"And you know this how?" Brent asks.

"I know a lot of things," Tara says. "Instead of asking me stupid questions, maybe you could just be glad that I do know." The tone of her voice makes it clear that she will not be messed with.

"So, Zariel, do you have any ideas for us?" Brent asks. There is no answer. "Zariel?"

He's gone. I never noticed him leaving. He's very sneaky that way.

"Well, tomorrow is Saturday. That should be a good day to start. If we know what we're going to do, then I'm going to look in on Jenny and Terry," Brent says.

"I need to go to the bathroom," Tara says.

They vanish, and I am standing in the sculpture garden of the Museum of Contemporary Art alone. Alone except for the statues. There is one of a headless boy riding on a turtle. The turtle turns its head to look at me.

Chapter 29
Hungry Ghost

"What is up, chickie?" the turtle asks.

"Nothing," I say, backing towards the gate.

I leave the museum grounds and find myself in a jungle. There are movements in the trees and eyes peer out at me from the bushes. I'm not afraid. I open my mouth to say, "Get out of my way!" but a jaguar's roar comes out instead of words. I look at my hands and arms, and see black cat fur. If I look very closely, I can see a spotted pattern underneath. I continue on my way. I catch the scent of something, a capybara. I can tell by the sounds it's making that it's coming my way. I slink off the path and into a clump of the tall ferns. I wait until I hear its footfalls on the dirt trail. I crouch, holding my breath. When it is almost past me, I spring from the undergrowth.

"Mimi?"

What is that noise? It has distracted me and I missed my target. The rodent squeals and runs into the brush.

"Mimi, wake up," the voice says again.

Something touches my shoulder and I swat at it, claws outstretched.

"Ow!" says the voice. "Good grief. Get up already. We have a lot to do today."

I open my mouth to roar, but words come out. How odd. "Fine. I'm getting up," I hear myself say. My eyes open and I discover that I am in a soft bed with pink sheets. I realize that I am back to being Mimi again. It's not even light outside yet.

"Are you always this cranky in the morning?" Tara asks.

"I was having this dream. I was a jaguar. I was just about to catch a three-foot rat when you started poking me," I say.

"A jaguar? How do you know it wasn't a leopard?" Tara asks.

"I just know. Besides, I was a black jaguar," I say.

"Make sure you tell the shaman about that. It might mean something to him. Especially, since you had the dream when you did," Tara says.

"Okay, so how do we find a shaman in Houston?" I ask.

"You start by brushing your teeth and getting dressed," Tara replies.

She is already groomed and wearing fresh clothes. It's barely six o'clock. Who gets up that early on a Saturday?

I stretch and crawl out from under the covers. "Are we going to at least eat breakfast first?" I ask as I strip off my pajamas.

"Sure, why not?" Tara says. "I'll meet you downstairs.

I'm in no hurry, and after I'm dressed, teeth and hair brushed and slightly more awake, I casually make my way down the stairs. It's only about half an hour later.

I write a note for my parents, telling that we're going shopping. Which, technically, is a violation of my parole. But because I'm with Tara 'Riverbirch Place' Berkman, they might let it slide. Or at least my mom will.

Tara gets her backpack from beside the door, and we head out to her car. I get in the passenger side.

"Hey, did you bring that crystal thingy?" Tara asks.

"No. I forgot my purse, anyway. Be right back," I say. I run back in the house and get my forgotten items. Can't leave my loser-phone behind, can I?

I get back in the car and buckle up. The car is so small, I'm not sure a seatbelt will help. If something larger than a motorcycle hit us, we'd be toast. Tara starts backing out of the driveway. I never heard engine come on.

"Is it always this quiet?" I ask, thinking it could be a great stealth vehicle.

"Yes. It's electric, remember?" she says.

I nod my head. I keep my mouth shut so that I don't say anything I might regret later. I don't want to have to call my mom to come and get me after Tara has left me God knows where.

"Will Brent know how to get to this place?" I ask. I don't know if he needs directions, or if he can just tell where we are.

"He's in the car now," Tara says.

"Is he? Hey, Brent. How are Jenny and Terry?" I ask.

"Terry is good. She is just starting to crawl. Jenny has started dating some guy named Chuck. I don't like him," Brent says, via Tara.

"You don't like him because he's with your baby mama, or because you have a bad feeling about him?" Tara asks.

"Maybe a little bit of both," Brent tells us.

I sense a detour coming.

Tara drives us to a, shall I say, 'vintage' strip center. There is a liquor store on one end, and, separated by several empty slots, a corner market on the other. A faded Lotto Texas sign hangs by one corner in the market's dusty window.

The woman sitting on a stool behind the tall counter doesn't look up from her tabloid. "Hello, Tara-belle. Myles said you'd be stopping by. There's some muffins and stuff in the back."

Tara-belle?

"Good. I'm starved. This is my friend, Mimi," Tara says.

Janet looks up. Her skin is loose and saggy, but her eyes are scary-sharp. If she'd been wearing a scarf, I might have wondered if she was Sthenno in disguise.

She's too far away to shake hands with, so I start to wave. But then I decide that just looks dumb, and curl my fingers, back into my palm. "Nice to meet you, Janet."

She nods, and keeps staring at me.

I try to keep my squirming on the inside. I don't want to dis Tara's friend, but she really makes me uncomfortable, the way she's looking at me.

"Myles should be back soon. The three of you can wait in the break room, if you want."

"Thanks," Tara answers, smiling.

It's the kind of smile that makes me want to smack her. She knows these people, this place. I know nothing, and I feel like that grin is taunting me.

I follow Tara through the Employees Only door next to the toilet. The back room is small, but clean. A coffee table squats on a Persian-style rug, more or less in front of a green loveseat that's seen better days. A small microwave sits at one end of a stained Formica countertop, which runs the most of length of the short back wall, before it stops at a dented harvest gold refrigerator. A stainless steel sink sits in the middle.

A folding card table is shoved against the back wall, and two wooden dining chairs are tucked neatly in at the available sides. A white bakery box sits in the middle of it.

Tara pulls out one of the wooden chairs and sits at the table. I wasn't hungry until she opened the box – now the muffins smell so good, I have to have one. I grab a blueberry one and plop onto the loveseat. I wonder if I have time for a nap before Myles arrives. Who am I kidding?

"So, am I the only one who can't see Brent?" I ask, peeling the paper off the sides of the muffin.

Tara swallows the mouthful of donut she's chewing. She looks at me, then cocks her head to one side, trying to gauge how serious I am. "Most people can't see him. He's by the door, in case you were wondering."

I nod. "Who, exactly, are Janet and Myles? Are they going to tell us where to find the shaman?"

"Oh? Is he lost?" asks an unfamiliar voice from the doorway.

"Uncle Myles!" Tara gets up and hugs the man who had just entered the room, holding her hands out awkwardly so she doesn't get donut glaze in his hair.

"How's my favorite niece?" he asks. "I see you've brought friends."

I study Uncle Myles. He's shorter than I am, dark hair and eyes, probably around my dad's age. I wouldn't call him fat, but he doesn't appear to miss any meals, either.

"Do I pass inspection?" he asks, eyes twinkling.

I shrug. I suppose I had expected someone more witch doctor and less genial relative. I pop the last bite of pastry into my mouth and lick my fingers.

Myles closes his eyes, takes a deep breath, and shakes himself as he exhales. "Shall we begin?"

Tara motions me over to the sink, and we wash the sugar off our fingers.

I turn to Uncle Myles, hesitating. "There's something Tara said I should tell you," I say. Seems a bit weird, in the daylight, to be talking about a dream. A pointless, ridiculous dream. "I dreamed I was a jaguar. A black jaguar."

"I see. Tell me about it," Myles says, opening a wooden box on the coffee table and taking out an incense stick.

"Not that much to it. I was a jaguar, I was about to catch a giant rat, Tara work me up. That pretty much covers it," I reply.

"Interesting."

I knew it was stupid to bring it up.

"Did you know," Myles continues, "that jaguars are guardians of the underworld? The black jaguar represents the sacred feminine, and that its element is water?"

The back of my neck goes all tingly as little hairs stand on end. "No. Never heard any of that."

I glance at Tara, who is still sitting at the table. Her eyes are closed. *What is she doing?*

"The jaguar's power is strongest at the new moon."

"When is that?" I ask.

"Last night. I would expect she's trying to tell you something. Since you were the jaguar, it is going to be something very personal to you. The underworld probably means death or transition. There may be another female involved, but the feminine aspect could be you. Jaguars love to swim – there is likely to be a pond or pool involved."

Hmmm. Death, female, pool. Where have I heard that story before?

Myles looks over at Tara. She opens her eyes and comes over to sit on the loveseat next to me. "Show him the crystal," she says.

I pull it out of my purse and set it in Myles' hand. He holds it up by the chain, and light glints off if it as it slowly spins over the table.

"Where did you get this?" he asks.

"Long story short, I borrowed it from Hades. It's supposed to change your vibrational level so people can see you in their dreams."

"That is cool! Meeting archetypes is rare," Tara says.

Nodding slightly, Myles puts the chain over my head, and the crystal hangs just over my heart. Suddenly, I hear Brent's voice.

"I'm tired and hungry, and I just want to go home," he says.

I can't see him, but his voice feels as if it's coming from off to my left, on the other side of Tara. I realize that I'm not hearing him with my ears, but inside my head.

"Brent? We're going to get you back to the Astral, okay? Just hang tight," I say, wondering if he can hear the thoughts careening around inside my head telling me this is too crazy to be real, and that I should just call my mom to come and get me.

"He's hungry?" Tara asks Myles. "He's a ghost. How can that be?"

"That's never a good sign," he replies. "He'll start borrowing, soon."

"What do you mean, 'borrowing?'" I ask. He's talking about my friend, here.

"There's a reason people take on meat bodies when they come to the Earth Realm. It's heavy and thick, and it takes too much energy to survive long if they don't have the buffer that the body provides. As the discarnate run low on fuel, they usually start to borrow energy from others around them. Most of them they don't mean any harm, and they don't take much, at least not at the beginning, but the more they borrow, the more they need. And they soon discover that a quick way to get a lot of energy is to terrify people. Once ghosts start borrowing, it's easy for them to become corrupted."

"Then let's get Brent home," I reply. The thought of Brent on the Seventh, much less the Eighth, Plane breaks my heart.

Myles pulls four candles – yellow, blue, green, and red - from the box where he got the incense. He puts each one in a glass holder and sets one at each corner of the coffee table, then lights the candles and incense. He starts singing to himself, barely above a whisper, as he goes to turn out the lights. I'm not sure I would understand his words, even if I could hear them clearly.

"Relax your body, close your eyes, and come with me," Myles says.

As soon as my lids shut, I find myself in a jungle. Unfamiliar birds make strange calls up in the canopy. Insects click and buzz in the undergrowth. Tara and Myles are to my right. Brent is just a little way off, on my left, looking grey and almost transparent. He opens his arms, and I run to hug him, but when I do, I start to feel a little dizzy.

"Stop!" Myles shouts, striding over to us.

Brent lets me go. "I-I am so sorry," he says. But he surreptitiously licks his lips as he looks down at the thin path through the jungle.

Myles glares at me. "Did you not hear a word I just said? If you want to help him, stay away from him."

I find myself at the head of the line, next to Myles. Tara is behind me, and Brent brings up the rear. It isn't long before we arrive at an oddly shaped building. I walk around it. It has ten sides, with colorful stained glass windows in four walls, almost evenly spaced around the building – window, wall, wall, window, wall, window, wall, window, wall, wall. If there's a door, I don't see it.

"Here we are," Myles says. "Tara, you go in first."

She smiles and turns. And walks right through the window, as if it is nothing more than a hologram.

"Next," Myles says to me.

I walk through the window. It's cool and refreshing inside. Smells like the star jasmine on our neighbor's fence. My mother would love the black and white checkered tumbled marble floor. For no apparent reason, a black pillar and a white pillar stand in the middle of the room.

And someone is waiting there to meet us.

"Zariel!"

"I've come to retrieve Brent," he says. "It is good to see you, as always."

Myles' head appears through the window. "We have a problem," he says. "Brent doesn't seem to be able to pass through."

Zariel frowns. He moves over to the stained glass and pushes his hand effortlessly through it. "Brent, take my hand."

I assume that Brent does, because Zariel starts to pull and tug as if he were trying to drag a reluctant rhinoceros into the room. He frowns and lets go. Then he steps through the window, and I hear him talking to Myles, but the words are unclear.

When he comes back in, he almost looks sad. "This is not going to work," he says. "He seems to have been contaminated."

Chapter 30
Gala

"What do you mean Brent is contaminated? Contaminated with what?" I ask Zariel.

"You," he answers. His flat tone still manages to accuse me.

"Wait. What? How is this my fault?" I stomp my foot, hoping to ground my frustration, by letting it flow out of me, through the floor, and into the dirt. But instead of a satisfying thud against hard tile, there is nothing.

"Even after you had just been warned about Brent's need to borrow energy, you still ran over and touched him. Are you telling me that you felt nothing, no transfer, when you made contact?"

"No. I'm not saying that. But if I willingly gave him some of my energy, you know, like a blood transfusion, how is that bad?"

I can see Tara over Zariel's shoulder, peering at the pictures in the stained glass windows. I can't tell if she's really fascinated, or just pretending, but either way, she's staying out of this discussion.

"Have you ever fixed anything with duct tape?" Myles asks. I hadn't noticed that he'd come into the room.

I think about that for a minute. If anything at our house gets broken, my parents just throw it out and get a new one. Everything is disposable, to them. "No," I answer. "I don't think so."

"Well, imagine that you had. It holds things together, but doesn't really fix the problem, not long-term, anyway. What you did was plop a big ole' strip of duct tape on the situation, and now Brent has a mixture of vibrational wavelengths and energy types."

"Fine. But if you thought he could get through the door, and I had no trouble getting through, why can't he get through, even though he got a little boost from me?" Despite the fact that I just saw Brent blocked from entering this room, there is some part of me that seems to believe that I can change reality, if only I argue enough about it. Works with my mother, anyway.

"Do you know how a polarized lens works?" Myles asks.

I have a vague recollection of hearing about polarized lenses in science class some time ago. But I'm too distracted by noticing that Tara and Zariel are whispering together in one of the far corner-ettes of this odd decagonal room. What could they possibly have to talk about? "No. I don't really remember anything about it." I cross my arms, guilt and paranoia colliding and exploding into anger.

"When light bounces off of something, the reflected waves go in all different directions, right? But very shiny surfaces, like water or glass have a glare because of a large amount of light being reflected horiziontally."

I shrug.

"Well, if you want to cut the glare caused by the horizontal light, you do what amounts to putting tiny Venetian blinds on the lens, so that only light that's coming in at a vertical angle gets through."

Tara and Zariel are still chatting away, while I'm getting a science lesson, and Brent is outside, doing who knows what. "Not to be rude, but is there a point to this?"

"It was rude, but the point is that you've depolarized Brent, and now he can't fit through the screen. You did ask."

So I did. "I'm sorry. I'm just frustrated. Seems like everything I do makes things worse. Maybe Tara and Zariel have come up with something. Let's go see."

I don't wait for Myles to reply as I stalk off across the room, feeling nothing under my feet, yet moving quickly, silent as snowfall.

"So how do we fix this?" I wedge myself into Tara and Zariel's conversation. "What do we have to do?"

"Nothing."

"Nothing? What do you mean 'nothing?' There's got to be some hocus-pocus thing like the Twilight Crystal or Persephone's

Remembering Dust that we can use. We can't just leave Brent trapped in between worlds." *Especially not when it's my fault.*

"Speaking of Brent, I think I'll go check on him," Myles says.

Tara follows him through the stained glass window.

"If he borrows no more energy, the problem will fix itself in time. But he will require watching. The temptation will be great for him."

I frown. "How much time?"

"As much as it takes. One day, or perhaps one thousand. I cannot say."

I'm tired of talking. I just want to go do something. Although, I don't really want to go face Brent after I just royally screwed up his life. Afterlife. Whatever. My bad.

"So. Do you want me to help you keep an eye on Brent?" It was the least I could do, after all.

"I did not create the problem." He smiles the kind of tight-lipped smile that said 'you screwed up' without him actually having to come out and say it.

"You mean me? I have to look after him? But I can't even see him!"

"As you have discovered, you are able to hear him when you wear the Twilight Crystal. Tara sees him clearly. I would suggest you enlist her assistance. I have pressing business to attend to. I shall take my leave now."

Fan-effing-tastic.

Zariel disappears through one of the stained glass windows.

I turn around. I don't suppose it matters which window I go through. They all lead outside, right?

Wrong.

I step through the closest one and find myself on the bottom of the ocean. In spite of not actually needing to breathe, I have a minor panic attack, especially as a dolphin comes swooping in towards me. Drowning will do that to a person. I hurl myself backward and through the window. Surprisingly, I'm not wet.

Tara's head is sticking out of the next window over.

"Are you okay?" she asks.

"Yeah. I'm good. Just took a wrong turn. No biggie."

I push myself out through her window and rejoin the guys.

"So did they tell you the good news?" I ask Brent.

"What good news is that?"

"You should be fine, soon. We can try again to get you back where you belong."

He nods.

I study his face. He looks the same as always, maybe a fraction paler. Or it could be my imagination. I don't think I could stand it if his face cracked and broke the way Lucas' had in the hospital when he held Deb and Anna hostage.

Myles starts back up the jungle path, and we follow him. Feels like we're going uphill.

"It's going to be okay, Brent. I promise. We can hang out and stuff until you're ready to go back." I almost manage to keep the pleading out of my voice.

"No," he answers.

Tara glances over her shoulder, but doesn't wade in.

"Wow, Brent. That's kind of hurtful," I respond.

"I didn't mean it that way. If I'm going to have to be here, I want to spend my time with my daughter. Terry needs me."

"Is that a good idea?" Myles asks.

"What's that supposed to mean?" Brent snaps.

"You said you were hungry," Tara says, meekly, as if she's worried about offending him.

Fair enough, since she's just implied he might eat his own kid.

"I would never harm my baby girl!"

Suddenly, we are back in the drab back room of Myles and Janet's convenience store. I'm disoriented for a moment, and I don't know where Brent is, now.

"But what about Jenny? And her new boyfriend?" I ask the blank wall, knowing that if he chooses to go to Jenny's house, there really isn't anything I can do about it.

"Chuck? All the more reason I should go watch over Terry."

Myles stands up and stretches. "You know," he says, "you're just another pitiful ghost here in the Earth Realm. If you really want to regain your strength, you have to get back to the Astral. The quickest way to do that is to stay calm and get your energies realigned. Then you can kick Chuck's butt, if he needs it."

I catch a blur of motion, a dark shape rushing past me, out of the corner of my eye. When I swivel my head to look, there is nothing to see. Could that have been Brent?

"Fine." Brent's voice sounds heavy in my head. "I'll stay with Mimi. But I am going to check on Terry now and then."

"Your mother will be fretting, Tara. You'd probably better be getting back soon," Myles says.

Tara rolls her eyes and looks at me. "My mom is hosting a charity gala for some organ transplant foundation – I forget which one. I told her I'd help her this afternoon. Which, to her, means 11 AM. Thanks again, Uncle Myles. See you soon."

"Thanks," I nod and half-wave as I follow Tara out the door.

Janet, still perching on a stool behind the cash register, does not look up as we approach. "Meredith has already called twice," she informs us.

"Okay. Thanks," Tara says, pulling out her mobile.

We're almost to the car. "Hi, Mom...Yes...I know...I know...Just have to drop Mimi off...Sure, I'll ask. Bye." She unlocks the door, and we get in.

"My mom says she has a couple of comp tickets wants to know if you and your mom want to come to the gala. You can help me serve dessert."

"Are you kidding me? My mother would kill to do that – something she can brag about to her tennis club."

The car starts silently and Tara backs out of her parking space.

"It's at that new Hotel Zephyr in the Museum District. The event starts at 8, so maybe be there 7:00ish?"

"Sure."

Saturday morning shoppers and errand runners are out in full force now, and traffic is almost as bad as on a weekday. I stare out the window. Finally, I get the nerve to ask the question I've been thinking all morning. "Is Myles really your uncle, or just a friend of the family that you call 'uncle?' I mean, he seems nice, but he doesn't look like...I don't know," I finish pathetically.

Tara makes a noise somewhere between a laugh and a snort. "Myles is Dad's twin. When they were in high school, my grandfather died of Cruetzfeldt-Jakob – Mad Cow Disease. They had different ways of dealing – Dad became a brain surgeon, Uncle Myles chose this."

"Makes sense, I guess."

We've finally made it to the entrance to my neighborhood. I have about a million more questions about Uncle Myles (and maybe one or two about Janet), but I don't want to annoy Tara and make her avoid me.

Tara pulls up to my driveway, and I hop out. "See you tonight. Come on, Brent."

He grunts to let me know he is there, but refuses to say anything else.

My feet are killing me, after spending the entire afternoon at The Galleria, shopping for dresses and shoes. Mom looks calm and composed now, but she had the emotional equivalent of an orgasm when I told her about the gala. "It's a $10,000-a-plate event," she gasped. I want to crawl under a rock. *Please don't embarrass me in front of my one and only friend.*

We're just about to make our grand entrance into Hotel Zephyr. We follow the event signs upstairs to the Borealis Ballroom. The double doors are made of pale wood with sparkling brass handles. Mom pulls one of the doors open, and we step inside.

"Whoa," I utter before I can stop myself.

The far wall is nothing but windows, and overlooks Hermann Park. I'm almost afraid to step on the floor. Near the entrance, it is white marble, gradually changing to translucent blue in the center, then the last third or so near the windows is clear glass. It looks like I'm stepping out onto the sky. I feel my pulse quicken as I enter the room. The floor seems less real than the floor of the strange Astral building I'd been in earlier today.

"Over here!" Tara calls. She's placing gi-normous vases of flowers on the buffet table off to our left. She looks gorgeous in her periwinkle taffeta and lace gown.

We head over, and I take tiny, careful steps, as if that would help if the floor gave way. From the buffet, I can see ducks swimming in the blue-dyed pond underneath the glass floor. Nobody's going to be looking up anybody's dress, not unless they've got SCUBA gear. Good to know.

An apple tumbles out of the colossal fruit basket and lands on the tile with a dull crunch, then rolls under the table.

"Oops," says Brent.

"Be more careful!" I hiss at him between my clenched teeth.

My mother turns to look at me, but I just smile at her.

A tall woman, Bluetooth in one ear, strides into the room. "No," she says. "The orchids didn't arrive…I'm not interested in snapdragons. It has to be orchids…I don't care if they went to the wrong store. Get them here now…Thank you."

She repositions her beaded clutch bag and extends her hand to my mother. "Sorry about that. I'm Meredith Berkman. Thanks for coming."

"Fran Sepulveda. The pleasure is all mine."

Dr. Berkman shakes my hand, too. "You must be Mimi."

"Y-yes," I stammer. Her grip is stronger than I expected, and she oozes authority from every pore. I can't help feeling intimidated. I probably should say something else polite and charming, but my brain is frozen.

The heels I chose were definitely too high. After all of the guests arrive, dinner is eaten, and I help Tara serve cake, I can barely walk. Everyone at the gala is at least as old as my mother, and besides, they are all listening to a speaker from the charity. With no one to impress, I slip off my shoes and stand on the cold glass near the windows. Relief.

I know that Brent is hanging around, because I can hear him complain every so often. The golf course looks surreal in the dark, surrounded by bright city. Movement below catches my eye. The ducks have all gone to bed, but something is swimming in the pond. I must be more tired than I think, because I'm sure I just saw a mermaid.

Chapter 31
Doctor's Orders

I rub my eyes. The mermaid waves at me, then slips under the water, flashing like silver just beneath the surface. At least I think she's a mermaid – it's a little hard to tell in the dark.

I catch Tara's eye and wave her over. "Look! In the pond! Do you see her?" I whisper.

Tara scans the glass floor. "See who?"

I looked again, but there was no sign of her. "I was sure I saw a – doesn't matter. Probably a reflection or something."

"No," Brent cuts in. "I saw her, too."

I am half grateful for his defense, and half annoyed that his voice randomly materializes from thin air. It's very disturbing.

"Who?" Tara asks, her voice tinged with frustration.

"A mermaid," I answer.

"Couldn't have been a mermaid," she replies.

"Why not?" *I know what I saw. I think.*

"They live in oceans," she says. "Probably a naiad or a lorelei. They live in fresh water."

"What are you, Creature-Pedia?" I ask. I should know Tara well enough by now to know she wasn't dissing me.

Tara shrugs. "I spend a lot of time helping Uncle Myles."

"What? Are you his apprentice or something?"

"I don't know about that…Apprentice seems –"

Applause interrupts our convo. Looks like the speaker just finished. People stand up and slowly collect their things, drifting into small clots in the aisles around the tables. My feet are still throbbing. I hope my mother hasn't noticed that I'm barefoot – she'd totally go off on me. But she's so busy yapping to a jewel-encrusted woman in a full-length fur that she doesn't even know I'm there.

It's Sunday morning. Barely. I open one eye because something's hissing at me.

"'Bout time," Brent says. "Were you going to sleep all day?"

"Go away."

"No. Get up. Please. This is important."

I sit up cross legged in bed, awake and not happy about it. "What? What is so important?"

"This Chuck guy that Jenny's dating. He's no good for her. I don't want him around Terry."

I suck in a deep breath to give myself a few extra seconds to think. The words are hard for me to say, and I frown. "Brent, you're dead. You can't be with her, not the way you want."

"Don't you think I know that?" Brent practically shouts at me. The lamp on my dresser thuds to the carpet. "This guy has to go. Why don't you believe me?"

I reflexively glance down at my midsection. Something seems to be tugging on me, but there isn't anything there. I look back to where I think Brent is. "What is it you want me to do? Go up to Jenny and say, 'Excuse me, I know you don't know me, but the father of your child (you know, the guy who said he didn't love you right before he accidentally stepped in front of a bus?) doesn't like the guy you're dating. So, maybe dump him? Have a great day.' How is that going to help?"

Silence.

"Brent? You still there?"

"Yeah," he replies. "Could you, maybe you and Tara, go watch them? You'll see what I mean."

"I seriously cannot believe that you're asking me to stalk your ex-girlfriend."

"She's not – never mind." He paused for a few seconds. "I'd do it for you."

His voice was so soft and quiet with pain that it almost broke my heart. "Fine. I'll see if Tara can be the wheelman, um, wheelgirl."

A soft knock sounds on my door at the same time as it opens. My dad peers in, as if he were looking for intruders. "Mimi? Thought I heard you talking to someone."

"Nope. Just…singing. You know how I love to sing first thing in the morning." Of course he wouldn't know that. He's never around first thing in the morning – always leaves early to go to the gym before work.

He nods. "Just thought I'd check."

I want to call after him as he moves down the hall, each step adding a little more distance; his self away from mine, his heart away from mine. But I sit silently on the bed, pretending it doesn't matter.

I shake myself. My mother hasn't added Tara's number to my loser-phone yet, so I go downstairs and call her on the landline. Lucky for me, my parents are old-fashioned, technologically speaking.

Mom was enthusiastic about me hanging with Drs. Berkman's daughter for the whole afternoon, so here we sit, outside of a coffee shop in in the mall, watching the children's play area. It's Sunday afternoon, and the place is mobbed, making it hard to spy on Chuck, Jenny, and Terry.

I had expected Jenny to be pretty, but not that pretty. She has huge brown eyes and thick, blue-black hair. If she'd been wearing fewer clothes, I could have believed that she'd fallen out of one of the ads from the Victoria's Secret a few doors down. It made me feel even weirder for watching her. Chuck is shorter than Brent, and denser, with hair that could either be light brown or dark blond. I do think the straw-colored highlights are kind of tacky, though.

Terry looks the way a baby should look, I guess. She's plumpish, with dark, wispy hair and no teeth. She giggles when her mother picks her up, or when Chuck tickles her. At least that's what I think she's doing. We're too far away to hear them. And I don't want to look pervy by hanging out in the kids area with no kids. That's all I need, for my parents to get a call from mall security.

Chuck and Jenny are there less than half an hour when they start packing Terry into the stroller. Tara and I pretend to look for dropped car keys as they pass, hoping they don't notice us.

"I skipped lunch. You want to grab something?" Chuck asks.

"What did you have in mind?" Jenny answers. Her voice is movie-star sexy. I think I hate her.

"Cheesecake Factory is kinda on the way to where the car's parked."

"Not in my budget right now."

"I can buy."

Their conversation is fading down the corridor, so Tara and I have to get up to follow.

"I said no, Chuck. It isn't very baby-friendly. Maybe we can get something in the food court."

They head towards the elevator, and we make for the stairs. By the time they arrive, we're pretending to consider soup and sandwich options. Although, I am actually kind of hungry. We take turns watching Chuck and Jenny – he orders pizza, she gets a smoothie – and then order sandwiches ourselves. Terry appears to be asleep, and Jenny pulls down the stroller canopy. We manage to snag a table on the other side of a column from them. Can't really see them, but we can hear them perfectly. I think I'm going to lose my mind listening to Chuck drone on about football.

"See what I mean?" Brent asks, from somewhere immediately to my right.

I jump and knock some chips off my plate. I scowl at the seemingly empty air for a moment before turning to Tara. "I don't really know what he's talking about. You? I mean, sure, that guy's got bad hair, and he's really boring, but still."

"Yeah," Tara answers. "Not my type, but he seems harmless enough. You hear her tapping her cup? I don't think she'll be with him much longer."

That wouldn't have occurred to me, but she's probably right.

"No!" Brent yells. "This is not right!"

"Brent Mitchell!" I hiss at him. "Chill. Out."

Again, I feel something tugging at me, just below my ribs. It's stronger this time, but I still see nothing.

"I can understand why he's jealous," Tara says. "But I don't think there's a reason for it."

Suddenly, one of the recessed light bulbs explodes.

Then another, and another, until they're all shattering and glass rains down on the food court. People start screaming and running, knocking cups and plates to the floor as they go, then sliding around in the mess. Some of them are bleeding, all of them are panicking. Chuck is one of the first out the door, leaving Jenny and Terri to fend for themselves. The stroller top is pulled down, so Terry isn't in any real danger. The restaurants' neon signs all began to flicker, and soda fountains gush random drinks that overflow their catch basins and puddle on the floor.

I feel light-headed. A fist-sized spot somewhere between my ribs and belly button feels hot and itchy. I have to grab the edge of the chair to keep my balance.

"Brent! Stop this now!" Tara shouts. She notices me and says, "Are you okay?"

I nod. Then I notice Jenny peeking around the column at us. "Brent, please!" I yell. "Having a tantrum isn't going to solve anything."

"Um, excuse me. But," Jenny asks, "Who are you talking to? Did you really say 'Brent Mitchell' earlier?" She has a white-knuckled grip on the stroller handle as she maneuvers it between herself and the column. "I used to know somebody..."

Tara and I look at each other for a long moment. "Named Brent?" I answer. "We also know Brent. It's...very complicated. You might not believe us if we told you how."

Tara looks at the Twilight Crystal, then into my eyes, then back to the crystal. I nod.

A fire alarm starts screaming, and I'm sure the mall security and the fire department will be here any second.

"Let's move to a calmer place, okay?" I say.

I stand up slowly. I'm not light-headed anymore, but I do feel much more tired than I ought to.

We help Jenny get the stroller through the broken glass and out into the second floor corridor. There's a flailing knot of people near the elevator, so we stop where we are. The clomp of heavy feet pounding up the stairs, followed by staticky voices over walkies, let us know the mall security team is on the job.

"This is probably good enough," Tara says.

"I'm sorry," Jenny says. "I just – I thought I heard you talking to someone named Brent. He died, and..." She trails off.

"We know. Terry's dad," I say. I wasn't expecting the look of terror that washed over her face. "It's a long story. There isn't time." I take off the crystal. "Maybe this will help."

She backs away from me as I try to put it over her head. "I'm not going to hurt you. Really. Brent can explain it better than I can."

She frowns, but closes her eyes as I put the necklace on her. I think she only let me because she was afraid I'd push her over the railing if she didn't.

Her eyes flick open, and tears stream down her cheeks. But she is smiling. Tara is smiling, too. Well. This is awkward. I turn and watch men in helmets and slickers crunch through the broken glass. One sees us, and comes our way.

"Sorry, girls," he says. "But you're going to have to leave. There's just been a severe power surge, and it may not be safe inside the mall."

"My friend! She'll never get the stroller down the stairs, and you can see what a disaster the elevator is," I say.

The man grunts. "Follow me."

He bulldozes his way through the mob at the elevators, then carries the stroller down the stairs for us. We thank him and head out the front door, trying not to get crushed or separated. We find a shady bench to sit on. The parking lot will be, well, a parking lot with hundreds of people all trying to leave at once.

I desperately wish for something to do, so that I don't have to watch Jenny crying and smiling, or Tara looking disgustingly benevolent.

Loser-phone says it's only been an hour and fifteen when we finally get into Tara's car, although it feels like several times that to me. I polish the Twilight Crystal with the bottom of my shirt for no real reason.

"Happy now, Brent?" I ask.

"He isn't here. He wanted to be with Jenny and Terry for a while," Tara answers.

"Oh. Who knew he could get so pissy?"

Tara scowls. "I think that's a bad sign. If he's using that much power, he's got to be getting it from somewhere, got to be stealing it. If he doesn't get back to the Astral soon, he's going to be in serious trouble."

I think of the utter horribleness of the Eight Plane and shiver. I have a very uneasy feeling about where Brent's been getting that power. I rub my midsection.

Tara drops me at my house around four, and I promise I will call her tomorrow. The last drops of adrenalin have just finished pounding through my blood. My hands are steady, now, and my heart isn't racing as I climb the stairs to my bedroom. Still feeling weak, though.

I dig out my old journal. Haven't written in it in over six months – I suspect that my mother had been reading it. Still, I get it out and start writing.

I look up when I hear Brent's voice. "Thanks."

"Dude! Did you really have to make a big scene at the mall like that? Seriously?"

"It worked. Jenny got to see what kind of guy Chuck really is. And I got to talk to her."

I slamm my journal shut. "Good for you. Not so good for everybody else. That was scary as hell, Brent. Never do that again. Never. Understand?"

"I'm not promising that."

"And another thing. Where have you been getting all of this energy all of a sudden?"

The door creaks. I look up and catch my dad lurking in the hall. "S'up, Dad?" *How long have you been listening at the door?*

He sighs. "You want to go out for dinner later? Just you and me?"

"Sure!" I immediately swallow my excitement. Don't want to seem like a baby. I shrug. "That'd be good."

"I just need to finish up a couple of things, then we'll go." He turns on his heel and leaves.

I wonder how much of my argument with Brent he heard. If he asks, I'll just tell him I was practicing some lines from one of the skits we did at opera camp. That should work. Maybe he won't even ask.

"Brent?" I whisper.

He seems to have left.

An hour later, Dad and I are in the turdmobile, headed down Briar Forest Drive.

"Where are we going?" I ask.

"You'll see."

"So, how's work?" I ask.

"Fine."

I don't understand why he wanted to have some 'us' time, if he won't even talk to me. I stare out the window, trying to guess where we'll end up.

After a while, he pulls into an oak-shrouded driveway, then stops at a wrought iron gate. He gives his name over the intercom, and the gate swings open.

"Um, Dad? What is this place?"

"It's very exclusive. It'll be fine."

I suddenly feel cold. Restaurants don't have security gates, no matter how exclusive they are.

A three story white fieldstone building sits at the end of the drive. As we get closer, I can read discreet brass lettering above the glass entry. 'The Silverman Clinic.'

"Dad?"

No answer. The car slows.

"Dad what is this place?" I can't keep the panic out of my voice, and it sounds more like screeching than talking.

"Trust me, Mimi. They can help you here. It's better this way. First, you've been hiding your drinking problem – you almost died, for God's sake – and now you're hearing voices. You'll thank me later, I promise."

Some men in green scrubs come out as the car stops. The locks click open as Dad kills the ignition. I push mine down and hold it. Through the tinted glass, I can see the orderlies frown. One opens my dad's door, and one opens the rear door on my side.

They've obviously done this before.

It takes them only a couple of minutes to drag me, kicking, screaming and biting out of the car and into the hospital. My father does not come upstairs with me to say goodbye. The goons in green slap wrist and ankle restraints on me, then strap me to the bed.

A man with frizzy grey hair and a lab coat comes in. "Dr. Angelus Silverman" is embroidered above the pocket.

"Hello, Mimi," he says. "I think we can help you here. But you have to help us. I'm going to give you something to help you calm down, then we'll talk in the morning. How does that sound?"

"I want to go home!"

"I hear what you're saying. But going home isn't possible right now. The sooner you cooperate, the sooner we can help you."

A nurse comes in with a metal tray with two syringes. "This may burn a little," he says as he plunges the needle into my thigh. It feels as though boiling coffee is being poured inside my leg. I struggle helplessly against the restraints. "Make it stop! Make it stop!"

It doesn't take too long before my muscles turn to jelly, and I can barely move. Dr. Silverman picks up the second syringe, and the nurse scrubs my arm at the inside of my elbow. I try to talk, but my jaws are stuck together, and it's just too hard to pull them apart.

The doc gives me the second injection, and my mind starts to go all fuzzy.

"You'll feel better in the morning," Dr. Silverman says as he walks out the door.

The nurse pulls out a clipboard with some forms on it. She takes the little silver studs out of my ears and writes on the paper. Then she removes the Twilight Crystal. More notes. "This is just an inventory of your valuables. We'll lock them in the safe for you during your stay."

She makes it sound as if I'm at a resort.

After she seals her form in an envelope with my stuff, she covers me with a sheet and a couple of thin blankets. She puts her hand on my forehead, as if she's checking for fever, before she turns out the light and leaves the room.

In the corner, near the window, I see something. My vision is hazing out, but it looks more or less like a person. A red person. And it's smiling.

Chapter 32
Parasite

My eyes close, and I feel as though I'm drifting through dark water, no need to breathe, just cool, dark pressure all around me. I gradually become aware of something caressing my foot. For some reason, I think it must be my mother. Who else could it be?

"Mom?"

There is no reply.

I fight to open my eyes. But it's incredibly hard work. I wish my hands weren't strapped to the bed, so I could use them to peel my eyelids open. But I finally manage.

The person touching my foot is facing away from me. Hard to tell if it is a man or a woman. Scraggly black hair sprouts from random patches on the scalp and hangs at almost shoulder length. Reminds me of when my mom's friend had cancer and started radiation therapy. I am suddenly scared that another patient has wandered into my room and is going to do something to me. I have no way of calling for help.

That's when I notice the hand that's rubbing my foot.

It makes me think of a chicken foot – three long, scaly toes that end in sharp claws.

I try kicking at it, even though I know I can't move my legs much. The person by my bed starts giggling. Sounds like a little kid. Totally creeps me out.

I jerk on the restraints again, hurting no one but myself. I try to yell, but the best I can do is a breathy moan. My vision starts to blur from the tears of frustration that form in my eyes. I blink them away with my sluggish eyelids.

The thing at my bedside holds up a scaly hand. Where the palm should be, there is a round rasping mouth, with a strange triangular opening. It looks a lot like the logo for a Mercedes.

I struggle uselessly as the hand-mouth brushes against the sole of my foot and latches on. Feels as though I'm being pulled out of my body through my leg. The only thing I can do about it is whimper quietly.

"Yessss. So pretty, young and tender," the creature mutters. It turns to face me. And I wish it hadn't.

Its eyes are black on dull white – no blood vessels, no moisture – nothing that makes them seem alive. But the pupils. The pupils glow red, as if there is a fire inside the thing's head, and they are the smoldering edges of it. These horrible eyes are set deep into its face, surrounded by dark circles, as if the thing never sleeps.

Two ragged holes puncture its face where a nose should have been. Its jaw is square and chunky, a few sizes too big. That awful face cracks into a toothless grin, a bad animation of a poorly drawn cartoon.

A tongue, a fat, wet tentacle covered in toothed suckers, shoots out of that over-sized jaw and latches onto my forehead.

I try rolling my head from side to side, but it's just too heavy to move. All I manage is a pathetic little shake. Now, I feel I'm being stretched between my foot and my head. It is unbearable. Inside my head, I scream for help. *Brent! Tara! Zariel! Somebody help me! Please! Help!*

The monster swivels its head towards the door. It lets go of me and dissolves into a red mist that moves into the far corner of the room, hovering like a cloud of unrepentant evil.

Squeak, squeak, squeak.

The door opens, and the nurse flicks on a dim lamp.

"Oh, I see you're awake," she says. She doesn't seem to notice the horror in the corner.

I groan at her.

"The best thing you can do is sleep, okay?" She smiles at me and checks my restraints. She frowns at the one on my left ankle and tightens it. "Just relax. Don't try to fight. We're here to help you."

Shut up, already.

She pats my foot, the same one the monster had grabbed, and I am surprised that it doesn't shatter. My body feels stiff and brittle. I think I know how a fly must feel, after the spider's been at it.

"What's this on your head?" she asks. She touches the spot where the creature had latched on with its tongue. "How on earth did you manage to scratch yourself?"

She wipes it down with an alcohol pad and tapes a piece of gauze over it.

If only I could ask her to leave the light on in my room. It might keep the thing in the corner away from me. I have to focus.

"Lllll-iii," I wheeze.

The nurse's body stiffens. "I'm not telling you a lie. We really want to help. I know this might seem harsh or unfair to you, but we have to make sure that you don't harm yourself or others until Dr. Silverman has a chance to evaluate you."

I want to smack her. Instead, I try again. "Llll-iii." I run out of breath. But this time, I look at the lamp, back at her, then back at the lamp.

"Oh. You want the light on, don't you? I should have known. Seems all the patients here do."

Can't imagine why.

"Please try and get some sleep. You're only making it harder on yourself by fighting. Things will be better in the morning."

The door closes behind her with a soft click, and her rubber-soled shoes squeak down the corridor. But at least she's left the light on for me.

The red mist in the corner is gone.

In no time, I'm asleep.

I know that I'm dreaming, because I'm walking down a run-down city street. Bits of trash blow past me in the breeze. A few blocks ahead, a decaying shopping mall slumps behind a row of dead trees.

I know exactly where I am.

I turn and sprint down the sidewalk, hoping that this time, I can find the Depot.

This time, for once, I'm right. There it is – the low grubby building. I burst through the dented metal door, and find Stan, sitting there, still reading his paperback, looking just like any other middle-aged security guard.

"You're late," he says, his lips hinting at a smile.

"Sorry." I'm so glad that I can move and talk and be heard that I don't care if he teases me.

I look around, hoping to see Zariel, or maybe even Brent. Instead, I see someone else sitting on the couch.

It's my dad.

For a second, I'm not sure whether to hug him or slap him. Then fear takes over. *Is he dead?*

"Dad?"

He turns to look at me. "Mimi? How did – what's going on?" He scowls at me.

I sit down next to him on the couch. "What happened, Dad? How did you get here?"

He looks so confused that I feel bad for him. "I don't …know. I was driving home…heard a horn blaring…huge boom…opened my eyes and here I was."

This can't be good. True, my father can be the most infuriating person on the planet – he had me locked up in the crazy crib, after all – but I never wanted him dead.

There is a flash of light, and suddenly Zariel is next to me. I have never been so glad to see anyone in my life.

Zariel ignores me and goes straight to Dad. "Walter, you cannot stay here. You have to go back."

And then Dad's gone.

"Thanks a lot!" I grouse at Zariel. "I needed to talk to him. Couldn't you have waited five minutes?"

"You have larger challenges at present."

Tell me about it. "Is my dad going to be okay?"

"Yes, but he will not be able to communicate with anyone for a few days, perhaps a week."

"And you're telling me this because…?"

"He is the only one who knows you are at the Silverman Clinic."

Crap. I cover my face with my hands, then slide them slowly down my cheeks. "There's a monster there, you know."

"Yes. It is a type of vampire."

Zariel puts his hands on my head and a cold, iridescent light shimmers around me. I feel as if I'm inside a quartz crystal.

"Never be in the dark, if it can be helped. But if it attacks you again, it will find you are armored against it. I have every expectation that it will give up."

I nod. I don't ask what will happen if it doesn't give up. What I don't know won't hurt me, right? "I'm worried about Brent."

"And well you should be. He is starting to become corrupted. You set up the link between the two of you when you fed him the first time. Now, he's taking energy from you as he pleases. He can't help himself. There is not much time left before he is consigned to the Seventh Plane."

"How much time?"

"Tomorrow," answers Zariel. "You may have until midnight. Possibly earlier."

"What?! You might have noticed that I'm stuck in the loony bin." My hands start talking for me, as if I'm doing some kind of modern interpretive dance. "Unless my mother comes to get me in the morning, I don't know what you expect me to do."

"Given that she does not know your whereabouts, that is unlikely."

Crap. "Seriously, Zariel. You're going to have to step in and do something here."

I get up and pace around the dingy room. Stan is still reading his book, intent on ignoring us. I feel a flush of anger at him, for no good reason.

"Mimi," Zariel says. "You should talk to Myles – Tara's uncle. He can get word to her. I can take you to his location.

Boom! The door crashes open and Hades comes striding in. "Not. So. Fast. I believe you still have something that belongs to me, and it's well past time you gave it back."

Chapter 33
Flight

"Hades?" I ask. "Hey. How's it—"

"Where is it?" His smile is polite, but not pleasant.

"The crystal? Yeah. About that. It's in a safe place."

Hades crosses his arms and raises one eyebrow.

"In fact, it's in a safe. At the Siverman Clinic. They took it when I, um, checked in."

"That makes it easy," he replies. I can see Zariel shaking his head slightly.

"Easy?" I ask.

"Easy for me to just take it. Anything in the ground falls under my domain." He starts to turn towards the door, then turns back. "Why did you not return it to Zariel as you were told?"

"I told her to use it. She is monitoring a liminal for me," Zariel says.

"A liminal?" Hades gives him a 'you've got to be kidding me' look.

My fists perch firmly on my hips. "He's my friend. It's not his fault he's stuck between realms," I say.

Then, faster than thought, Hades' right arm snakes out and he grabs my wrist. Fortunately, gravity isn't really an issue here, otherwise I would probably have fallen over on my butt, I jumped so hard.

Hades eyes close. He raises his head slightly, as if he's smelling something. Then he releases me. "That's unfortunate. I must have the Twilight Crystal. I'm certain you can find a work-around."

"But that's not fair! I need it to hear Brent."

Hades reaches out and lifts my chin, forcing me to look up into his face. "Do you presume to tell the God of the Dead what is or isn't fair?"

"No, sir," I squeak. The heat of his hand burns me.

"That's what I thought." He lets my chin drop. "I understand your predicament, but the Twilight Crystal is what keeps the Eighth Plane separate from the others. It's been away too long already. Any further delay could be catastrophic. As I said, I'm sure you can find another way to track your liminal."

"Wait!" I call.

"What do you want? I've wasted enough time here already."

"Could you please take the vampire that's attacking the patients here with you? If anything belongs on the Eighth Plane, it does."

Hades laughs. He doesn't bother going for the door, just blurs and vanishes. Guess you can do that when you're a god. *Did the laugh mean that he would snag that awful red monster on the way out, or that he thought it was a joke that I would ask him to do that?*

"Brace yourself," says Zariel.

Before I can ask why, a deep explosion rocks my body, rattling the bed and throbbing in my bones. I find myself back in my hospital room, strapped to the railings. An alarm whoops, and red lights from the hallway flash underneath the door. I hear slamming and thumping, and people shouting. Nurses' shoes squeak on the corridor tile. Sirens erupt in the distance.

A nurse, not the same one as last time, comes into my room. She starts unbuckling my restraints. "Just stay calm," she says. "There's been an electrical problem and we're evacuating the building as a precaution. Everything is fine. Just come with me, and then stay with the group. We're all going downstairs together."

I follow her out into the hall. My legs are still a little shaky, but they're good enough to walk. People clump together near the nurses' station. I guess these are the other patients – they look as disheveled as I feel. A few are in wheelchairs, and one man in a strait jacket barks and growls at the orderlies who are trying to carry him towards the stairwell without being bitten. I take a moment to feel grateful that I'm in street clothes, and not a hospital gown with my butt hanging out.

"Send the walkers down," barks Dr. Silverman, as he comes from the opposite end of the hall, followed closely by a burly orderly.

"That's all of them!" yells the nurse who unstrapped me. She looks around, and her eyes settle on me. "You! New patient. Come over here." She motions me over to an elderly lady in a wheelchair. "You drive. Help me get her down the stairs. Please."

I nod. "Mimi. My name's Mimi."

"Excellent. Thanks for helping."

Did I have a choice? "Sure. No prob."

The people who could walk were already out of sight in the stairwell. The first pair of orderlies and their wheelchair is just disappearing. Dr. Silverman, with his orderly and patient, roll along behind us.

It is hard work, getting a wheelchair down a flight of stairs. Lucky we are only on the second floor. The orderlies are strong enough to carry their chairs along, but we have to manage by bumping and sliding down each step.

Clouds of something hang in the air. It is hard for me to tell if it's smoke, or dust from the rubble where part of the building had collapsed. Yeah, that looks like a common electrical problem.

Four fire trucks, the Fire Marshall's red SUV and an ambulance stream up the driveway, red lights scattering off of every face in the crowd. The ambulance is an unpleasant reminder that my dad is in the hospital. Zariel says he'll be okay. I just have to trust him, because there was no way I could go to him right now. I don't even know where he is.

"Excuse me," says the lady in the wheelchair. I'm still standing right behind her. "But can you tell me what's happening?"

Is she blind? Oh. "Fire trucks are coming in. People are running everywhere. A back corner of the building is knocked down."

"Oh. Now, I understand. Can you tell me, though, is there a very tall cowboy in a blue vest standing in front of me?"

I take a little step away from her. "Not...that I can see."

The woman sighs and shakes her head. "I knew it. But he seems so all-fired desperate to tell me something. They just keep telling me he isn't real. But I see him all the time. I'm not sure who to believe."

"Velma?" The nurse from earlier steps over and repositions the wheelchair slightly. "Are you talking to that cowboy again?"

Velma sighs. The nurse steps away and the old lady leans back in her chair, toward me. "I have Charles Bonnet Syndrome, you know. I lost my sight years ago, can't see anything that's really there, but I sure see a lot of things that aren't."

I nod. I kind of know how Velma feels, but I'm not letting the nurse know that. She might think I'm crazy.

Dr. Silverman skirts the edge of the group, shouting into his cell. "Yes! I know that's impossible…The safe was just ripped out of the wall, then vanished. No tracks, nothing…How should I know? It was encased in concrete…" He trails out of range.

Hades' words pop into my head. "… Anything in the ground falls under my domain…" "…encased in concrete…" Well, that makes sense. Concrete is made of crushed up rocks and sand and stuff. I know exactly what happened to Dr. Silverman's safe. But I'm not going to give him the opportunity to write words like 'delusional' in my file. I suppose the missing safe is why the two police cars are now coming up the drive. Through the open gate. That no one is closing. *Thanks, Hades.*

I take advantage of the darkness and confusion to ease my way out of the crowd and use the bulky ambulance as cover. If I run, someone is sure to notice me. But if I just walk casually and quietly no one will be any wiser (I hope). So that's just what I do.

I am almost to the gate when someone shouts, "Hey you! Stop!"

A flashlight beam catches me in the face as I glance over my shoulder. Yep. He's talking to me. Feeling like Carmen heading for the smuggler's cave, I sprint the rest of the way along the driveway and down the sidewalk.

More than one set of feet is pounding the ground after me. And they're gaining. To my left, the traffic light changes. I dart into the street, barely missing getting run over by sleepy drivers. It isn't rush hour yet, but there are enough cars to keep the orderlies on their side of the street. I run down the median until I get a chance to cross. I dodge into the front door of a gas station mini-mart and out the back. Let them try and find me now.

Still, I know they won't give up, and it won't be long before the cops are looking for me, too. My house and the hospital will be the first places they check, so they're off limits. My cover of darkness is being pulled back by the rising sun. I've got no money, and I don't even have my loser-phone. I'm not exactly sure where I am. But I do know the general area, and Riverbirch Place isn't that far away.

I try to keep to the neighborhoods and avoid the main streets. The problem with that is most of them are designed to discourage people from cutting through, so there aren't any direct routes out once I get in. Rush hour has come and gone. I'm starving to death and I'm sticky and sweaty. But at least I only get turned around twice on the way.

Voila! There it is. White brick forms the guard shack and the wall around the place. The gates are black wrought iron with the spikey bits on the ends of the bars painted gold. A large black enamel-on-brass sign on the gate reads Riverbirch Place in fancy script. That's the good news.

The bad news is that if I walk up to the guard and ask to be let in to visit Tara Berkman, he'll probably call the police. I have to find a way in, and then I have to figure out which house was Tara's. This could take all day. Unless I have some help.

Brent? I don't know where you are, or if you can hear me. I can't hear you anymore. Maybe you already know Hades took the Twilight Crystal. But I need your help to find Tara. It's really, really important.

I feel the now familiar tugging at my midsection. Yellow snapdragons in the flowerbed to my right bend as if someone is walking through them. A bush moves back and forth, shaken by an invisible hand. Then another, a little further along, shakes.

Thanks, Brent.

I follow the moving shrubbery about two thirds of the way around the outer wall. Then it all stops.

Brent?

Nothing.

Please, please, please be Tara's house.

I start to look for handholds in the eight foot brick wall, or at least some way to lever myself over it.

"Mimi? Brent said you were out here." Tara's voice comes from the other side of the wall.

"Tara!" I whisper-shout at her. "You've got to please help me."

"Sure. First, we need to get you in the house."

"Got a ladder?"

"No, but if you walk down two blocks to the HEB plaza, I can pick you up. There are cameras all around the perimeter wall, and security will come looking for you if they see you trying to climb over."

Crap. I hadn't thought of that.

"Okay. See you in a few." I get away from the wall as fast as I can.

I figure there are probably cameras around the front of the grocery store, too, so I stay near the back. Close to the dumpsters. Probably a bad plan. When was the last time those things were emptied? But I'm not there very long before Tara's little electric car silently rolls into the parking lot.

"Jeez! What happened to you?" she asks.

"Great to see you, too. Long story – can I tell you after lunch?"

"Lunch? It's 3:30."

"Yes. That's why I'm so hungry. Can we please just go?" I scan the parking lot, scouting for any kind of official-looking vehicle.

"What's gotten into you?" Tara lowers the handbrake and the car starts to move.

"Cops are looking for me. Probably."

"What?"

I give her the Cliff's Notes version of my life for the past twenty four hours. I'm almost done by the time we pull into her garage.

"I could have my dad call and check on your dad," Tara offers, as we walk into a museum quality entryway.

"No! Then they'll know where I am, or at least that you've been talking to me."

I follow her into a kitchen that not only has a double width island, but a fireplace and a sitting area.

"Don't you think your mom might be worried about you?" she asks. She opens the fridge and gets some things out to make me a sandwich.

I sigh. "Probably. Zariel had said that Dad was the only one who knew I was at the clinic. But I'm sure they've called her by now."

"So what's the worst thing that can happen? Do you really think your mother will take you back to the clinic? I'm sure the police won't take you there – they'll just take you home, especially if your mom's filed a missing persons report." Tara passes a plate with two sandwiches over to me, then gets an apple out of a wooden bowl.

I suck in my breath a little too loudly. I hadn't thought about Mom doing that. Between visits to my dad at the hospital. Damn. I should have just called her to begin with, instead of wandering around subdivisions all day sweating like a pig and wasting precious time I needed to get Brent back to the Astral. *I'm such an idiot.*

"I think I've really screwed up. Zariel said we had to get Brent back tonight. But if I go home, Mom won't let me leave, not while Dad's in the hospital. But you're right. I should let her know I'm not dead." Idiot or not, I'm starved and I gobble the sandwiches. And the freshly washed apple.

Tara pulls out an envelope with some small white rectangles. Each one has a letter on it, written with a marker. She removed the one marked with a 'B.'

"These are SIM chips my parents use when they travel out of the US. Easier to have a local number when you're dealing with local colleagues. This one's from Brazil. Hang on."

Tara leaves, then returns with her phone. She takes the back off and swaps out the SIMs. "Call your mom."

I wipe the crumbs off my mouth before take the phone from her. I hold it for a moment, gathering my courage. I have to concentrate on the number – it's easy to forget when I have it in speed dial. After four rings, it goes to voice mail. "Hi, Mom. I'm fine. Please don't worry about me. I'll be home as soon as I can. Love you. Bye." I'm partly disappointed and partly relieved that I didn't get to talk to her.

Tara swaps out the chips and puts the bag away.

"So, what are we going to do about Brent?" I ask her. "He's getting kind of unstable."

"He says he is not unstable."

"Unstable people never think they're unstable." I frown. "I know where he's getting his energy."

"Where?"

"Me."

Tara's eyes widen. "Are you sure?"

I nod. "What were the ways your uncle said we could get Brent back where he belongs? The first one, the shaman thing, we tried and failed, and I've only made the problem worse, so we can cross that off the list. The next one was some kind of vertex in California, right?"

"Vortex, in Arizona. Even if we left right now, we couldn't make it in time. The last one was water fae. Like kelpies and mermaids."

Mermaids? "Mermaids! Remember, I saw one at the hotel?"

"That's probably a naiad, but sure. She counts."

"Then what are we waiting for? Let's go. Come on, Brent."

Chapter 34
The Naiad's Embrace

Tara frowns. "Brent says he doesn't want to go."

"What do you mean you don't want to go back to the Astral? You can't stay here – you know what will happen to you. Are you crazy?" I snap at him.

Tara stares at something off to her left. Her face is so pale, it scares me a little. "Brent, this is wrong." She shakes her head slowly, then looks at me. "He says he can make it work here in the Earth Realm. He has a good source of energy. Here, he can help Terry and Jenny. In the Astral, he can't do much for them."

I glare at Tara, even though it isn't her fault. "Yeah, I know where you're getting that energy, and it's not okay."

A deep growl fills the space around us. It's coming from everywhere. Something hits me in the stomach – it feels like a baseball bat, but there's nothing there that I can see. I hear myself cry out. It feels as if someone reached in and grabbed my insides with red-hot pliers and is trying to pull them out through my navel. I try to scream, but my lungs don't seem to be working. I choke and gasp, struggling for oxygen. Little lightning bolts flash all around my field of vision. I hear Tara screaming for Brent to stop as I collapse like a Jenga tower onto the cool tile.

The first thing I become aware of is the taste of blood. I lick my lips. Seems to be coming from the bottom one.

"Mimi?" Tara's voice sounds thin and high.

"Mmmm." I open my eyes, but quickly close them again. The room is over-bright.

"Can you stand up? We really need to get going."

I squint at her, then grab her outstretched hand. She hoists me off the floor. My knees are wobbly, and my ankles are loose and hard to control.

"What happened?"

Tara puts her arm around me to help me hobble along. "Brent says he's really, really sorry."

"What did he do to me?" I want to be angry, but I just don't have the energy.

"He got mad. Really mad. And he took too much energy from you. He didn't mean to hurt you. He hates to admit it, but you're right. He has to go back to the Astral. He's – let's just go, okay?"

I have to lean hard on Tara to make it out to her garage. My head is swimming by the time I buckle myself into her car. I lean the seat back a little and close my eyes. I just want to sleep. So I do.

The ceasing of the car's motion wakes me up. I'm groggy and not sure where I am.

"We're at the Zephyr," Tara says.

Zephyr? Oh, the hotel. "Okay. Now what?" I look around. It's dark enough for the parking lot lights to have come on, but the western horizon is still pale orange, where the hidden sun lingers at the edge of the world.

"Well, we need to figure out how to get to the pond, find the naiad, then convince her to help."

"That all?" I'm not sure I have the strength to get out of the car. "Maybe we could send Brent to look for a way to the pond."

Tara shakes her head. "No. When he had that big feed, he burned through all of that energy almost immediately. He's starting to fall apart, but he doesn't dare take any more from you. It would probably kill you."

Fantastic.

Tara looks around at the parked cars. "We're in the employees' parking lot." She twists around and digs through some things in the back seat. When she turns around, she has a pale yellow hoodie.

"I've parked as far away from the security cameras as I can," Tara says. "But I did notice a car on the way in with a maid's uniform hanging up in the back seat. I'm going to borrow it."

She puts on the jacket and pulls the hood up over her head. With that and her sunglasses, she could have been just about anybody. She gets out and opens the trunk. I notice something long and metallic glinting in her hand as she walks across the parking lot.

I watch her make her way casually over to a not-so-new green sedan that desperately needs a paint job. Tara looks around, then slips the slim jim down next to the window glass. In a few seconds, the door is open and the uniform is in her hands. She re-locks the car and slips back over to her own vehicle.

"I'm impressed. Where'd you learn to boost a car?" I ask her.

Tara smiles. "Well, I don't know how to hot-wire it. My Uncle Myles taught me how to pop the lock. His girlfriend, Janet – I think you met her at the shop – is always locking her keys in the car."

The uniform is enough sizes too big for Tara that she can wear it over her regular clothes.

"Somebody's looking out for us," she says, pulling a hotel employee swipe card on a lanyard from one of the pockets.

"Hope that's true." I think of Zariel. I'm starting to feel ever so slightly better, but not well enough to hike across the parking lot.

"I'll go have a look around, see what I can find, then I'll come back for you and Brent."

I nod. Me and Brent. I can't hear or see him. I just hope he's still holding together well enough to get back to the Astral. Wish I could talk to him, but I can't – so I stare out the window, looking at nothing. I fade into semi-consciousness as my mind wanders aimlessly through the recent past. I really hope my dad is going to be okay. Because not dead is not necessarily the same thing as okay. And Mom. What she must be going through. Soon. I'll be able to call her soon. I'll see my dad soon. Just as soon as Brent is back on the Astral. 'Soon' should be full of hope and promise – it's almost time for this to be over. Instead, it feels like a steel door with a deadbolt lock.

A rhythmic squeaking pulls me back into the present. Tara is pushing a laundry cart towards the car. When she gets to my door, I open it and try not to fall out. I notice she's got three large Gerber Daisies tucked into her hair.

"Get in the basket," Tara says. "We should hurry. If somebody sees us, they might think it's weird to have a cart out in the parking lot."

She helps heave me into the canvas hamper, then puts some towels over me. The canvas hamper smells slightly of stale sweat and mostly of cleaning chemicals.

"I found the maintenance entrance to the pond."

"Cool," I mumble from under the pile of towels. "How's Brent?"

"Not good. We have to hurry."

"Agreed."

We make it all the way to the ground floor of the hotel without being accosted. But just as we get inside, disaster strikes.

"Excuse me! Miss! Over here!" I hear a male voice calling

"Me?" Tara asks.

"Who else would I be talking to? I need fresh towels."

"Yes. Well, sir, as you can see, I've got a bunch I'm taking to the laundry room. It would probably be faster to call the front desk –"

"Well, I'd hate to interrupt your busy schedule to try and get you to do something so trivial as attend to your guests. What is your name, girl? I'm going to complain to the manager."

"Violetta Valéry."

"That sounds French. Are you some kind of foreigner?" I can hear the scowl in his voice.

"Have a nice evening." She starts to push the laundry cart again.

"I'm not finished with you!"

"I'm finished with you."

Tara keeps pushing, and the cart picks up speed. Behind us, I hear swearing, then a door slamming.

I can't help snickering "You know, Violetta and Mimi both died of tuberculosis at the end. Hope that's not a bad omen."

Tara laughs softly. "Well, what can I say? My mother loves her Verdi. Took me to Venice last summer to see *La Triviata*. Violetta was the first name that popped into my head."

"Yeah, well, Puccini's the man in our house. How much further?"

My knees are starting to hurt from being bent so tightly, and my calf is cramping.

"Almost there."

The cart turns right and Tara falls silent. That leaves me nothing to listen to but the wretched wheel. Squeak-a-week. Squeek-a-week.

Then it stops.

"We're here. I'm afraid this is as far as this thing's going."

Tara helps me out of the laundry cart. "This is the maintenance gate, so somebody can go in, feed the ducks, trim the grass, and whatever."

We enter through the narrow wrought iron gate. I have to lean on Tara to make it all the way to the back of the pond, under the opaque part of the floor. It wouldn't do to have a ballroom full of people watching us through the glass floor by the windows.

I lean against a support column underneath the ballroom. Tara scans the water. No sign of the naiad.

"Brent?" Tara asks. "I know it's hard, but you need to be here with us."

She smiles slightly, and I guess that means he's arrived.

"Hello?" She calls out to the water. She pulls the big daisies out of her hair – red, orange, and yellow – and drops them into the water.

Nothing happens.

"Brent, could you go closer to the edge?" Tara asks.

Oddly enough, even though I can't see Brent, I can see his reflection in the still, black water. His eyes are dark and hollow, cheeks gaunt. It hurts my heart to see him like that, and I wish I could hug him. But that's what got me in trouble the last time.

Seconds drag by, then minutes. "I don't think she's coming," I say.

"What are our other options?" Tara asks. "I think we should wait a little longer."

I sigh, then slide down the concrete column so I can sit. I know she's right, but I hate the feeling of helplessness. Either the naiad comes or she doesn't. And if she does show, there's no guarantee she'll help us. But she's the only chance we have.

So we sit in the dark, underneath the Borealis Ballroom with a party in full swing above us, and wait.

I watch the dancers' reflections on the glassy surface of the pond, some way in front of me. One of the reflections begins to move towards us. The impossibility of that movement takes a moment to register.

"Is that—?" I start.

"Shhh!" Tara cuts me off.

As the reflection gets closer, it starts to rise out of the water. It isn't a reflection – it's the naiad. In a moment, she stands before us, beautiful and naked, drops of water glittering on her pale skin. She doesn't glow, exactly, but we have no trouble seeing her clearly in the gloom. Her dark hair is long, past her waist, and clings to her face and body. Her eyes are solid aquamarine, beautiful and disturbing at the same time. She smiles at us.

"Are you here to swim with me?" she asks.

That actually sounds fabulous. If only I wasn't so tired.

"No," Tara replies. "We ask a favor, a boon."

The naiad's smile shrinks a little. "And what would you give me for it?"

"What would you ask?" Tara replies.

"What is the favor?"

Tara nods towards Brent. "We need to get our friend back to the Astral Realm."

"It is a small thing, I suppose. What am I offered?"

Tara hikes up the maid's uniform and digs in her pocket. She pulls out a small gold ring with a tiny fairy sitting on top of it, and holds it out towards the naiad.

"I have no use for trinkets. Swim with me."

"No."

"Why not?" I ask. Seems simple enough to me.

"Because naiads have a habit of drowning people." Tara replies.

Been there, done that. Think I'll skip it this time.

The naiad smiles and bats her eyelashes. "It seems we are at an impasse." She turns to leave.

"Arethusa! There you are." The male voice sounds familiar.

The naiad rolls her eyes. "Not interested. Go away."

"Don't be like that," he replies.

"Hades?" I ask.

The God of the Underworld steps from behind the other support column. His muscular arms cross his broad chest. One eyebrow lifts. "Mimi? By the Gods! What are you doing here?" He gives Tara an up and down scan and glances at Brent.

"I thought you were supposed to know everything. How did you not know I was here?"

Out of the corner of my eye, I can see Tara's hands fly to her mouth. Probably not the best idea to sass the God of the Dead, but I don't feel I have much to lose at this point.

Hades' lips curl downward slightly. "I'm not Zeus."

"Besides, he had something else on his mind," Arethusa sneers.

"That your liminal?" Hades ignores her and focuses in on Brent.

"That's my friend, Brent." I say.

"Our friend," Tara adds, softly.

"Looks like he'll be coming my way soon. I'll make sure he feels at home." His smile is icy.

"He's not yours yet!" I snap. I would lunge at him, but it's too much work to stand up, even with the help of the column.

Hades chuckles. "Yet." He turns back to the naiad, extending a hand to her. "Why don't you come with me, Arethusa? I can take you to a place you've never been before."

"Does your wife know you're here?" I ask.

I hear Tara gasp.

"What did you say?" Hades asks.

"Your wife. Persephone. Does she know you're up here chasing other women?" I ask again.

"Not that it is any of your concern, but no."

"You mean not yet."

Hades' face darkens.

I'm in for it now.

His lips begin to quiver.

I glance at Tara, then at Brent's reflection. I notice that it has gotten much more transparent. He's fading fast. *I'm so sorry I failed you.*

Hades bellows with laughter. It echoes off the cement underbelly of the hotel and ripples the water of the pond. Surely even the people dancing above us must hear it.

"I like you, Mimi. You amuse me." He turns to Arethusa. "I'll talk to you later."

He grins at me, then blurs and vanishes.

"I can't believe you did that!" Tara shouts, heedless of our location.

"Shhh. Someone will hear you."

"I believe," says Arethusa, "that I owe you a boon."

She wades out of the water, leans over and takes my hands in hers. She pulls me up as if I were a rag doll.

Then she kisses me.

I'm too stunned to move. That was the last thing I had expected. Now, every nerve in my body is singing, and my skin is alive. I can feel something cool flowing through me, like water, but not water. It swirls around, finding the parts of me that are broken and repairing them. But not just repairing them – making them stronger, more than human. The not-water ebbs away and Arethusa steps back. She smiles at me before she swiftly moves to Brent, wraps her arms around him, and vanishes.

Chapter 35
Wing and a Prayer

We will not make it to dinner at Tara's house on Saturday. I still go to opera camp, even though I'd missed Monday and Tuesday. Anything is better than being at my house right now. And at least I get to hang out with Tara.

Dad is home with his jaw wired shut and can only eat smoothies for at least six weeks. Mom is so angry with him for taking me to the Silverman Clinic without discussing it with either of us that she won't even speak to the man.

I'm not any happier with him. His betrayal was a sword straight through my heart. I think I know how Carmen felt when José stabbed her at the bullfight. It will take a very long time to forgive him, and I'm not sure I'll be able to fully trust him again, ever. But what am I supposed to do? He's my dad. It's not like I can just unfriend him and forget about it.

After the naiad thing, I feel better than ever. Physically. But I'm missing Brent, and yes, Deb, more than I thought I would. I don't even know if Brent made it to the Astral in time – I haven't heard a word from Zariel. In spite of seeing Tara every day at opera camp, I feel lonelier than I've ever felt in my life. If she wasn't there, I don't know what I'd do.

It's Thursday night, and I'm lying in bed, trying to sleep. The tears that burn my eyes are wet and cold on my pillow as I wonder if I would have been better off if Josh's dad hadn't pulled me out of the swimming pool.

I get up to go to the bathroom, and when I get back in bed, I close my eyes and lay in the dark, listening to the water fill up the tank. It seems to go on for a lot longer than normal, and it gets louder. I open my eyes and sit up.

I'm not in my room. I breathe in the spicy sweet smell of the flowers that surround the Fountain of Sirin. Then I see her.

"Deb?"

She looks so beautiful. To say she glows isn't quite right. She seems to be made out of light, only it doesn't hurt my eyes to look at her. As it would if I was looking at the sun.

"I made it, Mimi," she says. "Thanks to you."

I look over her shoulder at the fountain. I hate goodbyes.

"It wasn't just me. It was Brent and Zariel, too. And Master James. And Eurayle."

She smiles and it makes my heart ache. I'm happy for her, but I don't want to be left behind while she goes on to something amazing.

"Speaking of Brent," I ask. "Have you heard anything about him? Is he okay?"

"He is asleep, cocooned in the Seventh City."

I smile, just a little. "At least he didn't get stuck in the Eighth Plane. That's something, right?"

Deb nods. The flowers quiver, and little Sammie dog emerges, standing on her hind legs to be picked up. Deb scoops her up and holds her. They both start to shine so brightly that I can't look at them anymore, and I shield my eyes with my hands.

"Wait! Deb?"

I hear her voice, more inside my head than through my astral ears. "What?"

"Good luck. Maybe we'll meet up again?"

"No doubt about it. Later…friend."

"Later."

In a flash, they've gone. I sit under the overcast sky with my back against the fountain, and admire the fields of flowers. Little droplets of the cool water sometimes splash on my skin.

"You do good work."

I turn left, toward the sound of the voice. "Thanks, Zariel. That's me. Good work – except for how bad I screwed up with Brent."

"Brent made his own choices. He did not have to keep taking energy from you, especially after you told him to stop. Would you care to see him?"

"Sure!" Then I frown. "Deb said that he was cocooned in the Seventh City. What does that mean?"

"It means he is sleeping, protected by a shield of healing energy. You may still look in on him, if you wish."

I stand up. "Yes. I want to do that."

The instant I touch Zariel's hand, we're transported to the gate at Unadax, We have to walk the rest of the way to Airumel. Not too far inside the gates, we stop at a grey and stained building in. Half of a flickering neon sign lights up; the other half is dark. The word 'vacancy' in green neon flashes spastically underneath. A few blocks down, the rotting hulk of the mall where Lucas held Deb captive lurks like a slasher film stalker. In fact, the decrepit hotel in front of us looks as if it fell straight out of a horror flick.

Zariel pushes the dirty glass door open and we go into what is, at least technically, a lobby.

A man with thinning, greasy hair and a sweat-stained shirt looks up.

"Yo, Z! You here to check on your boy?"

"Indeed."

The man nods, and we go through to the elevator.

There is a large dent in the door, but it slides open easily enough. I can guess as to why the carpet is stained as the car lurches upwards, shuddering unsteadily on what I really, really hope is not a rusty cable.

The car jolts to a stop on the third floor and we get out. The hallway is dim, but I can still see how threadbare the carpet in the middle of it is. The whole place smells musty, with hints of cigarette smoke and beer. We make a couple of turns, and I get the sense that the motel is laid out in a big square, with Brent's room at the opposite side from the elevator.

Zariel stops at room three twenty two. A bare lightbulb dangles from a dusty wire just ahead of the door, and it gives Zariel enough light to insert the key he's suddenly holding into the lock. I brace myself for the squalor I expect to find Brent lying in.

When the door opens, I see a brightly lit, well-scrubbed room that could be from any modern hospital. I pause in the doorway, look out at the dingy hall, then back into Brent's room. This place will never make any sense to me. A young person in blue nurse's scrubs greets Zariel. I can't really tell if the nurse is male or female. I don't suppose it matters.

"How is your charge?" Zarial asks.

"He is recovering. He has far to go, however," the nurse replies.

I walk over to see Brent as they continue to talk about him. He's lying in a hospital style bed, with monitors and an IV that drips glowing green fluid into his arm. It even smells like disinfectant in here. I reach out to touch him, but my hand runs into a wall of energy, and blue sparks shoot around me.

"Ow!" I pull my hand back and shake it. That was much worse than static electricity. I turn and glare at Zariel. "You could have warned me."

"I did advise you that he was protected by a shield of healing energy."

That was true. But still. He could have reminded me. I turn back to my friend.

He looks awful. Brent is gaunt, and his papery grey skin has peeled away in some places, revealing bone and muscle. Anyone else would have looked at him and said, "Zombie!" But I know better. I know the sacrifices he'd made to try and help the daughter who would never know him, sacrifices that had reduced him to this. I feel a little sorry for myself, because I don't believe anyone loves me enough to do that for me. I wish I could touch him, but then, wasn't that what caused all the problems in the first place?

I am glad that Brent is being taken care of, but I'm starting to regret coming. I feel worse now than I had when I didn't know what had become of him. I had hoped, I suppose, that he'd be able to talk to me. Or something. I'm not sure what I thought would happen. I turn back toward Zariel and the nurse.

"I'm ready to go," I say.

Zariel nods. The nurse smiles, and I feel a little spark of warmth inside, like drinking hot soup on a cold day. I smile back.

Zariel and I head back out into the grungy corridor and down to the decrepit elevator. The door screeches open as soon as Zariel presses the down button.

"Are you sure this thing is safe?" I ask.

"As safe as anything can be in the Seventh Plane," Zariel replies as we step into the car.

"Well," I say. "That's reassuring." *Not.*

I hold the handrail, for all the good it will do, as the elevator jitters back down to the ground floor.

"How long will it take for Brent to be okay?" I ask.

"As long as it takes."

The elevator car jerks to a stop, and the door squeals open.

I want to kiss the ground as we step out. "So. What's next? Do you think the dream thing with Laura Samuels took? Should I go check on her, or something?"

"Later, Z," calls the sweaty hotel clerk.

Zariel waves at him as we pass. We hike back to Udanax. As soon as we are through the gate, he touches my shoulder and we are instantly at the Fountain of Sirin.

"You asked what is next," Zariel says. "Are you not content with returning to your normal life?"

How could I be, especially with the Cold War going on between my parents? "It's not that. After all this, I just wanted to make sure the Laura Samuels thing took, and thought you might have some fill-in projects to work on for now. That's all."

"I see. You are offering yourself as an apprentice?"

"I guess. Yeah."

Zariel cocks his head. "This would be something akin to what you would call an unpaid internship. However, it would be an expeditious way to cancel any karmic debt."

"So, it's all good, right? How do I sign up?"

"I will take it under consideration."

And that was that. I am back in my room. My alarm will go off in ten minutes, so I could get up for the last day of opera camp. I wouldn't miss the opera part, but I would miss Tara. Mom had finally gotten around to programming her numbers into my loser-phone. The problem was, Tara and her parents are leaving on Monday to go to Europe for a month.

Our camp schedule is to finish up the last bit of scenery building before lunch. Afterward, we get to be extras at the ball scene as the opera company rehearses *Die Fledermaus*. Hooray.

Tara and I work on painting the wainscoting of the back wall panel.

"My mom called your mom last night, don't know if she told you."

I shake my head. "She wasn't up when I left. Dad brought me."

"Well, my mom wanted to ask your mom if it was okay if we invited you to come with us on Monday. She said yes, and my dad's already bought your ticket."

I drop my brush and spatter periwinkle blue paint on my shoes. "Me, come with you to Europe for a month? Are you kidding me?"

"No. But if you don't want to…"

"Of course I want to!" I say so loudly that nearly everybody turns and looks at us. "It's just a huge surprise, that's all."

"We're not going anywhere that needs a visa, so as long as you have your passport, you should be good."

"Yeah. I've got it. I'm just kind of still in shock."

Tara smiles. "I can swing by on Sunday to help you pack."

"That'd be good."

The weekend passed by in a blur of shopping and packing, and I stand in front of the security gates.

"Have a good trip, Mimi. Don't hesitate to call any time if you need something," my dad says through his wired-shut jaw. At least that's what I hear, anyway. He hugs me stiffly – he's still having some problems from his car wreck last week.

"Be good, baby," my mom says. "Love you." She has tears in her eyes, and she nearly squeezes the breath out of me.

Even my brother hugs me. "Have fun," he says.

I pass through the x-ray machine and meet Tara's family on the other side. I have the window seat, and Tara is next to me. After a few hours and a semi-edible meal, I fall asleep.

I suddenly become aware that I am floating at the top of the plane, looking down. I see myself, asleep, and Tara may be asleep, or she may be listening to music with her eyes closed, in the middle seat. The plane suddenly drops about thirty feet, then rolls side to side in heavy turbulence. We're in the middle of a thunderstorm, and the pilot tries to pull up and take us above it, but the air is too bumpy. Lightning flashes over the plane like liquid fire.

I realize that Tara is floating next to me. One of the passengers stands up and looks at both of us. But it isn't a passenger. It's Zariel.

Here we go again.

Mythic Personalities

Hades and Persephone

Hades was the brother of Zeus and Poseidon, and the son of Cronus and Rhea. When the Olympians overthrew the Titans, the brothers drew lots to divide up the cosmos. Hades drew the short straw and became the ruler of the Underworld. Not only did he have dominion over the dead, but also the earth's hidden wealth – everything from seeds to gold and diamonds. Zeus arranged for him to abduct Persephone as his wife, but her mother, Demeter, was so angry that she froze the earth until her daughter was returned. Hades let Persephone go, but because she had eaten six pomegranate seeds, she was obliged to live in the Underworld for six months out of the year. Some stories portray Persephone as an unwitting victim, but, according to Homer, she was the proud Queen of the Underworld who relished both her husband and her power. Like his brothers, Hades was not a faithful husband, and fathered children outside of his marriage to Persephone. The nymph Arethusa wass the one to discovered Persephone's whereabouts in the Underworld and reported them to Demeter.

Rhiannon

Rhiannon was a fae woman (or possibly a goddess) who married the prince, Pwyll, and even though their relationship got off to a rocky start (she was betrothed to someone else who did not at all appreciate her running off with another man), they were deeply in love. When she failed to produce an heir in the first two years of marriage, Pwyll was strongly urged to choose another wife, but he refused. In the third year, she gave birth to a son. However, the baby disappeared, and the maids, frightened of being punished for losing him, smeared the sleeping Rhiannon with dog's blood.

She was accused of killing and eating her baby. Even though Pwyll was again pressured to choose another wife, he again refused. Rhiannon remained his queen, but she must do a penance for the disappearance of the child – she was required to sit on a white horse at the gates of the city and tell her story to travelers. Eventually the missing child was found and returned to his parents, and Rhiannon was vindicated and redeemed. Her story is one of perseverance in the face of tragedy and injustice.

If you enjoyed this book, please consider leaving a review on your favorite book sharing site.

Artemis Greenleaf has always been fascinated by the mysterious, and she devoured fairy tales, folk tales and ghost stories since before she could read. In 1995, she had a near-death experience which turned her perception of the world upside down. She lived to tell the tale (and often does, in one form or another). Artemis lives in the suburban wilds of Houston, Texas with her husband, two children and assorted pets. She writes novels, short stories, and non-fiction, and her work has appeared in magazines and anthologies. For more information, please visit artemisgreenleaf.com.

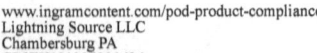